P9-DWD-583

A BETTER GOODBYE

A Novel

JOHN SCHULIAN

TYRUS
BOOKS

Published by
TYRUS BOOKS
an imprint of F+W Media, Inc.
10151 Carver Road, Suite 200
Blue Ash, OH 45242. U.S.A.
www.tyrusbooks.com

Hardcover ISBN 10: 1-4405-9204-7
Hardcover ISBN 13: 978-1-4405-9204-1
Paperback ISBN 10: 1-4405-9205-5
Paperback ISBN 13: 978-1-4405-9205-8
eISBN 10: 1-4405-9206-3
eISBN 13: 978-1-4405-9206-5

Printed in the United States of America.

10   9   8   7   6   5   4   3   2   1

Library of Congress Cataloging-in-Publication Data
Schulian, John.
  A better goodbye / John Schulian.
    pages cm
  ISBN 978-1-4405-9204-1 (hc) -- ISBN 1-4405-9204-7 (hc) -- ISBN 978-1-4405-9205-8 (pb) --
ISBN 1-4405-9205-5 (pb) -- ISBN 978-1-4405-9206-5 (ebook) -- ISBN 1-4405-9206-3 (ebook)
1. Triangles (Interpersonal relations)--Fiction. I. Title.
  PS3619.C473B48 2015
  813'.6--dc23
                          2015022658

Cover design by Sylvia McArdle.
Cover image © iStockphoto.com/Meinzahn.

This book is available at quantity discounts for bulk purchases.
For information, please call 1-800-289-0963.

Let the bell toll for

Johnny Lira, the toughest guy in the neighborhood,

and

Jim McCarthy, who believed because that's what friends do.

They all have a plan until they get hit.

And I wonder where you are
And if the pain ends when you die
And I wonder if there was
Some better way to say goodbye

1

Too bad Barry lived in Santa Barbara. Suki would have told him her real name if he'd been local. Or maybe she would do it anyway, her resistance wavering as the two of them lay naked in the master bedroom. He smelled like soap and had a nice ass. Best of all, he was mature, not like the last client she'd dated, the loser whose cell phone bill she was still paying. Even with the curtains drawn in the middle of the afternoon and the only light coming from the candles beside the futon, she could see that his short black hair was going gray fast. He'd said he was forty-two, twice her age practically, but she didn't mind.

The last song on her Mazzy Star CD had ended a while ago, and now it was just Barry talking about his new car and generally acting like an hour with her was more enjoyable than the massage or the happy ending.

"It's a Rolls," he said. "Convertible."

"Really?" Suki didn't know much about cars, but she did know that a Rolls-Royce cost a fortune. "Did you just buy it?"

"It was part of a business deal."

Barry always talked about business, but he never said exactly what it was he did. Other guys would let you know right away that they were lawyers or doctors—lots of weird doctors out there—or producers or writers or the one thing Southern California must have had more of than any other place in the world, entrepreneurs. But Barry kept it vague. Suki wondered if he was a drug dealer.

"You look like you're freezing," he said, not waiting for a response as he reached down to grab the comforter and pull it up over both of them.

"A little, I guess," she said, relishing the sudden warmth. Even snuggled against Barry, she'd felt like she was turning blue.

"How much longer are you working?"

"Like I'm supposed to get off at seven, but I don't have any more appointments scheduled. Unless the other girls booked something while I've been with you."

"They do that?"

"No, usually, if someone asks for me, they say I'm off, or I don't work here anymore." Suki couldn't help laughing.

Barry frowned.

"Come on," she said. "It's funny."

"It wouldn't be in my world."

"Girls are always bitches to each other."

"They are, huh?" Barry was smiling now. He looked like he wanted to say something else when there was a knock on the door.

"Suki?" No mistaking Contessa's voice. She could offer you ice cream and make it sound like you'd stolen her favorite earrings. "Time's up, baby."

"Be right there," Suki said.

She sat up quickly, her long hair tumbling over one of her small, perfect breasts, her smile turning into a pout. "Sorry," she said. She scrambled off the futon, grabbed her black Trashy Lingerie mini dress off the floor and tugged it on. "I always forget the clock when you're here."

Barry nodded in a way that made Suki think it was the same for him, and he never took his eyes off her. He'd told her he liked her with clothes on as much as he did naked. It was the kind of thing guys always said, but he made it sound real.

"Do I have time for a shower?" he asked.

"Sure. I put a clean towel out for you."

She was just about to open the door when he stopped her with a question: "Would you like to go for a ride? I was going to ask you before but . . . " He nodded toward the door and the lingering menace of Contessa's voice.

The guys who were sprung for Asian girls, the rice chasers, would see Suki for the first time and ask her out almost before she'd told them to turn over—dinner, a concert, a weekend in Vegas—but not Barry. He'd started seeing her when she worked for the Russian couple on Laurel Canyon, and only now, eight months, three apartment complexes, one guesthouse and her own place later, was he making his move. "Cool," she said, her smile big and genuine. "I'll find out."

When she stepped into the living room, she made sure the door was closed before she turned to face the stare she knew Contessa had waiting for her.

"Look at you, all smiley and shit. Musta fucked him."

"No way," Suki said, pissed that she'd forgotten to lose the damn smile. A hand job was as far as she ever went when Contessa was on the other side of the wall.

"Bullshit." The word sounded extra bad because Contessa was so pretty, with her milk chocolate skin and her hair dyed honey blonde and braided. She had huge boobs too, real ones that looked more enormous than ever now, as she crossed her arms beneath them and they bulged out of a white negligee that wasn't meant to contain them in the first place. "You in there for an hour and twenty minutes, got to be some fuckin' going on."

"Well, I hate to disappoint you," Suki said.

"Uh-huh," Contessa said with an accusing smile.

Any other time, Suki would have been trying not to laugh. Contessa made no secret of the fact that she screwed every client who asked for it. It didn't matter if they were players flashing gold or uptight white businessmen out to prove something to themselves. She did them all, even a guy who looked like a grandfather and had to be risking a heart attack every time he saw her. And here was the thing none of the clients knew about Contessa: she never cleaned herself afterward. Didn't douche, didn't shower, didn't do anything but count her money—three hundred for full service—and wait for the next guy with his sights on the health hazard between her legs.

"Do I have any more appointments?" Suki asked. "I'd kind of like an hour off. Maybe a little longer."

"With that dude in there?"

Suki flushed and looked away from Contessa's stare. "You know it's always slow the next couple hours. I'll be back by the time the phones get busy."

Contessa wasn't the boss or anything. The boss was a real-estate guy named Derek who always had a massage operation or two on the side, for the unreported income and easy sex. Derek couldn't turn down the volume on his salesman's yada-yada-yada, which was all the reason Suki needed to go deaf when he came around. But she tried not to leave the other girls hanging no matter where she worked. Sometimes they reciprocated.

Contessa glanced over at the sofa. A blonde who called herself Brooke was curled up on it, worrying a strand of her streaked hair as she worked one of the two phones on the coffee table in front of her. There wasn't any other furniture in the room, and Suki always thought the relative emptiness made their voices sound different.

"Security code's five-oh-seven," Brooke was saying. "Same as the apartment." She flashed Suki and Contessa a smile as she listened. "Great. Then I'll see you at two-thirty." Another smile, bigger this time. "I can't give too many details on the phone, but I promise you'll leave very satisfied, okay, sweetie?"

Brooke put the phone down and stood. She was tall and willowy, like a model, just not that pretty; she needed a lot of makeup to camouflage her ravaged complexion. "New client," she said.

"You tell him about a two-girl?" Contessa asked.

Brooke got the same guilty look on her face she'd had when she told Contessa she watched *Buffy the Vampire Slayer*. "I will when he gets here," Brooke said.

"Yeah." Contessa nodded slowly, letting her know that would be a damn good idea.

Suki was starting to fidget. She hoped Barry would wait in the room until she went back in, the way unwritten protocol said he was supposed to. If he came out now, before a decision was made, Contessa would know what was up even if he never said anything except goodbye.

"I think I'll wear my red negligee," Brooke said. "From Victoria's Secret."

"You sure?" Contessa said. "Makes you look titless and shit."

"Really?" Insecurity strangled Brooke's voice. "I better go see what else is in the closet."

She started toward the master bedroom, where the girls kept their things. Suki had to stop herself from reaching out and grabbing her.

"Brooke, my client."

Contessa went back on the offensive instantly. "She been fuckin' him and won't say."

"Well, he is really cute," Brooke said. She was so consistently nonjudgmental in her ten-watt way that Suki couldn't help liking her.

"Nothing happened, believe me," Suki said. "Let me see if he's ready." But she stopped at the door and looked at Contessa hopefully. "So, you think it would be all right? I'll only be gone for, like, an hour."

"Fuck it," Contessa said.

Suki took that as a yes and ducked back into the master.

✢ ✢ ✢

The only other Rolls she could remember seeing in Sherman Oaks belonged to Barry White, and Sherman Oaks was loaded with phat rides, especially when you went up in the hills south of Ventura Boulevard and the houses got fancy. At least, someone had told her the Rolls was Barry White's—probably a client old enough to remember when he was making all that "Take off your brassiere, my dear" music. To Suki he was just this bloated black dude with a Jheri curl head who looked like he could barely squeeze behind the steering wheel. Or maybe it was his driver who had the eating disorder. If you could afford a Rolls with a root-beer-colored body and a cream-colored convertible top, it would be cool to have a driver.

The few times Suki had seen the Barry White–mobile rolling down out of the hills, she'd never imagined riding in one. Now here was her own Barry, Santa Barbara Barry, opening the passenger door of his Rolls for her. It had a pale yellow body and a white ragtop, and he was saying it was a '97 Corniche. *Six years old*, Suki thought. In her world, that made it practically hot off the assembly line. But this wasn't the time to change the subject. Barry was having too much fun talking about how much horsepower it had and how it was so heavy—indestructible, even—that it went through brake pads like they were Kleenex.

He was cuter than ever when he was wound up this way, but there were only two things about the Rolls itself that really mattered to her then and there. First was the sound the door made when he closed it behind her, like the door on a velvet bank vault. And then there was the leather upholstery, so soft it made her wish she were wearing shorts instead of jeans.

She was still running her hands over it when Barry climbed behind the wheel. "Can't stop giving massages, huh?" he said.

"What? Oh . . . " She pulled her hands up into her lap and smiled at him uncertainly, not relaxing until his deadpan expression gave way to a smile of his own. "It's just that these seats are, like, totally amazing."

"I've got to tell you this is the nicest car I've ever driven," Barry said, "and I've driven a lot of nice cars."

"I'll bet." She glanced at the dashboard. "Is that real wood?"

"Yeah. The guy I got the car from told me what kind, but I forgot." He laughed at himself. It was another thing she liked about him.

He was one of those clients who made her forget the life that had brought them together, the life she led in the apartment complex in whose shadow they were still parked. She wasn't ashamed of what she did there, although she did try to stay away from neighbors' prying eyes. She just liked being with a guy who made her feel like they could have met anywhere. That wasn't how it usually was.

Suki didn't know the engine was on until Barry eased the car away from the curb.

"Wow, quiet," she said.

As they went around the block and got on Sepulveda, the noise from outside the car was still there, but it was filtered through privilege.

"Know what one of these costs new?" Barry said.

"How much?"

"Three hundred and two thousand, five hundred dollars."

"Really? Wow." Suki laughed self-consciously. "I keep saying wow all the time. Sorry."

"I'll take it as a compliment."

Barry looked at her as if he expected her to say something else. "What?" she said.

"Don't you want to know what that twenty-five hundred dollars is for?" he asked. "I mean, you'd think three hundred K would be a nice round number everybody could live with, right?"

Suki said, "Sure," with as much enthusiasm as she could muster.

"Floor mats."

"Really?"

"No."

When he began laughing, she joined in, punching him lightly on the arm and saying, "I thought you were serious." Then she settled back, content, thinking his sunglasses were way nicer than hers and liking how the lines around his eyes crinkled when he smiled.

"It's got a killer sound system," he said. "Listen." He pushed a button and a couple of seconds later a woman's voice was filling the Rolls with yearning: "I envy the rain that falls on your face, that wets your eyelashes and dampens your skin . . . "

"Who's singing?" Suki said.

"Lucinda Williams."

"I didn't know you liked country music."

"I'm not sure I'd call her country. I mean, that's how she started, but now she's got lots of other things going on. Blues, rock-and-roll, even gospel sometimes."

Suki nodded. "She's good. I like her." It wasn't a lie, either. It was just that Suki didn't know much about music except Coldplay and what she put on during massage sessions. Most of her friends were into rap and hip-hop, and that was cool too. In fact she thought the funniest song she'd ever heard was "Smack My Bitch Up." But she wasn't going to tell Barry that, not yet anyway.

By the time they were heading east on Ventura, Lucinda was singing about a jukebox getting her through the long nights of the heart, and Suki was back to thinking what a great day it was to be in a car like this. Seventy degrees in the middle of January, and the air was clear the way it never was in the summer.

"Can we put the top down?" she said.

"Absolutely," Barry said. "I should have done that right away."

He pushed a button on the center console, and slowly, seductively, the top began to rise and move back. With the first crack of blue sky overhead, Suki felt the sun's warmth.

"Let's go up to Mulholland," Barry said. "It'll be beautiful."

"I haven't been up there in, like, forever."

They'd been hitting green lights all the way and the traffic wasn't as thick as it usually was, all in all a perfect afternoon. Nothing for Suki to do but ride the good feeling wherever it took her.

Then Barry said, "Shit."

Suki had only heard him swear a time or two before. When she looked over, his smile was gone and he was leaning on the button for the convertible top. The convertible top. That was the reason for his mood swing. It was sticking straight up as they rolled past Tower Records, a block from Van Nuys Boulevard. They were supposed to turn there and head up to Mulholland. But right now Mulholland was the furthest thing from Barry's mind.

"Goddammit," he said.

Lucinda Williams was still singing, but the only sound that registered on Suki was a low grinding noise. When she looked around, she saw other drivers staring and two Asian guys in a jacked-up Honda Civic pointing at her and laughing, like this was what she got for hanging out with a rice chaser old enough to be her father. Her first impulse was to flip them off.

Then Barry said "shit" one more time, and she turned her attention back to him. "What should we do?" she asked.

He had both hands on the wheel now and he was moving into the right lane, hunting for a parking place. He didn't look at her when he said, "You should get me a brain transplant."

"No, don't say that."

"I was fucking stupid enough to try putting it down when we were moving. Should have parked."

"It'll be all right."

"Not if I fucked up the goddamn car."

He hit the brake when he saw a Lincoln Navigator pulling out of a parking space. But it stopped halfway onto the street because the woman behind the wheel was busy yakking on her cell phone. "Fucking bitch," he said.

Suki flinched. She didn't like the side of Barry that was emerging any more than Barry liked sitting here knowing that everybody who saw his Rolls's convertible top waving in the breeze thought he was a rich idiot. She would have thought the same thing if she'd been driving down the street. And she had to stifle a giggle when she realized she couldn't wait to tell someone about what had happened. Not Contessa, but maybe Brooke. No, not Brooke either, because she'd turn around and tell Contessa. Then they'd both dis Barry the way they dissed most clients, and Suki felt too protective of him for that. But she had to find someone. This was just too good, you know?

✣ ✣ ✣

Stepping into the apartment, she didn't hear anything except the icemaker in the fridge. There was no sign of Contessa and Brooke—they were probably still in session. She walked toward the living room and saw that the coffee table's glass top had been knocked sideways. A closer look told her it was cracked. One of the cushions had been pulled away from the sofa, too. Suki, starting to feel strange, off-balance, moved to straighten things up, the way she always did, and almost stepped on one of the phones. It was lying on the floor, smashed, as though someone had jumped on it.

She glanced around the room, the sun sinking in the west, its light streaming through the vertical blinds. There was a dark slash on one of the walls that hadn't been there when she left. Below it lay what she guessed had put it there: the other phone, now cracked and useless.

Suki's breath caught in her chest. The cops must have busted Contessa and Brooke. Alarms were going off in her head as she wondered if there had been anything with her name on it lying around. And were the cops waiting for her to come back? This was all new to her. The only other time she'd thought she was going to get busted, she was working in a musician's guesthouse on Beverly Glen and another masseuse got all cocaine paranoid and started playing head games. Suki had forgotten her purse in her rush to get out of there, and when she went back to get it she was so scared she almost wet herself. That wouldn't happen now.

Purse in hand, she was starting to leave when she heard something besides the fridge and the hum of traffic out on Sepulveda. Crying, maybe. Or a moan. Wait, there it was again, coming from behind the master bedroom's closed door: "Motherfuckers." Definitely Contessa. But she didn't sound nasty, the way she usually did. There were tears in her voice. And pain.

Suki reached for the doorknob as if it were a coiled snake. When she finally made herself turn it, she opened the door an inch at a time. Six inches in, she was greeted by a scream and Brooke shouting, "No, go away! Leave us alone!"

"What are you talking about?" Suki said.

Then she stepped inside and saw for herself.

Brooke and Contessa were on the futon, both in their robes, sheer little things that were their greatest concession to modesty. Contessa was lying on her side, looking back over her shoulder at Suki, a pillow pulled tight against her chest, the towel beneath her stained with something dark. Brooke was kneeling beside her protectively, eyes wild and desperate. Her hair was a tangled mess, and there was a mark on the left side of her face and what looked like dried blood under her nose.

"They raped us," Brooke said.

"Who?" Suki asked, barely able to get her voice above a whisper.

"That new client. I buzz him up and he's all well dressed and everything, and before I close the door behind him, his friend comes charging in."

"Niggers," Contessa said.

Brooke sank back on the futon and started to cry. "They said they'd kill us. Oh, Suki, they had guns."

"We've got to call the police," Suki said. She was fishing around in her purse for her cell phone when Contessa stopped her with a derisive snort.

"And tell 'em what, a couple ho's got raped? Yeah, those cops'd love that. We can tell 'em the motherfuckers stole all our money, too. And you know what they gonna do, little girl? They gonna laugh and say it's the price we pay for peddlin' our pussies."

"At least call Derek."

"Bitch, all that motherfucker want us to do is clean up our mess and disappear."

Suki tried to think of what to say next. Contessa beat her to it.

"Just get the fuck outta here, all right?"

Suki looked at Brooke, hoping to find an ally but knowing that now more than ever Brooke wouldn't stand up to Contessa. She wouldn't even raise her head.

"Goddammit, go," Contessa said.

Suki hurried from the apartment without so much as a good-bye, shedding her name like a second skin. By the time the elevator stopped in the underground parking garage, she was back to being Jenny Yee and nobody else. She doubted the process would be that easy for Contessa and Brooke, cursed now with their terrible secret. And she wondered, as never before, what their names really were.

2

The Mexicans woke Nick Pafko at six straight up, the way they always did, their radio blaring music that was heavy on happy accordions and *ai-yi-yi-yi*'s. They were gardeners who lived in the termite palace next door, anywhere from four to six in a one-bedroom. Nick had watched them come and go, probably back and forth across the border with as many Yankee dollars as they could squirrel away while tending the lawns of anybody with enough money to afford them. The only ones who never left were the guys who drove the two trucks, both of them in their fifties and easy to imagine respectfully taking off their ball caps when the lady of the house came out to say bugs were eating her roses. Once they figured out Nick didn't work for La Migra, they stopped watching him out of the corners of their eyes. They'd smile or nod, sometimes offer him a beer, as though they understood he wasn't any better off than they were. Good guys, but they couldn't keep it down in the morning.

Nick rolled out of bed and into the chilly March dawn. The rising sibilance on the 405 let him know that last night's rush hour was already turning into morning drive time without a break. The trick with the traffic was to pretend it was the ocean, waves washing up on a concrete shore. He didn't hear many people spoiling the illusion by honking, the way they did back home in Chicago. With nothing between him and the freeway except the two apartments up front, a street the city never fixed, and a half-assed wire fence, Nick took his blessings where he found them.

Sleep had come hard last night, refusing to budge until exhaustion got the best of the voices in his head. The voices had shouted loudest when the rest of him was ready to shut down, and now, looking at himself in the bathroom mirror, he could see the weariness in his eyes. There were still women who liked his looks—they liked his smile too, though a smile was a sometimes thing for him. It was as if his mind was always focused on what he saw now, scars above and below each eye and a broken nose that had never been set properly. At least those wounds had healed. It was the deeper ones he feared never would, the ones he was forever struggling to keep at bay.

As he walked out of the bathroom, he shook his head disapprovingly at how he'd slept in his sweatshirt and jeans. That wasn't his style. His apartment proved it, everything squared away, no matter how big a mess his head might be. The place wasn't much, but it was all he needed. That and the money to keep him in it for another month. He was trying to think of a way to come up with it when the phone rang. It was Coyle, sounding like a call so early made him some kind of a comedian.

"Yeah, I'm awake," Nick said. "What's going on?"

"It's time I did you a favor," Coyle said.

"Why do I think there's something in it for you?"

Coyle had never been a fanatic about his marriage, and this time he wanted Nick to drive his beer truck for a couple of hours while he boned a liquor store clerk he'd met on his route. For his part Nick would make two hundred bucks in cash, more money than he'd seen in a day since he'd maxed out his unemployment.

"Big spender," Nick said.

"It's what I pay when I'm paying for it," Coyle said, with the confidence of a man who had a job he wasn't going to lose.

"Yeah? Well, I'll try not to think about what that makes me. Looks like you got a deal."

"Man, I'm gonna fuck her so good I'll wish I was her."

Coyle had used the same line when they were throwing bags for Delta at LAX, but Nick let it slide. It was easier just to picture Coyle's leering face and oddly canted posture. He always looked like he was going to fall in your lap, but somehow the ladies didn't seem to mind. Or maybe he just concentrated on those with low standards.

It wasn't like he'd had a lot of time to explain his philosophy of chasing tail to Nick. On a big day before the 9/11 horror show, they would be part of a three-man crew that turned seven or eight planes—bring 'em in, unload 'em, load 'em, and push 'em, one after the other. The repetition drove Coyle nuts, but Nick welcomed the numbing predictability, letting it swallow him whole for twenty-two dollars an hour.

The only time he came all the way out of his trance was to save Coyle's ass. First, Coyle pissed off one of the two-to-eleven shift's king-sized Tongans, then he got holier-than-thou with a do-ragged, corn-rowed gang kid who was stealing bags. The gangster backed down because his spine was made of what Nick suspected it was—chickenshit. But the Tongan was one of those guys who thought brawling was fun, until Nick froze him with a shot to the liver and then walked away rather than throw any more punches.

He offered no explanation, and he didn't want Coyle's thanks. Coyle, being Coyle, however, couldn't shut the fuck up. The guy stayed grateful even when the terrorist-freaked airline industry went into the toilet and Delta laid them both off. Sometimes Nick thought Coyle was embarrassed that his brother-in-law had gotten him on at Budweiser, except embarrassment wasn't his style. It was more like he felt bad for Nick, which made Nick the one who was embarrassed. It was hard enough on his pride to find out that nobody was hiring, grab day work where he could, and count on $666 from the state every other week to keep him in a studio apartment with peeling paint and cancerous-looking carpet. Unemployment was only supposed to last six months, but he got a three-month extension, and then another. After that, the law ordered him off the public tit.

So here he was, driving toward a score that would help him make his rent—$825 for another month in a dump that was all wrong for the Westside, where everybody was supposed to be a movie star and every car was supposed to be a Mercedes. His pickup was a fourteen-year-old Chevy S-10 with a transmission that slipped and an odometer that had gone around the clock. It said 17,000 miles, but 217,000 would have been closer to the truth. The only thing on the truck he didn't worry about was the burned-out catalytic converter that used to light up the CHECK ENGINE sign. He had pounded the dash until the light bulb broke.

There were lots of trucks like Nick's in Highland Park, a neighborhood of people who knew from necessity how to make do. The fact that they all seemed to be Hispanic barely registered on his consciousness when he got off the Pasadena Freeway at Avenue 43 and rolled north on Figueroa. The city didn't belong to the gringos anymore, and the proof could be found in one sign after another, from *Lazaro Bateria de Serviço* to *Clínica Médica y Dentista* to *El Pescador*, where he'd had seafood tacos the last time he'd traveled this far east. Up ahead he could see the marquee for the Highland Theatre. Across the street, there was an old-time bowling alley. Coyle had said he'd be waiting in the parking lot behind it.

Nick turned left onto Avenue 56 and started looking for the entrance to the lot. What he saw first was a guy crouched beside a beat-to-shit Pontiac, using a sander to finish a Mexican patch. The guy had probably told the owner he could fix a dent, then plugged it with Bondo without bothering to pull the dent or grind down the metal. First time the owner hit a bump, the Bondo would fall out. It happened all the time. But people kept getting Mexican patches.

The parking lot's entrance wasn't quite halfway down the block. As Nick hung a right into it, a hooded figure in black caught his eye and he instinctively slowed down. It was a gangbanger who wanted to make sure everybody knew it. He was going up the steps of an old Victorian with a ragged front lawn and drooping window shutters. Even if he'd been in his underwear, his walk would have told the world he was trouble, shoulders hunched, legs wide, stride filled with slow-motion menace. Take that hooded sweatshirt off him and you'd undoubtedly find a shaved head and tattoos on his arms, back, and chest. He probably had them on his legs, too. Nick was getting the picture in his mind when the banger caught him staring. No big whirling gotcha or anything like that, just a subtle turn of the head, the banger peering around the corner of his hood and meeting Nick's stare with one of his own, his eyes like black ice.

The challenge was unspoken: What you lookin' at, mother-fucker? Once it had been a staple of Nick's existence, whether he was asking or answering; now he could barely summon the enthusiasm to do either. It was only habit that made him return the banger's stare for a beat longer. Then he looked back into the lot and saw Coyle standing beside his beer truck, radiating impatience. Time to move on, but Nick could feel the banger watching him all the way into the parking space next to Coyle's. When he climbed out of his pickup, he looked back toward the Victorian. The banger was nowhere to be seen.

"Something the matter?" Coyle said.

"Nah, just some guy."

"Somebody you know?"

"Forget it." Nick nodded at Coyle's truck. "This what I'm driving?"

"Yeah, if my afternoon punch shows up."

"A smooth operator like you, how could she resist?"

"Hey, fuck you," Coyle said.

Nick liked yanking the man's chain. Some days it was good for the only smile he got.

"You're on time, one-thirty, she should be too," Coyle said. "She's the one that wanted it like this, but I'm the guy putting out the money to make it happen. You, a motel room—"

"You could call her, you know."

"And act like she's got me on a leash? Fuck that."

"Maybe we better talk about what you want me to do. Get your mind off your problems."

"You brought your trucker's license, didn't you?"

"Yeah." Nick was damned if he would show it unless Coyle asked.

"I wasn't sure you'd have one. You must get out of that shitty apartment more than I think."

"Coyle, the truck . . . "

"You sure you've driven one of these?" Coyle slapped the side of his Mack. It had a five-speed Maxidyne, three hundred and twenty-five horses, and handled like a car as long as you were careful backing up and taking corners. "They can roll on you."

"I'll be fine," Nick said. "As long as you loaded it right."

This time they both smiled. Then Coyle pulled a key from his pocket, slid it into the lock on a bay door, and rolled the door up like a Venetian blind. Inside, cases of cans and bottles—half Bud, half Bud Light—were stacked and waiting to be unloaded. "Good enough for you?" Coyle said.

"Tell me my first stop and I'll get rolling."

"Right there."

Coyle pointed at a building with BOWLING painted on it in large, faded blue letters. Beneath it was more: "Air Conditioning— Open Bowling 3 Games—8AM to 5PM." There was a door with an orange vinyl sofa and a dilapidated easy chair beside it. Over the door was an arrow aimed at the door with the words "Mr. T's Bowling" on it.

"They like to bowl around here, huh?" Nick said.

"Fuck, no," Coyle said. "Lanes haven't been used for years. It's a bar and coffee shop now. Nights they have music."

"Yeah? What kind?"

"That punk shit." Coyle thrust the key at Nick. "Don't lose this. Door'll lock by itself when you pull it back down." He took a sheet of paper folded in quarters from his hip pocket. "Here's the other addresses you're going to, size of the delivery, all that good shit."

Nick studied the note while Coyle rattled on like he was certain his replacement couldn't read. "Only four stops besides this one, no big-assed unloads and everything's in Highland Park. You oughta be back here by three forty-five, four at the latest. Any problems—you got a cell phone, right?"

"There a reason why I should?" Nick asked.

"It's the fucking twenty-first century."

"Maybe I want to see how the century works out before I get carried away."

"Jesus Christ on a crutch."

"Relax, Coyle. It's right here."

Nick gave Coyle a glimpse of his cell phone, then stuffed it back in his Levi's. He loved messing with Coyle. Push the right button and you could spin his head around. Just as Nick was about to do it again, he spotted a dirty red Jeep Cherokee pulling into the lot. "This your ride?" he asked.

"She's my ride all right," Coyle said, leaning on "ride" just hard enough to make it sound dirty. As he walked toward the Cherokee, he looked back at Nick and said, "I'll give you a call so you can listen to her scream when she comes."

"What if she yawns instead?"

Coyle gave Nick the finger and kept walking. The woman picking him up flashed a big smile that made her prettier than she had first seemed behind her sunglasses. "Hi, Ray," she said, just loud enough for Nick to hear.

Nick hadn't heard many people call Coyle by his first name. He wondered if Coyle's wife did. He was still thinking it over when he began taking cases of beer from the truck and stacking them on a dolly. He'd start with six, three on the bottom, three on top. It might take longer that way, but he didn't want to lose any beer if he could help it. He didn't need Coyle bitching at him. He just needed two hundred bucks.

✣ ✣ ✣

By the time Nick found his last stop, he was running late and praying to God he was done with pissed-off store managers and postage-stamp-sized parking lots. Paisano Groceries sat next to a locksmith that told the world where it was with a large yellow sign shaped like a key. The store's windows were papered with hand-drawn signs for brands of soda that supermarket chains couldn't be troubled to carry—Big Red, Nehi Peach, Root 66 Root Beer. There was a beat-up Chrysler Fifth Avenue, its color a cross between dirt and Bondo, parked across the two handicapped spaces in front of the store's double doors. Nick nosed in beside it, and by the time he had walked to the front of the truck, a small round man wearing a grocer's apron was coming out to greet him.

"Only ten cases of regular today," the round man said. "Nights are too cold for my beer drinkers, I guess."

"Ten," Nick said. "You got it."

"But still five Light."

"Right." When Nick saw the round man looking at him, puzzled, he said, "Coyle's taking some personal time."

"Oh, okay. I wasn't sure what to think. You're not wearing a Budweiser shirt. I'm Eddie."

"Nick."

After they shook hands, Eddie told Nick the girl at the register would have cash waiting for him and went back inside. As Nick wheeled in his first dolly load, he heard Eddie talking soda pop with a customer. Something from North Carolina called Cheerwine. "I don't know what it is about the South—they like high carbonation. Sometimes the bottles just explode. I come in some mornings and there's glass on the floor and soda all over the place." Eddie shook his head. "The carbonation."

Nick wouldn't have minded staying a while, maybe have a sandwich from the deli counter and wash it down with one of Eddie's recommendations. But ten minutes later he was pushing the last cases of empties out the door. He had the envelope with the cash in his hip pocket. He didn't bother counting it.

The parking lot rang with the laughter and shouts of three Hispanic kids who were buzzing around the truck. The oldest of them was no more than twelve. He was riding a peewee bike with oversized gooseneck handlebars, and his two buddies were laughing and chasing after him, so naked in their yearning for the bike that Nick felt it in his gut.

"How you guys doing?" he said.

The oldest kid skidded to a stop by the rear of the truck. "Give me a beer," he said. His buddies snickered, watching their leader with something approaching reverence.

"A beer?" Nick took the first case of empties off the dolly and held it as he looked at the kid with a smile. "What do you want with a beer?"

"Drink it. What else?"

The kid smirked while his buddies erupted in laughter.

"I better see your ID first," Nick said.

"Left it at home," the kid said. "Come on, man, just one—" Then his eyes got wide. His buddies' eyes did, too. "Shit," he said, and spun away on his bike, pedaling furiously as his buddies scrambled to catch up with him.

Nick was watching them disappear behind the truck when he heard a voice at his back: "Your money, man, and no fockin' around."

"Just let me put the bottles down," Nick said.

"Nice and easy or I'll kill your ass."

Nick lowered the case to the ground and turned around slowly. It was the gangbanger he'd seen when he was pulling in behind the bowling alley, still in black with his hood up and that life-is-cheap look on his face. The only accessory he had added was the pistol he was pointing at Nick, holding it flat instead of up and down, like he'd learned everything he knew about guns in the movies.

"You'll kill me?" Nick said, more curious than afraid.

"Goddamn right I will." The banger was coming toward Nick, not too fast, not too slow, every move a message that he had done this before.

"What if I told you I don't care?" Nick said.

"You must be fockin' crazy."

But something in the banger's voice betrayed him. Not doubt, really. More like discomfort at having to think in a situation where he was confronted by a kind of victim he'd never had before, one whose expression stayed as blank as the parking lot they were standing on.

"Keep talkin' and you're dead, motherfocker. Swear to God you are." The banger stopped a step away from Nick. "Now quit fockin' around and give me the money."

The pistol, whatever kind it was, was pointed at Nick's belly, and Nick could see the banger's finger tensing around the trigger.

His stomach muscles tightened reflexively, and everything after that became instinct. There were footsteps coming out the store's front door, letting him know there was still a world beyond the gangbanger's threats. Then a voice: "Hey, Nick, hang on a minute." Sounded like Eddie. The banger glanced over to see who it was, maybe even flashed on shooting a second moth-erfucker if that's what it took to get the beer man's money. That instant was all Nick needed to unload a left hook straight out of his past.

His hands were at his side, so the punch had to travel farther than it would have in a boxing ring. Four inches, six inches, that was the ideal. But beggars can't be choosers. Distance be damned, everything else was the product of all those years in the gym—calling on the muscles on his right side to torque his left side, pivoting on the toe of his left foot, keeping his left shoulder back as long as he could until he brought his arm whipping around and unleashed a punch that crackled with violence. He caught the banger turning back to him, a lot of jaw, a little bit of that stupid fucking hood, and the contact sent a lightning bolt all the way to his armpit. The air filled with a crack—maybe it was the banger's jaw breaking, maybe it was Nick's imagination. Thought, consciousness, even precious seconds of breath ceased for the banger. He pitched to his side, motionless, and landed with a sound that was soft and wet.

Like shit from a high-flying bird, a voice in Nick's memory said. Nick didn't want to hear any voices. But Eddie was standing over the banger, yelling, "Jesus Christ, I think he's dead," and Nick knew it might be true—he'd seen it before—and it scared him more than the gun had. He was still scared when the cops showed up, uniforms first, then two in plain clothes. Even when the banger finally sat up and the cops cuffed him, Nick couldn't silence the cacophony in his head.

Eddie and his customers were chattering among themselves, saying they'd seen a lot of crazy shit in the neighborhood but never anything like this. The locksmith from next door kept wishing out loud that he'd had a video camera—he'd watched the whole thing—and the kids came back to stare at Nick with more awe than Anglos usually got from the locals.

Nick wanted to make it all go away, as if getting rid of the talk, the people, and the cop cars would bottle his memories back up.

But the only thing he could do was watch one of the plainclothes cops walk up frowning and say, first thing out of his mouth, "I hope you realize that asshole could have killed you."

"Yeah, he mentioned the possibility," Nick said.

"Guess you weren't impressed."

"That's one way to look at it."

3

She liked to sit up front in class. The girls she had made friends with at school, the ones who had no clue about her other life and knew her only as Jenny, said she wanted the professors to see she looked like Lucy Liu, only cuter. Though she never said so, she enjoyed the flattery. But she certainly wasn't glammed up for Modern American Poetry, no makeup, her hair pulled back in a ponytail, wearing jeans and a cotton sweater. On the first day of spring quarter, she was raising her hand with a question she couldn't wait to ask, and not because she wanted to score points, which might otherwise have been her strategy. This time she really wanted to know something.

The instructor, a middle-aged woman in the midst of dropping the country's big names in poetry—Frost, Plath, Berryman, Schwartz, Jarrell, Lowell—looked mildly amused by her eagerness. "Yes, Ms. . . . ?"

"Yee," Jenny said. "Will we be reading anything by Elizabeth Bishop?"

"Are you an admirer of Bishop?"

"Kind of, I guess. I mean, I read 'One Art' and . . . " Jenny searched for the words to describe the way the poem had hit her, and haunted her.

> *I lost two cities, lovely ones. And, vaster,*
> *some realms I owned, two rivers, a continent.*
> *I miss them, but it wasn't a disaster.*

It was ironic the way Bishop had written about mastering the art of loss, insisting that you could lose anything in your life and get on without it. Jenny knew from experience that wasn't true, and she knew Bishop had known it, too. That was the connection she had made with a poet who was a lesbian, an alcoholic, and dead, three things Jenny wasn't, but this didn't seem like the time to be baring her soul.

"And it was just, like, really beautiful," she said at last, taking refuge in the inarticulate.

"It's a villanelle," the instructor said.

"Excuse me?"

"'One Art' is a villanelle, a nineteen-line poem consisting of five tercets and a final quatrain in two rhymes."

Jenny couldn't resist smiling. "If I promise to remember that, can we read Elizabeth Bishop?"

"I'm afraid that's a promise I can't make," the instructor said. "We're dealing with a finite amount of time and I'm forced to exclude some poets whose work I truly admire."

"Like her?"

"Afraid so."

"That's okay," Jenny said, and she sounded so sympathetic that the class erupted in laughter.

She was the only Asian, so maybe they didn't expect her to have a sense of humor. They probably couldn't understand why she wasn't with all the other Asians, studying computers or math and science. But like almost everybody else—Caucasians, Latinos, African-Americans, Russians, Persians, maybe even the students in their forties and fifties—she wanted to move on to a four-year school. Bay City College was a way to get there, a two-year stepping stone to UCLA, although this was actually the third year she had taken classes there, off and on. She kept telling herself she was finally getting it together.

Sara and Rachel, the girls she went to have coffee with after Modern American Poetry, assumed she always had it together. Sara was the first to get that idea because she and Jenny were so crazy about video games that they once spent an entire weekend, nearly sixty sleepless hours, killing the zombies and dragons that populated *Gauntlet: Dark Legacy.* They finally beat the game around ten on a Monday morning and celebrated by calling Rachel and convincing her to skip class so they could go shopping for lingerie.

All Jenny bought was a fishnet teddy, but it was enough to make Sara and Rachel attach themselves to her because they thought she knew something about guys they didn't. The best Jenny could say on the subject was that she had reached the point where she could take them or leave them.

It was kind of boring but Sara and Rachel would practically break out in a rash if they had an inkling that they were on a guy's radar. Jenny assumed it was partly because they were always struggling with their self-image, although right now both of them had lost weight and looked pretty good. The other thing was that they were so much more innocent than she was. When a guy checked them out, she could practically hear the girls' hearts thumping. With her it was like whatever, one more moron on a mission to get her naked and prove his manhood. It had got so every time she saw the private-caller ID pop up, her eyes rolled. Talk about jaded.

This morning, when she was still trying to wake up, her latest ex-boyfriend had called all pissed off about his cell. "What happened?" he whined. "You didn't pay the bill," she said. It was the same message she had been delivering for the last six months, since he'd confessed that his credit was so lousy he couldn't get a cell without putting down a thousand-dollar deposit. She had opened a Verizon account for him in her name, even agreed to pay half the bill, but it wasn't because he was a great lover or anything. He was just a cute guy she'd met doing massage, back when she was going through a lonely spell, before she learned he was still living with his parents.

She wondered if they'd been listening this morning when he told her, "I'll go pay it now," and she had told him, "It's okay, it's already been paid—and the phone's turned off." After he got all the "fucks" and "goddammits" out of his system, he'd uttered the magic question: "I mean, shit, how could you?" And she'd said, "You don't need a cell phone. You don't deserve a cell phone." And it felt good.

Now Jenny's cell was ringing again, another private call. It seemed like her entire life revolved around that phone, her worth as a human being measured by the enormity of her monthly bill. She would use her cell to get together with somebody, and when they were finally at the same club or party or whatever, she would talk to someone else on the phone about getting together with them. She wondered if life was like that everywhere, or just in L.A.

"Excuse me," she said to Sara and Rachel, who were in deep yenta mode, talking about their respective hair colorists, giving no sign that they heard her.

It was Jeff calling. He ran a small construction company and dealt drugs on the side. She'd met him at a party when she bought Ecstasy from one of the girls he called his elves, twenty dollars for a few hours of guaranteed mindless entertainment.

"Hey," she said. "I thought you were in New Zealand."

"Just got back."

"So soon?"

"No point in staying. I sold all my tabs."

"You're joking me. The whole bible?"

"Yeah. I cut it up and told the Kiwis, 'Here, take the word of God.'"

Something in Jenny's laugh made Sara and Rachel start sneaking looks at her, really straining their peripheral vision. Their curiosity always soared when they sensed that Jenny had a man on the line. Sometimes she thought it was adorable, sometimes annoying.

"You must be rich now," she told Jeff.

"I couldn't spend all the money I made down there."

"What about up here?"

"We should hook up and see. You and me, you know?"

"Is that right?"

Coy or not, Jenny couldn't help thinking about a weekend in Vegas. Or a trip to Mexico, maybe Cabo. It had been two months since her last job ended ugly and she still hadn't taken the time to unwind. Maybe Jeff would come through for her.

"Let's check out some boxing," he said.

"I'm really not so crazy about boxing," Jenny said, too bummed to keep the disappointment out of her voice.

"It's not that Oscar De La Hoya bullshit. I'm talking about, like, underground boxing. In a warehouse or something. They won't even tell you where it's going to be unless you're tight with somebody. The guy that runs it gets his drugs from me. I don't know where he finds the fighters, jail maybe, but you wouldn't believe how these crazy fuckers fuck each other up."

Jeff was laughing, but Jenny said, "It doesn't sound funny to me." That was when Sara and Rachel stopped pretending they weren't eavesdropping and started staring.

"Come on, lighten up," Jeff said. "It's just a bunch of assholes who'd be kicking the shit out of each other anyway."

"I've got to go, okay?"

"What's wrong?"

"Nothing. It's just, I'm being rude to the friends I'm with and—"

"Aw, you gonna be like that? Okay, fine. But sooner or later we're getting together, and you won't be sorry, I promise." Jenny didn't take the bait, so Jeff plowed ahead. "This is your cell, right?"

"Right."

"I'll call you tonight."

"Cool," Jenny said, hanging up without a goodbye and knowing he wouldn't call because guys in his world never did.

Now she had to deal with Sara and Rachel, incredulity frozen on their faces by the chill she had put in the air.

"I can't believe you blew that guy off," Rachel said.

"I was talking to a guy?"

"You are such a bitch," Sara said.

"I thought you'd never notice," Jenny said, smiling sweetly.

"Well, we did," Sara said, "but you can make up for it. Tell us about the guy you were talking to."

"The truth wouldn't be half as fun as what you're imagining."

"No way," Rachel said. "The truth will set us free."

"Sorry, you'll have to set yourselves free."

"That gets old," Sara said as she and Rachel burst into laughter.

"I've got to go." Jenny was on her feet, shrugging on her backpack. "You're like totally obsessed with guys and I want to talk about poetry."

"You mean you were serious about Elizabeth what's-her-name?" Rachel said.

"Bishop. You should read her poems. They'll improve your dirty little minds."

"I'd still rather hear about the guy you blew off," Sara said.

Jenny heard her but kept walking, content to let Sara and Rachel conjure up their own fantasy about her life. Most likely the fantasy would never include massage, and yet massage was out there waiting to be discovered by anybody who looked hard enough. It was as obvious as the ad in the campus paper that Jenny had answered two and a half years ago, the one that said, "Cute Asian Girls Wanted—Lots of $, Lots of Fun." She was sure she wasn't the only cute Asian girl at Bay City who'd answered it.

They were everywhere, hotties who looked like they were majoring in nightlife on the Sunset Strip or in Koreatown or Little

Saigon, shaking their asses and searching for sugar daddies who plied them with Crown Royal. The Trendy Asian Bitches shopped at A|X and Bebe, wouldn't wear shoes that weren't platforms, did their makeup like movie stars, and hunted for boyfriends who drove Ferraris. No Benzes or Beemers for them.

Then there were the hoochie TABs, who took everything one step further. If their hair was colored, they wouldn't settle for mere blonde, they would look to L.A.'s chemical sunsets for inspiration and go red or purple, even orange. Their boob jobs were a revolt by girls too long dismissed as the young and the breastless—massive protuberances on tight little bodies, whose owners would go on cigarette-and-bottled-water diets the instant they hit a hundred and five pounds. It was the hoochie TABs who were most likely to do massage—they cultivated a look that screamed horny—but some straight-up TABs had done massage too, when they were fighting with the boyfriends or parents they counted on for money.

Jenny didn't feel like she fit in either category. Her hair was the color it had always been, black, and she was frightened by the thought of what one client had called "bolt-on tits." Globs of silicone inside her? No, thanks. She couldn't fathom spending a fortune on clothes either, and it was a rare day that she could be bothered to do her makeup according to the teachings of her TAB girlfriends. Her lone concession to fashion was that two-thirds of the things in her closet were black. All right, she liked shoes, too, especially stilettos and platforms, even though they made her feel like she was going to tip over.

But she read way too many books to be a genuine TAB or, God forbid, a hoochie TAB—and the books weren't romance novels. The only time she'd been tempted to dive into those was when a masseuse she worked with swore that reading them would make her better in bed. She didn't have a boyfriend then, so being great in bed didn't matter. The time she would have spent screwing was devoted to reading all the Dickens she hadn't got around to in high school. Halfway through *Oliver Twist*, she knew she had made the right choice.

If people wanted to say she was a little odd, that was fine with Jenny. She lived in a world of her own making, with her books and her extended periods of seclusion, and there was no sense in changing now. She felt safe, secure, even when the occasional troubling thought slipped through her defenses.

Sometimes doing massage bothered her, no matter how much she loved the easy money. But it wasn't a moral issue—some guys just needed to get off, others craved a little tenderness, and if they were married, well, maybe having a stranger pulling their plugs was what they were looking for. What gnawed at Jenny was that she knew she should be doing something with her life besides wondering how to spend her money while jerking off a guy she had never seen before and might never see again. She wasn't a rocket scientist, but she was bright—lots of clients had told her so, lawyers and writers, even a UCLA professor whose class she wouldn't have minded taking—and she appreciated her gifts enough not to want them to wither and die. It was a curse, kind of.

So were the thoughts that dogged her about those girls at the apartment on Sepulveda. Even when their massage names blurred in her memory, names being as changeable as fishnet tops and crotchless panties, she remembered the pain and terror on their faces. And the ominous stain beneath the black girl, the one who was so nasty in so many ways—Jenny remembered the stain most of all. At every recollection she scorned herself for not standing up to them, for not calling the cops or taking them to the hospital. Where had the nearest hospital been, anyway? She had no idea because she had never imagined needing one. But she should have loaded those girls into her car and found it. Instead, she had caved in to the black girl's orders—Contessa, that was her name—and she had been relieved when she ran, glad to have her money and her safety, never pausing to consider the unseen baggage she was taking with her.

The baggage was here now as she went through the contents of the safe-deposit box she kept at a Bank of America branch on Santa Monica Boulevard. She had other boxes at other banks, but this was the one where she stored most of what she saved in cash from massage. Her checking accounts made her nervous. She felt self-conscious when, two or three days a week, she deposited piles of money straight out of an ATM, and she worried about the IRS, too. Some weeks she made thousands of dollars and didn't pay a penny in taxes. She knew she should have saved more, but she was still comforted by those stacks of twenties, fifties, and hundreds, so neat and precise, right down to the rubber bands around each of them.

As she counted fifties in a private alcove, she began to wonder if any of them were from her last day on Sepulveda. It left her feeling disoriented, even queasy, as if the dark stain had somehow spread to her.

Jenny put the money on the table and tried to think of something else, but something else turned out to be the calls she had received after the rapes, all from girls in the business who were scared to death. When it got to be too much, she canceled the number they were calling. Just a few good friends had the number she kept, most of them unaware of what had happened or the life that had provided the money she was visiting now.

She took a deep breath and resumed counting it, wondering how long it would last, and what she would do when it ran out. She knew, of course. She just didn't want to admit it. Not while she was feeling like this.

4

Onus DuPree Jr. strolled into Skybar, on the roof of the Mondrian Hotel, and right away started feeling seriously antisocial. Even with the city lights twinkling below on the Sunset Strip and standup heaters keeping the customers nice and toasty, he wondered what it would be like to rob the movie stars he rarely saw there but always heard tourists gossiping about. He wondered, too, about making victims of the singers who had just gone platinum and the moneychangers who were forever inviting presidents and would-be presidents to their big-assed houses for cocktails and campaign contributions.

And here was the thing about DuPree: with his shaved dome and a navy blue turtleneck under his suede windbreaker, he could have passed for Skybar royalty. In fact he would have, at least on this night, if some sissy hadn't waltzed over the minute he got there and asked did he really produce Mary J. Blige's last album. "Get away from me, faggot," he said, knowing his words would spread through the bar like napalm, and not caring. For DuPree, half the fun of a place like this was fucking with the clientele.

He ended up at the bar with people giving him plenty of room as he sipped his cranberry juice and club soda and thought about the work he'd be putting in later. Three seats down was a porcelain blonde who had seen the guy she was with abandon her for some buddies, all of them turned out like lawyers or agents and big on laughs and high-fives. While DuPree shook his head at the waste of prime pussy, the blonde looked his way every now and then.

When he finally looked back, she held his gaze. He took it as an invitation.

"Shouldn't never be an empty seat next to you," he said as he slid onto the stool. "Hope you don't mind."

"You haven't heard me scream for help, have you?" she said.

"You a screamer?"

She raised her eyebrows and drained the last of her white wine.

"You better have another," DuPree said, and moved to flag down a bartender.

"A little on the assertive side, aren't we?" the blonde said.

"Got to be. I'm workin' against the clock."

"Oh." She feigned a pout. "So you're going to go off and leave me too."

"I'll come back—if I'm invited."

The blonde smiled and made a purring noise. An instant later, DuPree felt a hand clamp his right shoulder.

"Move along, LL Cool J," the hand's owner said. "The lady's spoken for."

DuPree turned in his seat and found himself looking at the guy who must have just remembered the blonde was with him. Had one of those dents in his chin and a tan he probably got on a boat of his own. He wasn't in any hurry to let go of DuPree's right shoulder.

"You don't take your hand off me," DuPree said, "I'm gonna give it back to you in pieces."

"You can talk all you want on your way out the door," the guy said.

"Marty?"

It was the blonde, trying to get the guy's attention. She'd seen the change in DuPree, how he wasn't the charmer who had sat down beside her any longer. Now he was what you never want to see step out of the shadows. But the guy was too wrapped up in his own drama to realize he had no chance against DuPree. None at all.

"Marty!" The blonde was close to losing it.

The guy turned to her, annoyed, and DuPree came off his stool, uncoiling like a rattler. He turned his left hand into a club that broke the grip on his shoulder, spun the guy a hundred and eighty degrees, and put him in a hammerlock so cruel it buckled his knees.

DuPree leaned close and whispered, "My name ain't LL Cool J, motherfucker."

The only response the guy could muster was the strangled sound of someone in severe pain. It fell to the blonde to say, "Don't hurt him, please." But that just pissed DuPree off more. And then he saw the guy looking desperately for his buddies.

"Ain't nobody gonna help you, bitch," DuPree said, grabbing the first finger he came to on the guy's hand and twisting it like a swizzle stick. The guy tried not to scream, but people nearby still heard him. DuPree didn't care about them. "Please," the blonde said. DuPree didn't care about her either.

The guy was whimpering now, and there had to be bouncers on the way. Maybe the guy's buddies were coming, too. DuPree looked the blonde up and down once more. "Damn, you are fine," he said. Then he snapped the guy's finger like a no. 2 pencil.

The guy's scream filled the air as DuPree shoved him to the floor face first and started toward the elevator. He had to wade through the gawkers who were already gathering. Those who saw what he'd done stepped out of his way. And all the while he kept telling himself to be cool. Just take his time. No need to run, no need to even walk fast. He was the king of the fucking jungle.

✣ ✣ ✣

A little before ten-thirty, as lights started to go out all along Hollyridge, DuPree pulled up beside the fence behind Chuck Berry's old house and parked looking down the hill. The night was too dark and the shrubbery too thick for him to eyeball things, but he knew from the changes out front that there had been a lot of work done on the motherfucker. It needed some serious beautifying after the way the bands that rented it had trashed the place, thinking they were honoring old Chuck by living like pigs—empty bottles, dirty needles, and women's stained drawers everywhere.

White boys acting like that's what it took to be black, DuPree thought. It hurt to contemplate the enormity of what they didn't know. Of course, being partial to Nas's bad-assed rap, DuPree might not have known either if the old man hadn't told him. Not that the old man was tight with Chuck or anything, but he had been to parties here even before he signed with the Dodgers, just out of Fremont High and acting like there wasn't any kind of shit he couldn't get away with. Said he shared the first white woman he ever had with Chuck himself, a bad-talking blonde straight out of that old-time porn where hairy ofays never wore anything except black socks. Of course it could have been bullshit, too. DuPree's old man threw bullshit around like he was running for president. But that had been his time back then, the fifties turning into the sixties, and Chuck Berry riding high before he took that underage Apache girl across a state line for what the law said was immoral purposes.

Thinking about it made DuPree glad he wasn't famous. Better to be a clean, well-dressed African-American criminal sitting in his black 5 Series BMW, a ride just right for looking like it belonged in the neighborhood. If any of the neighbors peeked out their windows and saw his car before going nighty-night, they'd most likely assume he was visiting somebody on the block. The fact that he was black wouldn't upset them as long as he wasn't coming through a window and pinning them to the wall with a spear.

DuPree was wiggling his toes comfortably in a pair of Bruno Magli cordovan loafers, the O.J. touch in his wardrobe, when his man came around the curve off Bronson and headed up the hill, driving too fast in his Acura MDX for such a narrow street. It didn't look like he noticed DuPree, which was what DuPree was counting on. Just keep everything normal, let the man do his home deliveries, like the one he'd be making to an actor in another minute or two.

The actor had struck it rich in the early nineties as a lovable goof in a sitcom that made being stupid look like a good thing. He had celebrated his good fortune ever since by shooting as much smack as he could without killing himself. The times he had tiptoed to the edge of the abyss, his standup girlfriend had been around to dial 911. Barely half his age and she was the adult in the equation, until she wound up loving heroin even more than he did. It figured he wouldn't be in any condition to call for help when she OD'ed. Now he sat up in a three-million-dollar house with a view of the Hollywood sign and a rat problem, grieving and staying as fucked up as he could, coming down just long enough to sleepwalk through another TV or movie gig that would finance his drug habit.

DuPree wondered if the hopeless motherfucker even remembered his dealer's name. He should have, seeing as how the dealer made deliveries three nights a week, always right around this time. But the important thing was, DuPree remembered.

He'd seen Teddy George for the first time six or eight months ago playing bass for Esther May at the House of Blues. Other than having a big head of rock-and-roll hair and pants so tight he must have been castrated to squeeze into them, George was nothing special musically, no Flea or Stanley Clarke. But DuPree started getting interested when one of the guys in his party said Esther had been a stone junkie back in the 50s, when she was taking R & B mainstream with a song called "Midnight Moan." Then someone else, a Latina with glitter on as much of her titties as DuPree could see, said if Esther was still using, she probably got it from Teddy George.

Turned out he dealt an upscale high to writers and directors in the Hollywood Hills, producers and lawyers in Beverly Hills, and agents, record executives, and moguls of every description in Bel Air, Brentwood, and the Palisades. The only time he didn't make his appointed rounds was when he was on the road; then his kid brother hauled the tar heroin, rock cocaine, weed, crystal meth, Ecstasy, Vicodin, and OxyContin. But with Esther May looking like she would spend her golden years nodding off, George had more and more time to devote to his nightly magical mystery tour.

DuPree had spent the past month figuring out the man's stops and which night was the busiest. He had time on his hands after the bank robbery in Porter Ranch, way the hell out there in the Valley. There might be even more downtime if he stayed away from the armored car job that was getting talked about. Armored cars seemed like too much trouble—more partners, more chance of gunfire and bloodshed, and the last thing he wanted was a piece of a shootout like that B of A shitstorm, two crazy motherfuckers with full body armor and insane firepower, and they still got their asses blown away. When it came to pain, DuPree was about giving, not receiving.

So he had gone solo, liking the feeling as he followed Teddy George partway one night, then partway another, piecing things together until here he was, waiting to cash in on a Thursday night. Thursdays were the heaviest with cheddar, George's clients most likely stocking up for the weekend and George not running a credit card operation. As DuPree wondered what that dumb-fuck actor up the street paid for his smack, George came rolling back down the hill and disappeared around the curve.

DuPree started his car and pulled out, punching up *Stillmatic* on the CD player, listening to Nas kick the shit out of Jay-Z and all the other Nee-groes too fucking stupid to realize that the flag is red, white, and blue, no room for black. An hour of this and DuPree would have his blood up right where he wanted it.

✢ ✢ ✢

The colonial's porch light was on, and DuPree could see the front door open and George step inside the way he'd done the other times DuPree had followed him to the Palisades. He'd stay four minutes, five tops, just long enough to conduct business.

DuPree used the time to ease his Beemer up two houses without turning on its lights. Then he snugged up his leather driving gloves and picked up his Luxeon Hand Torch from the passenger seat, $89.95 worth of flashlight straight off the Internet, approved by SWAT teams and the military, now on the verge of being tested in a criminal endeavor. He made sure the interior light was off before he opened the door and eased onto the street. He closed the door softly, then checked the nine-millimeter Glock tucked in the back of his pants and stepped to the other side of his car. If anyone should come along and ask—a cop, for instance—he had his big-assed flashlight out so he could say he was checking a tire that had been making some bad noises.

A minute later, as the porch light went off behind him, George came back down the walk without the grocery bag he had taken in. He was humming a tune that DuPree couldn't put a name on. George unlocked his MDX by remote, and when he started to open the door DuPree made his move, hurrying across the street toward his target, flashlight in his left hand and raised to shoulder height.

"Yo, Teddy," he said.

George grunted in surprise and turned around just as DuPree clicked on the flashlight, aiming the beam at his eyes. George threw up his left arm to block the glare.

"Who is it?" he asked, having no success whatsoever at keeping the uncertainty out of his voice.

"It's me, man."

"Who?"

DuPree, still advancing, could see George running through the file of black male voices in his memory bank, trying to find one that belonged in a neighborhood full of rich motherfuckers. That ruled out most of the musicians he had played with, drunk with, maybe even sold drugs to.

"Shit, get that fucking light out of my eyes so I can see you, dude."

Just as George came to the realization that he had never seen the black guy who was almost on top of him, DuPree said, "Yeah, sure." And he turned off the flashlight and clubbed George on top of the head with it, making a noise that sounded like a drum he had heard once in a reggae band.

George's knees buckled and he grabbed his open door to stay upright. DuPree skull-thumped him again, hard enough to draw blood and send the batteries flying out of the flashlight. George lost his grip on the door and did a face plant on the street.

DuPree kneeled and turned him over. Motherfucker had a bloody nose now, to go along with that gash on his coconut. DuPree dug through George's pants pockets, pulling them all inside out. His first discovery was a glassine bag containing cocaine, no shake, all rock, a little something to help him celebrate later. Then he moved on to George's faded Doobie Brothers tour jacket, wondering who the fuck the Doobie Brothers were until he unzipped an inside pocket and pulled out the night's grand prize. It was a wad of bills the size of his fist, and DuPree had a big fist.

The clock in his head told him to wait on counting the money. He straightened up and climbed behind the wheel of George's MDX, checking everywhere he could think of for more to steal. The glove compartment contributed a vial of pills and there was another, smaller roll of bills under the passenger seat. The only other thing of interest he found was a CD with "Britney Demo" written on it with a girlish star over the "i." Britney Spears? What self-respecting musician would have anything to do with her? Was George doing session work? Auditioning for her band? He couldn't be a fan, could he? All that cracker bitch was good for was bending over, and DuPree was positive he'd had better white pussy at Uni High, those little rich girls giving it up so nice for the football hero.

He pulled the CD from its diamond case and snapped it in half. Then he got out of the MDX, took a look at George on the ground, blood still oozing from his head and nose, and kicked the motherfucker in the ribs hard enough to hear one of them breaking. Then he kicked him again, trying for another. Fuck Britney Spears.

5

Kill someone and he never really goes away, not if you have a conscience. Alonzo Burgess had haunted Nick since that night in Oakland, toppled by one last four-punch combination and doomed to hit his head on the bottom rope. The result was the worst kind of whiplash, his brain stem snapping and the lights going out on his life.

Fourteen years later Burgess still ghosted through Nick's dreams and shadowed his waking hours, and the only time Nick got to come up for air was when trouble found him. He'd lost his blood-lust, and yet he had felt whole there in that parking lot, the gang-banger in a post-knockout fog and Eddie the shopkeeper pressing a hundred-dollar bill into Nick's hand and telling him to take his wife or girlfriend out to dinner. "Both if you got 'em," Eddie said. For just a few minutes, Nick embraced the return of his capacity for violence. But soon enough he was alone again, alone except for the specter of Alonzo Burgess.

Sometimes Nick would swear it was Burgess's voice in his ear, though he didn't remember hearing him speak even at the weigh-in, when boxing protocol smiles like a death's head at fighters with big mouths. Nick didn't remember saying anything either. They were just two warriors out to make seventy-five hundred apiece, him on his way up, a fight away from Las Vegas, thinking he'd be a champion someday—promoters would cut off body parts for a good white fighter—and Burgess the old campaigner, who had to sweat and spit and starve to make one-sixty. A human stepping stone, that's all Burgess was supposed to be, a middleweight education for a kid with eleven knockouts in eleven pro fights. But this was the thing Nick never told anyone, the thing he had a hard time admitting to himself even now: Until he saw Burgess's leg start twitching, he'd wanted to kill him.

Boxing could do that to you, make you forget everything nice you ever did outside the ring and turn you into a treacherous motherfucker. The man in the ring with you was intent on destroying you, and you had to destroy him first. Forget just beating him, even if you respected the guy. You wanted that son of a bitch on his back and the referee counting ten over him.

Alonzo Burgess sure as hell had that in mind for Nick, though you wouldn't have known it from the way he pawed and shuffled through the first four rounds. Then, not quite a minute into the fifth, as Nick peppered him with punches that puffed up his eyes and impressed the judges, Burgess dug a right hand into Nick's liver. Everybody in the arena must have heard him grunt with pain. But nobody except another fighter could have imagined the instant paralysis he felt or the breath he was gasping for and not getting.

To the half-filled house that was suddenly on its feet and howling, the next punch Burgess threw looked like a left hook that missed Nick's chin. It was the elbow trailing the fist, however, that was meant to do the damage, and it did, knocking Nick's mouthpiece halfway out. He had just enough of his wits left to tie up Burgess and waltz him into the ropes, reflexively throwing punches but far more eager to find a moment's peace before the referee made them break. He rested his head on Burgess's left shoulder, looking away from those unshaven jowls, treasuring every second he had to regroup.

Burgess responded by turning his shoulder into a weapon, abruptly bringing it up into the side of Nick's face. Nick reeled backward, unable to protect himself against the overhand right that Burgess brought crashing down on his head. He dropped like a sack of potatoes. It was what he deserved for getting suckered, and it would have been worse if he hadn't unscrambled his thoughts and climbed off the deck at the count of eight. The referee warned Burgess about the shoulder, but there was no disqualification, not even any points taken away. *Fuck it*, Nick thought, he'd take care of the dirty motherfucker himself.

He was so wrapped up in his anger that he scarcely realized his left eyebrow had been split until he was back in his corner and Cecil Givens, his trainer, was closing the cut with a mixture of Vaseline and adrenaline 1:1000. All the while, Cecil kept telling him not to let Burgess work him that way—just hit and run and let the old son of a bitch wear himself out. And don't fall for any more of his damn tricks.

Burgess just missed thumbing Nick's right eye in the sixth, and he tried stepping on his feet too, but Nick was too nimble, or maybe Burgess was too slow. Every round seemed to take a little more out of him, depleting any quickness he'd had to begin with, stealing the sting from his punches. What the hell, he was thirty-eight years old and he worked days on the docks. Motherfucker had a right to be slowing down as the sixth round bled into the seventh, the seventh into the eighth, and the eighth into tragedy. No fight of Nick's had ever lasted this long, but he was twenty-two then, and young legs trump old ones every time. Old legs turn to stone.

If Burgess saw any openings, he was a split-second late getting to them. The openings Nick saw, he filled with the punches that were his vengeance. And his vengeance began with a right to the heart that stopped Burgess where he stood and turned him into a statue to be disassembled. Nick followed with a right to the ribs. Was that a death rattle he heard somewhere inside Burgess then? No, he would tell himself later, just his imagination giving him a preview of the tape loop being embedded in his memory. And the beating went on.

He kept moving, always moving, striking from angles Burgess was no longer able to defend, throwing "punches in bunches," the way Cecil liked them, the phrase so innocuous that it sounded like something out of a nursery rhyme. Nick double-jabbed Burgess, stepped to the right and shot an overhand right to his head, stepped to the left and ripped a left hook to his ribs, back to the right for a right uppercut, back to the left for a hook to the body and another to the head, before tying a ribbon on the package with another double jab.

The whole time Nick was thinking, *You pulled that dirty shit on me, you motherfucker, and now I'm kicking your ass and you can't stop me. How do you like that, you motherfucker? You can't stop me.*

Cecil said later it was the referee who should have stopped it. Nick's manager, Frank Delzell, said it too, but he wasn't talking out of love, the way Cecil was; he was just trying to protect an investment. They wanted to blame everything on the ref, like he was a second-rate bum who froze at the worst possible time. And, okay, maybe he should have seen how Burgess's head was lolling helplessly, unprotected, a perfect target. But it was Nick who didn't scream, "Stop it or I'm going to hurt him!" Didn't do it even once, the way he had heard other, better fighters beg for mercy on their victims.

He kept his silence and put together that last four-punch combination. It was far from his best of the night, but by then it didn't matter. Burgess already looked soft and helpless when Nick finished with a straight right hand and watched him fall. When his head hit the bottom rope and his right leg started to twitch, Nick stopped wanting him dead.

Everybody kept telling him afterward that Burgess would be fine. But Nick had known different as soon as he saw the referee not bothering to count and the ring doctor scrambling through the ropes and the EMTs clamping an oxygen mask on Burgess's face. Those weren't images that could be erased just because a pretty girl at the Holiday Inn rubbed up against him later, wanting to kiss his boo-boos all better. Nick said no and uttered a silent prayer. In the morning he went to Mass and prayed even harder, him and Cecil. Delzell had a meeting to go to. When he heard that Burgess's wife was holding his hand at the end, Nick wanted to tell her he was sorry and try to explain how things had gotten away from him, how what a fighter fights for doesn't always turn out to be what he really wants to happen. But Cecil wouldn't let him see her.

Nick supposed that was for the best, if only because it gave him one less painful memory. He had learned over time to fight to a draw, stepping lightly, holding back in and out of the ring when the occasion called for violence. He'd lost at least a couple of women because he was too remote for them, and only when there was more at stake than self-interest did he tap into the reservoir of savagery that had made him a boxer to be reckoned with. The gangbanger opened the floodgate, but Nick would pay for it. The days ahead would be filled with the shopkeeper's cry—"Jesus Christ, I think he's dead"—and the nights would be a bed sheet twisted by regret.

And then there was Coyle groaning with worry when Nick told him about the gangbanger. All he could talk about was how his job would be toast, and his wife would kill him, and the skank he had nailed that afternoon would mark him as more trouble than he was worth. He barely paused to ask Nick if he had shit for brains, going up against a Pancho who wanted nothing more than a teardrop tattooed on his cheek for killing somebody.

"I would have given him the money," Nick said, "but I was afraid it wasn't just me he was going to shoot."

Coyle's expression turned to dismay. "You're going to be on the fucking news, aren't you?"

"I don't think so."

"Yeah, you are. Channel 9 or some shit. Like you're a goddamn hero."

"But there weren't any cameras there. Nobody talked to me. Reporters, I mean."

"You sure?"

"Why would I lie?"

"Everybody lies."

"I'm not lying."

"This when you hit me?"

"I'm not gonna hit you. Have I ever—" It was then that Nick realized his fists were clenched. He opened them and tried to smile. "You're my friend, man. I don't hit my friends. I didn't even want to hit that kid with the gun. He didn't give me a choice, that's all."

Coyle looked at Nick for a moment before he said, "Whatever. I got to get this truck in."

"You got to pay me, too," Nick said.

He was ready for another argument. Maybe he'd even get screwed over. It wouldn't have been the first time, picking up work the way he had lately, here and there, always in cash. Coyle practically radiated the sad story he wanted to tell about how the gangbanger had changed everything, but he caught himself before he could start.

"Two hundred, right?"

"Yeah," Nick said.

Coyle dug a roll of twenties out of his pants pocket. As he peeled off ten of them for Nick, he said, "I can't believe you're not going to be on the news."

But TV let the story slide, and the next day's *L.A. Times* gave it maybe two hundred words, identifying Nick as a former boxer working as a fill-in truck driver and letting it go at that. If it hadn't been a busy news day locally—an eight-year-old girl killed by a stray bullet in South-Central, the new chief of police raising hell about gangs, poor people dying in a hospital that was supposed to heal them—it might have been different. But Nick didn't keep up with the news.

The cops from Robbery-Homicide had him come downtown to give his formal statement. One of them said he'd seen Nick fight, and they all talked boxing, asking him to show them how he'd thrown the punch. He ducked that one by mumbling something about digging up an old Joe Frazier fight on tape if they wanted to see a hook that was really a wrecking ball. Next thing Nick knew, the cops were laughing about how that dumb fucking gangbanger's head was still ringing. But that didn't spare him from worrying someone would bring up Burgess until he was out of there and on his way home.

A couple of days later Coyle called, sounding like there weren't any flies on him. Said his wife was none the wiser: "If it's not *Survivor* or J. Lo and Ben, she don't want to know about it." There hadn't been any trouble at work either. Coyle had concocted a story about how he thought he had appendicitis so he called his buddy Nick to cover for him while he went to the *clinica* on Figueroa.

"Like I just happened to be in the neighborhood?" Nick asked.

"I said you lived around there." Coyle didn't give Nick a chance to protest. "Hey, we're talking about my brother-in-law here. It's not like he's going to ask for your address."

"If you say so."

"Matter of fact, he wants you to stop by and see him. Next time he has an opening for a driver, you could be at the top of his list, you play your cards right."

Nick said he would. What the hell, he didn't have anything else going for him.

✢ ✢ ✢

As soon as he heard someone knock on the door, Nick remembered that the security gate was broken. Going on four months now and the landlord hadn't laid a glove on it. Another knock and he decided that whoever was out there wasn't going away.

He opened the door and found himself staring at a man in a faded Hawaiian shirt that was just right for a day that was sunny and seventy. He was a couple of inches taller than Nick, but his watery blue eyes negated any danger in the size advantage. There was a hopeful smile beneath a badly trimmed gray Fu Manchu mustache that told the world he had worn his hair long before he lost it.

"Nick?" the man said.

"Yeah."

"I thought it was you, but there wasn't any name on your mailbox." The man extended his right hand. "Andy Rigby. From the *Times*."

"Oh, right. Andy." Nick shook with him, more polite than glad to have a visitor. "I didn't recognize you. Been a long time."

"For both of us," Rigby said, laughing self-consciously.

Nick thought he smelled alcohol when he invited Rigby in. Pretty early for that. And there was what looked to be a fresh scrape on Rigby's forehead, the kind he might have acquired falling off a barstool.

"How'd you find me?"

"Asked around. I don't live too far from here actually. Over in Venice."

Nick wondered which of the old fight guys had an address for him. It might have been Cecil. Nick had heard he was back in town.

"Still writing sports?" Nick asked.

"Whenever they let me," Rigby said.

They were sitting now, Rigby on the sofa, Nick on a kitchen chair that he had turned around so he could prop his arms on its back.

"I thought you were a big deal at the paper," Nick said. "Columnist or something."

"Used to be—you know how it goes." Rigby looked like he had a sad story he wanted to tell, but thought better of it. "They've got me doing local stuff now, small colleges mostly. Some boxing too, except there aren't many good fighters around anymore."

Nick shrugged. "I don't pay much attention."

Rigby nodded, biding his time, hoping Nick would go on. But everything Nick might have said stayed in his head. There was no forgetting how Rigby had gone to bat for him back in Chicago, when his manager was fucking him over, making side deals with promoters. Even when Rigby moved to L.A., he stayed in touch, calling Nick every six months or so, covering himself in case the kid won a title. He called after the Burgess fight, too, but Nick never got back to him. Now Nick was watching Rigby fidget nervously under the weight of those years of silence.

"I'd like to write about you," Rigby said at last. "You know, after what happened the other day."

"That's old news, isn't it?"

"What was on the police blotter, yeah. But I was thinking there's more to the story."

"Like human interest."

"Exactly."

Nick could see Rigby getting confident. Pulling a notebook from the hip pocket of his jeans. Extracting the ballpoint he had clipped inside his shirt, between the second and third buttons. Looking at Nick with an expression that would have been condescending if it hadn't been rooted in such obvious neediness.

For all the time Nick had been away from it, the game between sports writers and their subjects remained the same. They used you, you used them, and everybody profited—unless, of course, they were tearing you a new asshole. But most fighters talked even then, forever rooted in poverty, beholden to the writers who might help them tunnel out to a better life. Hell, Rigby knew about Nick's father stealing from him to keep a bookie's leg-breakers at bay, and Nick's mother walking out on his old man, and his kid brother Frankie getting shot to death when he tried to rob a chop shop. Rigby knew all the Pafko family secrets, which was why Nick could hardly believe it when he heard himself say, "Sorry, Andy. Not this time."

Rigby's watery eyes looked ready to spill over. "Think about it. A story like this, it might help you. You never can tell."

"Help someone else," Nick said.

✧ ✧ ✧

Two days later Coyle was on the phone so early the Mexicans hadn't even cranked up their radio yet. "You see the paper?" he asked.

"What paper?" Nick said, fogged in by sleep.

"The one that says you're some kind of hero. The fucking *Times.*"

"Oh." Nick had been afraid this would happen.

"'Oh' is right. As in 'Oh, shit, this is going to get back to Mrs. Coyle somehow and she's going to realize her loving husband has been fucking around again.' Jesus Christ, you telling me you couldn't have stopped this asshole reporter from writing about you?"

"What did you want me to do, Coyle? Tie him up and throw him in the ocean?"

"Well, he makes it sound like you're old friends or something."

"I know him from Chicago, that's all. Now let me ask you something: Is your name in the story?"

"No."

"So why are you bitching?"

"I'm just—"

"Go back to sleep."

"Can't. I'm already at work."

"Okay, then I'll go back to sleep."

Nick was about to hang up when Coyle said, "You don't talk much about fighting. Were you really as good as that story says you were?"

"How would I know?" Nick said. "I haven't read the story yet."

But he did later that morning, though not from top to bottom. He zeroed in on words or phrases that grabbed his attention, then looked elsewhere when they began to make him uncomfortable. He nodded at the mention of the two fights that had made him a contender, and he scarcely remembered some of the anecdotes that were intended to prove he was flesh and blood. Had he really strutted around Chicago's North Side shouting, "Who's the toughest guy in the neighborhood?" Had the raggedy kids who'd made him their hero really answered, "You are, Nick"?

Rigby had squeezed the essence of Nick's life as a boxer into seven hundred words. Nick couldn't make himself read the last of them, though. It hurt too much to be reminded of the days when he had a chance to be someone special. But there was no holding back the memories. There had been promises of big paychecks, and women had lined up to get in his bed, not girls from down the block or barroom sluts, but the kind you shine your shoes for. And then the good life that was supposed to be his went away in the time it took to send a man to his doom.

Now Nick sat with a hollow feeling in his chest and the sports section in his hands, consumed by thoughts of what might have been. It was as close to self-pity as he allowed himself to come, and he always beat it back with guilt and embarrassment. Alonzo Burgess was dead—no way the toughest guy in the old neighborhood could feel sorry for himself. What kind of joke would that have been? Nick smiled ruefully. He even laughed. There wasn't anything else for him to do until a reason to live came along, and he hadn't had one of those since the night the lights went out in Oakland.

6

Scott Crandall wondered if the Pink Dot geek had run over old ladies to show up so fast. Okay, geek was harsh, but really, what else could the guy be, fighting Westside traffic all day to deliver smokes and groceries, wine and home pregnancy tests? He might even have been driving one of the original Pink Dot VW Bugs, with the royal blue body, the Pepto-colored dots, and the pink-and-white propeller hat on the roof. Honest to God, a propeller on the ugliest car the sixties ever saw. Scott had heard Pink Dot still had a few of them on the road. Geekmobiles. And he knew there was only one species that could drive them. Geeks.

He handed over three twenties and a ten and told the geek to keep the change. Then he closed the door without waiting for a thank you and carried his two bags of goodies back to the IBM ThinkPad he'd fired up as soon as he had dragged his ass out of bed. He kept his computer on the dining room table, not that there was a dining room in his one-bedroom. It was more like a place to eat if he wasn't standing at the kitchen counter, wolfing down cold pizza or takeout Thai or—talk about inescapable for the man who couldn't cook—something from Pink Dot.

In fact, he planned on having a late breakfast/early lunch/ whatever there before he headed to Warner Bros. for a 1 P.M. casting session. So would it be spaghetti with marinara sauce or the Southwest taco salad? Better go with the salad. The spaghetti felt like it was frozen solid. Good thing it was in the same bag as his Smirnoff vodka and Twix candy bars. That would be everything for the evening if he spent it at home. Well, maybe he'd have a Twix now. Just one. And a cigarette.

Scott was chewing the last bite of his candy bar when he lit up an American Spirit. He swallowed, took a drag and returned his attention to tailfeathers.com. With *Daily Variety* and the *Hollywood Reporter* out of the way—took you twenty minutes to get through them and two hours to get over them—it would complete his Internet reading for the day. His only reading of any kind, not that anybody cared.

Tailfeathers was devoted to hookers and johns all over the country who preferred to call themselves providers and hobbyists. There were masseuses in the mix as well, very few of them certified by any board of health, more and more turning tricks the way masseuses never had a decade ago, when a pretty girl could bankroll her education or her lingerie and drug habit with hand jobs. Now they joined escorts under the imagined protection of the euphemism "provider." Scott supposed that such self-deception came into vogue after the people who ran Tailfeathers prefaced their home page by saying, "This site was created purely and solely for entertainment purposes." Still, the announcement always made him laugh, because it was partly bullshit and partly the absolute truth. He'd always found pussy entertaining.

Once a week or so, he would scan the L.A. escort reviews on Tailfeathers to make sure his girls weren't in there. He'd given them specific instructions not to draw attention to themselves that way. Vice cops probably spent more time reading Tailfeathers than the perverts did. Worse, the guys who wrote the reviews—assuming it wasn't the girls doing it themselves to drum up business—couldn't resist exaggerating golden showers, rim jobs, and ass banging. Back when he didn't care about reviews, Scott had checked one of his girls on Tailfeathers and saw that a guy had created a friend for her: "Sometimes one girl would fuck the other with a vibrator while simultaneously fucking me." The girl in question was a psych major from UCLA—killer body, desperately broke—who had shown up a virgin, so naive that Scott had to have a redheaded porno washout teach her how to jerk a guy off. When the virgin quit three weeks later, the other girls still hadn't seen her naked, much less getting creative carnally.

No time for Scott to read reviews today, though. No time to use the links on the reviews to check out the competition, either. He still hadn't taken a look at the scenes for his audition, and he wanted to do that before lunch. But the one thing he couldn't ignore was the discussion board. The board in L.A. was Tailfeathers' liveliest and busiest, hobbyists and providers exchanging sometimes surprisingly insightful notes on everything from STDs to falling in love on the job. Clients were warned when cops started busting massage operations, girls coming from out of town could line up business, and the rip-off bitches got outed.

Scott scrolled down the page, seeing the same names he saw on posts every time he checked Tailfeathers, not noticing anything out of the ordinary until he reached the bottom: "Providers Beware: Real Criminals Resume Rampage, LE Wants to Help." LE was shorthand for law enforcement. Everything else spelled trouble. "Shit," Scott said, clicking on the post with no more enthusiasm that he would have had for walking on hot coals.

The poster was a guy who called himself Concernedcitizen, a know-it-all douchebag who really did know a hell of a lot. Scott skipped the part where Concernedcitizen complained about having been called a grandstander for his previous warnings to providers. Nor did Scott want to waste his eyesight reading when Concernedcitizen got all liberal and sensitive, writing, "I'm sorry the men in question are African-American, but I have a moral obligation to report the reality as it has been reported to me."

"Yeah, yeah, yeah," Scott said. Then he arrived at the heart of the matter. These assholes had spent the last year raping and robbing massage girls all over the city, bouncing from the Westside to Los Feliz to the Valley, striking twice in a month, then crawling back under a rock until you damn near forgot about them. It wasn't the kind of story the straight media was going to pay attention to—Christ, they didn't have the time or space to chronicle all the murders in L.A.'s ghettos. So this unholy tag team came and went at will, and now they were back at it, having turned a two-girl operation on Beverly near CBS into a nightmare.

Concernedcitizen was on the case. "These predators may be responsible for as many as ten attacks," he wrote. Some of the victims apparently had gone to him instead of the police because he was a lawyer who would counsel them, not sell them out. But he made it sound like the cops sided with the girls this time: "While LE is our opponent on the issue of prostitution, LE is with us in deeming these two criminals far more dangerous than the hanky-panky of the providers. Should a well-dressed African-American gentleman show up at your door saying he works for a bank, he may have an accomplice waiting out of sight. Please do not let him in. Even call LE if he bangs on the door."

Scott skimmed the responses to Concernedcitizen's post—lots of outrage and indignation from other hobbyists, nothing from any girls. But he knew that in the provider community the drums were already beating. Hookers and hand whores read Tailfeathers devoutly, pissing about clients whose reviews made them sound like sluts and moaning about girls who claimed they were twenty-two when they wouldn't see thirty-five again. He'd heard that providers had their own website too, talking shop and rating both clients and bosses, but he'd never taken the trouble to track it down. That was more bitching than he could handle.

He caught enough shit every day from his own girls. There were seven of them now—the number seemed to go up or down every few weeks—and he knew they were primed to freak out at the bad news Concernedcitizen had passed along. At times like this, rampant fear was as much a part of the business as eye shadow.

When Scott had set up his first operation three years before, there had been a little accountant-looking dude who would take masseuses up on their offer of a shower and come out of the bathroom waving a gun and demanding all their money. The next year it had been a carpenter who preyed on skinny blondes, trussing them up, throwing them in the back of his van, and driving out to Palmdale to go animal on them. The carpenter wound up killing himself, although there was still talk that one of his victims' boyfriends had pulled the trigger. As for the accountant, who knew? He had vanished into the ether that seemed to consume most of the crazies who declared open season on girls who, when you got right down to it, were all but defenseless.

Not that the girls didn't try to do something. Scott knew that some of them hugged first-time clients coming through the door, thinking they could feel hidden weapons. There were probably also girls who carried Mace or even a small pistol—if wide-load pro football players could pack, why not hundred-and-five-pound hand-job artists? But Scott didn't want to think about a gun in the hands of some of the women he'd employed. Too many of them were so scary stupid that they'd wind up shooting the wrong person, and the wrong person might be him.

Scott's first impulse with the latest maniacs to descend on the business had been to call them the Love 'Em and Leave 'Em Bandits, but his girls didn't laugh, they just became more skittish than ever. Now it was clear that the only way he'd be able to stop them from getting any crazier was to hire security. He'd done it before, but that didn't mean he liked it or anything he had heard about it. There were stories of off-duty LAPD providing muscle for a girlfriend in the business, but that could have been bullshit. What your average massage operation got for security was several cuts below the knuckle draggers who worked as rent-a-cops at shopping malls and car shows. The best Scott had come across were an apartment manager's kid brother, a recovering car salesman with a speech impediment, and a guy in one of his acting classes who wanted to be a professional wrestler.

His head swimming at having to choose from a pool of morons, Scott lit another smoke off his old one, flipped open his cell, and dialed. One ring later, he heard the voice he was counting on to reassure him that things would be cool.

"What?"

DuPree never turned off the attitude for a second. Sometimes Scott was tempted to call him Junior just to annoy him, but even on the telephone, the motherfucker was intimidating. One word and Scott could picture him, elegant and dangerous at the same time, shaved head, high cheekbones, ropy muscles, and a stare that could shrivel your balls to the size of raisins. Scott was sure he'd done time.

"Where you at, yo?" Scott couldn't help himself. He lapsed into black-speak every time he talked to the guy.

"Having my morning latte, checking out the foreigners." DuPree started most days at the Coffee Bean at Sunset Plaza, Eurotrash central. "You going to waste my time with questions you know the answer to, or you going to tell me why you're calling?"

"You know me too well, man."

"So?"

"So you hear anything about a couple brothers robbing trick pads? Raping the girls?"

"Brothers?" DuPree was keeping his voice down, making sure nobody could overhear his business. "As in African-American males?"

"Yeah, that's right."

"And you sure that's what they are? Brothers, I mean."

"Well, it's what they're saying on the Internet."

Scott tried to sound cool. It should have been easy; he was an actor, after all. But DuPree was the shit, and sometimes Scott couldn't get around that.

"They?" DuPree asked. "They who?"

"Some lawyer. That's what he says he is, anyway. On Tailfeathers. You know, the website. Said he'd heard from some girls that these motherfuckers—"

"The brothers."

"Yeah. They're out there running around, menace to society and all that shit."

"Okay. Okay. It's clearing up for me now. You make these assumptions, and then you come to me because I'm what, your connection to the thug life?"

"Look, man, I'm not dissing you." Scott hated to backpedal. It happened every time they talked about something serious, and DuPree never broke a sweat. "I'm just trying to see which way the wind is blowing, that's all."

"I didn't even know it was blowing. You want something specific, you better call up the"—DuPree's voice dropped to a sinister mocking whisper—"Bloods and Crips, ask 'em yourself, 'cause I got nothing to do with them. You hear what I'm saying?"

"Hey, I'm sorry. I just thought—"

"I know what you thought and it was wrong. Now, we done?"

Hardly, Scott thought. He wanted to ask DuPree if he knew any guys—okay, thugs—who could provide security at the apartment. He'd hoped DuPree might be interested himself. The guy had never passed up a session with one of the girls, free, of course. But all Scott could say was, "Yeah, I guess so. We're still cool, right?"

And for the first time since DuPree had picked up, Scott heard him chuckle. "You know we are," DuPree said. "You my nigger."

✤ ✤ ✤

He didn't shave for his audition, but how many actors did anymore? He didn't bathe either, which was a private joke on Hollywood that he shared with Steve McQueen. He'd heard that

69

anybody who wanted McQueen back in the days of *Bullitt* and *The Thomas Crown Affair* had to be willing to scrub his unwashed ass because he wasn't going to do it himself.

That was how Scott wanted it, too. Obviously, suits from every studio trampled each other to do the honors for McQueen. Scott's ass, meanwhile, wouldn't have meant anything to anybody important if it were stuffed with silver dollars. And yet Scott maintained the fiction of his spiritual connection to McQueen. It helped get him over the rough spots careerwise, of which there had been many for, oh, the last decade or so.

The other thing Scott hadn't done as he drove his 1988 Porsche Carrera onto the Warner lot was give the sides for the casting session so much as a glance. His agent had faxed them over last night, but out of habit and a severe lack of enthusiasm, he had put off reading them for this morning. Then the Internet gossip about the rapes had screwed things up, and DuPree had done absolutely nothing to unscrew them. DuPree had spoiled his appetite, too. Scott had planned on using the time he was stuck in traffic to get his head around the scenes he was supposed to do, but the 405 was wide open, and so was the 101, and he couldn't remember the last time that had happened.

He couldn't celebrate being twenty minutes early, though, because if he showed up now, he would just look desperate. And he wasn't desperate, not for a guest-star gig on yet another cop drama, this one called *Stringer*. He was pissed off was what he was. How could he be anything else at the prospect of his ten thousandth audition? Even with a career at low tide, he thought he deserved better. He should be taking a courtesy meeting with the executive producer and the director, and the job should be his if he wanted it.

This was TV, for Christ's sake. He'd done it, been a star as a matter of fact. Well, a little bit of a star. Fifth lead on a young doctors-in-love show at the end of the eighties, one of those ensemble things loaded with actors who were still turning up in big-budget features and playing leads in artsy-fartsy indies. He, on the other hand, had gone on to play the title character in *Stormy Weathers*, which was what the trades called "a syndicated actioner." Translation: off-network, non-prime-time junk. If the show contained one legitimate surprise, it was that Scott didn't lose his mind doing it for three seasons and sixty-six episodes. His salvation was the fifty grand he made per ep, just about what he needed to afford his bad habits, an ex-wife, and two kids. And he'd assumed his price would go up as soon as he jumped back on the prime-time gravy train. But the only train he found was the one that hit him with the news that he didn't count for much anymore.

He was thirty-one then, and now it was ten years later and all he had to show for the passage of time were two failed pilots, twenty or so guest-star gigs, a handful of bad cable movies, and a spreading girth that told him he needed to get to the gym more often. He still had his hair, though, as well as enough ego to believe he was better than any of the other clowns who were there on the second floor of Building 9 to read for the part of—what was this scumbag private eye's name? Grondyke, that was it. Al Grondyke. He sounded about right as fodder for *Stringer*'s hero.

After killing time smoking and feeling sorry for himself, Scott checked in with a pleasant middle-aged woman who must have been the executive producer's assistant. Then he scoped the waiting area for actresses who had worked massage for him—didn't want any embarrassing moments—and actresses who gave off a vibe that they might. It was a no on both counts. There were two girls who looked like they should play nuns; everybody else was male, and at least two of them had to be up for the same part as Scott. The moment he looked at the lines for his first scene, another prospective Grondyke walked in, talking loud enough on his cell phone for everyone to hear and sucking the energy out of the room.

"Yeah, I just did a twenty-minute short. Corporate espionage, definite Hitchcock overtones. It was some kid just out of USC. He was going to use it as his student film, but it screened at Harmony Gold and now they're trying to get it in some festivals. Dante Spinotti took a liking to him. How's that for being anointed, a genius cinematographer like him? Anyway, Dante called over to Paramount and arranged camera packages. We were shooting every day with two- and three-camera setups, ten different locations around town."

The show's casting director shut up the energy thief by calling him in ahead of everybody who had gotten there before him. By then, there was a bad echo in Scott's head, courtesy of the lines he was trying to memorize. "You're playing on my front lawn, Stringer. I want you off." Hadn't he given Sonny Crockett that warning on *Miami Vice*? "If you get any deeper in this mess, you might as well say, 'Goodbye, cruel world,' and pull the flusher." That was *Hunter*, wasn't it? Or maybe *Silk Stalkings*, not that anyone remembered *Silk Stalkings*. No wonder reality TV was on fire—all those old cop dramas had been the same show, just different actors, settings, and budgets.

It wasn't the first time he had thought of that, but he had never done it with a job within reach. This was when he was supposed to call on his powers as a thespian to defeat the sameness of the material, to spin the stereotypically sour Al Grondyke in some new and unforeseen way. God knew Scott needed the fifty-two hundred dollars he could make on *Stringer*—and he'd ask his agent to demand final position on the acting credits, the one where it would say "And Scott Crandall" like he was a big deal.

Quite frankly, though, he was beyond caring. Without even thinking about it, he rolled up his sides and let the crushing monotony of his career drive him deep into his seat. He neither moved nor let the name Grondyke enter his consciousness again until the casting director summoned him for his three minutes in front of *Stringer's* producers. As he walked through the door, the infinite wisdom of his decision to tune out was validated. The casting director was pulling aside the actor who had just read, a guy Scott actually liked. "The producers want you to come back later and meet the director," she was telling him. "And don't change a thing—you were perfect." Scott knew instantly that he was dead on arrival.

He didn't bother getting upset when he saw that the three producers he was reading for were far more intent on their lunches, one very crunchy salad and two sandwiches dripping with what looked like Russian dressing. When the casting director asked if he wanted to do his scenes sitting or standing, he had to resist the impulse to say, "Standing—on my head." But he managed to annoy her anyway by reading every one of his lines and hardly bothering to make eye contact with her. She was staring death rays at him as he left. Of course that might also have been because of his response when one of the producers, the young one naturally, couldn't have been out of his twenties, confided that he still had a *Stormy Weathers* T-shirt. "No shit?" Scott said.

He would deal with the inevitable fallout from the casting session later. All he wanted to do now was get to Patys in Toluca Lake and dig into a hot turkey sandwich with mashed potatoes and gravy. Those fucking producers had reminded him how hungry he was.

He headed toward a table that an older blonde waitress was clearing. She had her hands on an abandoned copy of the *Times* when he snatched it from her, an act of daring that earned him a nasty look and a little advice: "If you want it that bad, make sure you take it with you." He flashed a smile that sent her to the kitchen muttering and flipped through the ketchup-stained paper until he found the sports section. Shaq and Kobe were getting along for a change—what was up with that? And then it didn't matter because he saw a story about a fighter he remembered seeing back when both of them had futures. By the time he finished reading it, he didn't care that the waitress hadn't come back yet. He'd had an epiphany, and if the producers who never hired him anymore didn't know the meaning of the word, they could look it up.

7

Jenny wanted to see how high she could bounce off the sofa, treating it like a trampoline, her long hair flying and her laughter filling a designer-perfect living room. Up she'd go, her eyes pinwheeled by the blur of Impressionist paintings and Moroccan pottery, and when she descended she would see her friend Rosie bouncing up toward the stratosphere she'd just left and loving it as much as she had. Rosie did massage too. Gentle and willowy, she was a Singapore fantasy right down to her broken English. But she was self-conscious about her accent until she took a hit of Ecstasy. Jenny, on the other hand, did E because it made her feel so good, even now when the guy who had invited Rosie and her up to the Hollywood Hills was running back into the room, screaming at them.

"Get the fuck offa there! That's a two-hundred-thousand-dollar sofa!"

"What?" Jenny said, unable to stop bouncing on demand, just hoping she wouldn't go as high as she had before.

"The fucking sofa! It cost two hundred thousand fucking dollars!"

"No way," Rosie said, laughing harder than ever.

"Goddammit, I'm not fucking around!"

The guy looked as angry as the music he and his band played. He wasn't the lead singer—if he was, he probably would have been in jail or rehab—but he was supposed to be this great guitar player. He even had a contract with a major label to do a solo album. At least that's what he had told Jenny and Rosie at the Falcon in Hollywood when they were making up their minds to take off with him. His house sounded great, Spanish, built in the twenties, featured in *Architectural Digest* the year before he moved in. The drugs sounded even better.

They were still making Jenny smile as she rummaged through her brain for the power to reason with someone who was seriously pissed off. The best she could come up with, besides the good sense to stifle a laugh, was a meek, "We're sorry." Every other part of her was begging to start bouncing on the sofa again. After all, she and Rosie were still standing on it.

"Fuck sorry," the guy said. "You gotta leave. Now."

That struck Rosie as the funniest thing she had heard all night. "Deported," she said in her own special way.

"What?" the guy said.

Jenny offered a translation and gave Rosie a look that begged her to shut up. Rosie started giggling so hard that it looked like she was having a seizure. Before the guy could go off worse than he already had, Jenny said, "She was making a joke."

"Well, I'm not laughing, okay?" he said. "And Jesus Christ, get down from there before you fuck it up any worse."

"We took our shoes off," Jenny said. It was the best defense she could muster.

While the guy was saying he didn't give a shit, she grabbed Rosie, who was still having a giggling fit, by the hand, and the two of them stepped carefully onto the dark wood floor, like they were afraid it would move.

That was when Jenny was reminded of how tall the guy was and how small they were. There must have been more than a foot difference, and the guy's tats and piercings made him scary even though he was concentration-camp skinny. Then he spoiled everything by saying, "If you silly cunts ruined that sofa, my parents are going to kick my ass."

For the first time in her life, Jenny didn't frown at being called a cunt or fight back by saying something equally nasty. She was too busy recoiling with surprise. "Your parents?" And then she burst into laughter. Rosie, who may or may not have understood what the guy had said, resumed laughing along with her. Mr. Rock-and-Roll Drug Fiend still lived with Mom and Dad. That was some funny shit.

✤ ✤ ✤

By the time she dropped Rosie off at her boyfriend's place in Los Feliz, they had stopped laughing. They said they would have to hang out again soon, but Jenny wasn't so sure about that. It wasn't like they were big friends or anything. Rosie had just happened to call when Jenny was starting to feel the walls of her apartment closing in on her, and one thing had led to another.

It had been fun but only in the fast-evaporating way that Jenny always had fun with the girls she met doing massage. Most of them weren't very ambitious, or smart even, and they always seemed to be stuck with boyfriends who were only too happy to live off what they brought home. Jenny tried to think better of herself, but maybe she was a snob. Maybe she was the same as them. *Oh, God,* she prayed as she drove home, *please just let this be the depression that always follows Ecstasy.*

Here was this drug that gave her more pleasure than anything she had ever taken. It was like a serotonin overload, an orgasm for the pleasure center of the brain, but two or three hours afterward, it always felt like the world was caving in on her. She wondered if she got depressed because the makers put rat poison in it, and if the urge to jump around like a maniac was just a side effect. The only thing she was positive about was that E shouldn't be legalized. The law was the way it was to keep stupid people from doing too much of something. She knew she wasn't stupid—okay, sometimes maybe—but she didn't want to think about that now.

It was almost 4 A.M. when she walked in the door of her apartment, a one-bedroom on the first floor of a homely stucco building northwest of Sawtelle and Olympic. On the table by the front door were the schoolbooks she'd had every intention of reading before Rosie called. She had a paper due Monday in her Vietnam War class, and had planned to work on it tonight—well, it had been Thursday night but now it was Friday morning. She would go to sleep, and when she woke up she would start working on her paper.

Thinking about it made her wish she had stayed in touch with Tran, a Vietnamese girl she'd met doing massage in North Hollywood. Tran's family had escaped the Communist takeover on a rickety little boat, and sometimes when Jenny looked at her, with her delicate features and gentle eyes, she imagined Tran surviving the storms at sea by clinging to her dream of America. But what kind of dream was it that had led her to a jack shack with a rotting carpet? The answer to that question was unhappy, and Jenny didn't do unhappiness. It cut too close to her own life and to the shadow world she was trying to leave behind.

Massage was supposed to be a means to an end, not a defining experience. She wasn't even doing massage now, so why should it be on her mind so much? She didn't want to know the answer. Better she should climb into bed—a mattress on the floor, really, with lots of pillows—and treat herself to a couple of Elizabeth Bishop's poems before she went to sleep. She pulled the covers up to her chin and leafed through *The Complete Poems: 1927–1979* until she found "Squatter's Children." It was a favorite of hers, but before she got to the second verse, the one with the storm gathering behind the house where the girl and boy are playing, she was asleep.

She rejoined the living ten hours later with her good intentions intact. They stayed that way through a breakfast of green tea and strawberry-banana yogurt. She knew she should have real fruit around, oranges or apples or something, but she really didn't like fruit very much. It sucked that Gummi Bears weren't good for you. If they were, she would have been the world's healthiest person.

She grabbed a handful anyway as she sat at the kitchen table that doubled as her desk, fighting off the urge to read more Bishop or play *Tiger Woods PGA Tour 2003*. When her eyes fell on one of the books she'd gathered for research on Vietnam, she was afraid she would never open it if she didn't do it now. Her self-imposed guilt trip sent her to the book's index, where she began looking for something about Ho Chi Minh and his relationship with the United States before the domino theory warped American thinking. She found it with the greatest of ease, but before she could start feeling virtuous, her private line rang with classical music. She could never remember the title or the composer. It was probably because the only people who had the number were two masseuses, an ex-boyfriend who wasn't an asshole, and the girl who was calling now.

Lindsey was a friend from high school who had stayed in touch, and when she moved into her own apartment a year and a half ago, the first person she'd invited over was Jenny. It was a gesture that still made Jenny feel good, so now she found herself answering the phone and getting an earful from Lindsey about the other women at the boutique where she worked. "One of the girls keeps farting in the changing rooms," she said.

But a little stink was nothing compared to what her boyfriend was putting her through. She said he was a gaffer, like Jenny was supposed to know what that was, and for the last two months he'd been working on a movie in North Carolina. Lindsey thought he was cheating on her. When she called his motel room, a woman answered, and he got on right away and said it was somebody he worked with and they had just wrapped shooting. Lindsey didn't believe him because the three-hour time difference meant it was almost midnight back there. Jenny said they'd probably been doing night scenes—"Movies have them, you know"—but Lindsey didn't want to hear it. She was too bummed. She didn't have the money to fly to North Carolina to confront her boyfriend, and if she wasn't careful she was just going to buy a couple of pints of Chunky Monkey and eat them both.

"You don't want to do that," Jenny said, remembering how Lindsey had boasted of losing twelve pounds the last time they had talked. Was that really two months ago? Maybe Lindsey had already gained the weight back. She was tall, five-ten at least, and she had admitted to weighing as much as a hundred and sixty-five pounds. It was probably more, since women rarely told the truth about things like that. But what mattered now was that Jenny could relate to what Lindsey was going through with her boyfriend, so she said, "You want to hang out?"

Lindsey wasn't like Jenny's Korean party-doll friends, who thought the only place they could have a good time was in a K-Town nightclub the size of an airplane hangar. Lindsey was beyond safe; she was sane. She wouldn't think it was cool to have a waiter drag her over to a table full of socially inept guys who blew cigarette smoke in her face and thought drinking gallons of watered-down Crown Royal made them charming. She might even laugh at nerds who were scared that Jenny, at twenty-two, was too old for them.

And Jenny thought she would be in good shape to work on her paper on Saturday and Sunday even if she blew off tonight. She believed it right up until the moment she walked into Lindsey's Culver City apartment and Lindsey said, "I want to get laid tonight."

✤ ✤ ✤

Lindsey got what she wanted in the spa at a condo complex in Marina del Ray. It was sometime after midnight and Jenny was a witness. She had seen people have sex before, but both times had been in two-girl massage sessions and the incentive was cash. This time, judging from the sounds coming from the other end of the spa, it was all about pure animal lust.

Jenny and Lindsey had hit a series of bars in Venice and the Marina before Lindsey found Mr. Right-for-a-Night. He was a web designer named Randy who had a gap between his two front teeth and knew a lot about *The Simpsons*, which impressed Lindsey and meant absolutely nothing to Jenny. Randy wasn't quite as tall as Lindsey, but that didn't matter, especially when they were in the water.

"Somebody's having fun," Randy's muscular, red-haired friend Doug murmured to Jenny.

Doug seemed like more of a puppy dog than a horndog, which was why Jenny found herself with him at the other end of the spa, the two of them as naked as Lindsey and Randy, watching the steam rise off the warm water. Jenny could feel Doug's breath on her neck, and then his lips, small kisses, more like nibbles really, and not altogether unpleasant. He wasn't her type—she liked guys who were older or cuter, or both—but just to show she wasn't antisocial, she turned her face to him, flashing a smile that was an invitation to a kiss. He gave her one—and then he grabbed her left breast and twisted her nipple like it was the dial on a combination lock.

"Ouch," she said, trying to keep her voice down as she pushed his hand away.

Doug looked confused. Either he couldn't get his head around Jenny's lack of enthusiasm or no woman had ever suggested that the work he obviously did with weights didn't translate into a lover's touch.

"Sorry," he said.

But his hand went right back to her breast, and he moved in for another kiss, this time adding some tongue. Jenny pulled away, leaving it hanging in midair for a second before he put it back in his mouth. "Gross," she said.

At the same time Lindsey was going into overdrive. "Yes, yes, yes," she said. Or maybe it was "Uh, uh, uh." Jenny had noticed that passion took a toll on enunciation. Doug, meanwhile, was using the love noises as the cue to make his big move. More kissing, more groping, everything in his master plan to get Jenny to do it in water she had every reason to believe was a germ hatchery.

"You know you want to," he said, breathing heavily.

"In your dreams."

Suddenly she was under water. Doug's hand was on top of her head, holding her there, and she wasn't going to get back to the surface until he let her, no matter how hard she flailed her arms, no matter how fervently she wished she'd had time to take a deep breath. At last she stopped thrashing and started wondering how long he was going to keep her there. Twenty seconds must have gone by already, maybe thirty.

Just when she thought she had hit her limit, he pulled her back to the surface, flashing a smile that she thought looked idiotic and that he probably thought was seductive.

"Are you on crack?" she gasped.

"I want to fuck you," he whispered.

"And I want to scream for the cops."

Down she went again. *Oh, my God,* she thought, *he really is going to kill me.* At last she started fighting back, hitting him, scratching him, twisting and turning to get his hand off the top of her head. She thought she had succeeded when he let her resurface, but as soon as she called him "asshole," he pushed her back under. It happened twice more like that, and then she heard the voice that became her salvation.

"Dude, give her a break, huh?"

It was Randy at the other end of the spa, leaning around Lindsey, who was still riding him to glory, not missing a stroke.

"What are you talking about?" Doug said.

"Like, you're trying to drown her," Randy said.

"I'm just fucking around."

"You stupid motherfucking motherfucker!" Jenny shouted, wishing she were more fluent in profanity.

"Hear that, man?" Randy said. "She doesn't like it, so cut that shit out."

It looked like he wanted to say more, but Lindsey pulled his head back to where he could bury it between her breasts.

"Whatever," Doug said, his shoulders sagging.

Jenny couldn't believe what she was seeing. "You're pouting? Why, because you didn't kill me? Jesus, you've got to be the biggest asshole in the world. Maybe the biggest asshole in the whole history of assholes."

Doug looked up as if he was going to defend himself, only to stop before he started. Even if he had said something, though, no one would have heard him, because Lindsey came with a scream that must have awakened the entire complex.

As soon as he got out from under her, Randy made his way down to Jenny. "Hey, you're really cute, you know that?" said the guy she thought was her hero. "We should do a threesome, me and you and your friend."

"You don't even remember her name, do you?" Jenny said.

"The moment's more important than what we call ourselves," Randy said, leaning forward to kiss her.

Jenny turned her head, giving him nothing more than a cheek. Then she stood and said, "I am so out of here."

"Come on, don't leave yet," Randy said.

Jenny had her gaze locked on Lindsey. "You got what you wanted," she said. "Can we go now?"

"I guess," Lindsey said.

One by one they climbed out of the spa, the girls leading the way. When Jenny glanced back, she saw a condom floating on the water.

✤ ✤ ✤

Two-seventeen A.M. Home again. Her hair was still wet and her Vietnam War project was still waiting to be done. Wondering if she should forget about sleep and start working on the paper, she sorted through the mail she hadn't bothered to look at for days. There were notices for shoe sales she would never go to, two-for-one offers from pizza joints, pleas for donations from charities, credit card bills, and offers to get new credit cards. It was all stuff she had seen before until she reached the bottom of the pile and found an official-looking envelope from the DMV. What did they want? Her license renewal wasn't due until summer. She opened the envelope and what she found inside left her feeling like she was back under water, drowning, with no one to save her this time.

8

On the days when work didn't find him, which was most days, Nick walked. The only thing that could keep him inside was one of those special-effects storms L.A. had when it got any rain at all. Otherwise, he would hoof it west on Olympic, then south on Bundy, and down to Pico, where he would head west again. The closer he got to the ocean, the more homeless people he saw. They seemed to him a reminder that things always balance out: You want the Pacific, you have to take the human flotsam and jetsam. Poor bastards. Sometimes Nick would give one of them his spare change when he grabbed a sub at the Italian deli he liked on Lincoln. Problem was, there were always more of them than he had change.

He'd sit at one of the outside tables and ask himself how he was going to get out of the dead end his life had become. When it came to work, if there was any baggage to be handled, he couldn't find it. There didn't seem to be any nails to be pounded or ditches to be dug, either. Trucks to be driven, well, he'd find out about his one shot at that soon enough. He knew he should keep looking just the same, but he'd reached the point where most days he couldn't stand to beat his head against that particular wall. The best he could do was try to come up with something he hadn't thought of. When he'd gone without an answer for as long as he could stand it, he'd eat the last of his sub and head for home along Santa Monica Boulevard.

He could kill a good three hours that way, always walking, never running. Running reminded him of roadwork, and road-work reminded him of boxing, and boxing intruded on his thoughts often enough without his encouraging it.

Some days he made it back to his apartment wishing he were still on the move. More than once, he turned around and went back out the door, walking up to Westwood for a glimpse of the pretty girls from UCLA. Then it would be down to Rhino Records, where he'd heard "The Dark End of the Street" for the first time. It was about cheating lovers who can't stay away from each other, and it sounded melancholy enough to be played at a funeral for their good sense. Nick hadn't been in a jam like that in years, but the song touched something in him just the same.

When he was out of places to go, he sat in front of his twenty-one-inch Toshiba, the nicest thing in his apartment though he hadn't paid a cent for it. The previous tenant had left it behind when he fled without paying his rent for four months. He had pirated cable service too, so Nick found himself with more chan-nels to stare at numbly than he'd previously known existed. Ball-games ate up time the best—didn't matter which sport—and old movies were good too, particularly when Bogart was in them. Or Gregory Peck, the one his mother had always had a crush on. Nick thought it was because Peck seemed like the kind of decent guy his father had never been.

He was watching *To Kill a Mockingbird* the night Cecil Givens called, first time in five or six years, saying they should get together for a meal. Cecil's voice was still deep and mellow, a touch of the South in it even though he'd never done anything there except fight and catch the first thing smoking out of town. Cecil said to meet him at the Pantry. There was a cook there he wanted to see, a Latino guy who had done some boxing before he got in trouble with the law. Cecil needed to ask if the guy could help a friend of his get a wait job. His friend was a reformed burglar, and when

Cecil said reformed, Nick could picture the laughter in his heavy-lidded eyes.

The laughter was still there when Nick spotted Cecil watching him make his way down the line that seemed to form outside the Pantry every minute of the twenty-four hours it was open daily. Cecil looked a little thicker through the middle and his forehead was higher—what the hell, he had to be in his sixties—but he still had a tidy mustache, a soul patch, and a silky way of moving. Before he'd turned to training, he had been a damned good middleweight. With a better manager, he might have been a champion—or maybe not, because no manager could have kept him from getting shot. His kid brother had beat up some crazy son of a bitch in a street fight, and the crazy son of a bitch was determined to spill the blood of someone in the Givens family, didn't matter who. Cecil never fought again.

There would be no hugs now, no backslapping or pronouncements that it had been too long. "Good to see you, man," was all Cecil said. It was enough. He had always been about efficiency, in the ring and in life.

"I thought you were still in Vegas," Nick said.

"I am, most of the time."

"With Bettina?"

"Most of the time." Cecil frowned. "What the fuck you smilin' about?"

"How some things never change," Nick said.

The frown disappeared as Cecil rolled a toothpick on his tongue. "I like my freedom, man. She knows it."

"This where you come for freedom?"

"L.A.?"

"Yeah. You got a place here, right?"

"Over by Crenshaw, uh-huh."

"She know about it?"

"There's plenty in Vegas that keeps her busy."

Cecil smiled, and Nick felt himself give in to the rhythm their conversations always had. Nick was the puncher and Cecil the counter-puncher. Nick had just been away from him for too long, that was all.

Once they were seated, a waiter as grim as a seven-year jolt at Chino slung plates of coleslaw and sourdough bread in front of them. If they wanted something in the way of vegetables or an appetizer, there was a lazy Susan filled with radishes, carrots, and celery sticks. "No fairy food," a cut man once told Nick. The menu was on a wall that was the only color it could be, the color of grease. Maybe it had been painted since a former mayor had bought the place, but it hardly mattered with all the meat that got cooked there every day. The place wouldn't have looked right any other way. Nor would the waiter have fit in if he had brought them their Bud Lights and taken their order—a porterhouse for Cecil, a New York for Nick—with anything other than a look that suggested he had a shank in his belt.

Once he was gone, Nick asked Cecil, "The guy you're helping out, he have as much personality as our waiter?"

"He gettin' there," Cecil said.

"Better not count on a lot of tips."

"Man needs the job. Up to him what he does with it."

"Yeah, I suppose. You said he was a fighter."

"Not much of one. Heart like a blister."

"And you trained him?"

Cecil took a bite of unbuttered sourdough and chewed it thoughtfully. "Favor to his daddy. Remember Bolo Garcia?"

"Saw him fight on TV a couple times," Nick said. "He was finished by the time I came around."

"A true-life ass-kicker. Only thing that beat him was lies. Take a dive down in Texas, they said, and he'd get a title shot."

"Never happened, huh?"

"Hell, no."

Nick let Cecil have a moment with his thoughts. Then he asked, "You hear from anybody I used to know?"

"You the only one I don't hear from since you ain't at the airport," Cecil said.

"So, give me some names," Nick said.

"John-John Causion, he thinks he a trainer now; ain't bad, either. And that crazy muthafucka Simmie Watkins got him a storefront church in Detroit." Cecil started laughing. "You hear about the stripper Rico LaPaglia married?"

"No."

"She shot his ass."

"Dead?"

"Not unless she shot him again since he told me."

Now Nick was laughing too.

"You still a good-lookin' kid, you laugh that way," Cecil said. "Oughta try it more often. Might get you some pussy."

"Probably the wrong time for that."

"There's never a wrong time. How 'bout that story in the paper?" Cecil asked. "It do you any good?"

"Andy Rigby's story?"

"Uh-huh."

"Not really. I mean, the buddy I was driving for that day—when the kid jumped me—he keeps saying his boss will have something for me. A month, two months, when one of their drivers moves out of state. But every time I'm supposed to meet the boss, it gets postponed."

"On account of you or him?"

"Him. Christ, Cecil, I got rent to pay, you know? I need a job."

There was a flash of mischief in Cecil's eyes. "You want, I could put in a word for you here."

Nick couldn't help smiling. "No, thanks."

"Yeah, these sour muthafuckas, I can't blame you. But you gonna let me say I'm sorry, ain't you?"

"For what?"

"For tellin' that shitass Rigby where you was," Cecil said.

"Don't be sorry, man," Nick said. "You couldn't read his mind. Besides, I didn't talk to him much when he came around. All he did was dig up, you know—" He shrugged rather than say more. No sense having Alonzo Burgess at the table with them even if it was in name only.

"Yeah, I know."

"He could have written the same thing if he'd never found me. Looked like he was pretty desperate for a story. He a drinker?"

"Might be. Was a time all them newspaper cats boozed pretty hard."

"Forget about him," Nick said. "I'll get by."

"Just the same," Cecil said, "muthafucka better not come askin' me for no more favors."

He looked like he was still brooding on Rigby's betrayal when the waiter plopped their steaks in front of them, their orders reversed. As they switched plates, Cecil said, "You eatin' regular?"

"Regular as I can."

"Don't look like it."

There was always something that felt right to Nick about Cecil ragging his ass.

✥ ✥ ✥

It was Cecil who had introduced him to soul music, to Otis and Aretha and obscure singers like James Carr and Howard Tate—anything to mellow him out after sparring. And it was Cecil who worked with him for nothing after his old man stole damned near every penny he'd made in his first seven pro fights. Fucking Matt Pafko—Nick tried not to think about him anymore, but when he did, he always wondered how a father could let gambling become more important than his son or anybody else in the family. Good thing Cecil had been there when Nick came west to Vegas to see if he could pick up the pieces.

Cecil took him to Johnny Lupo's gym for the first time, saying this was paradise for any fighter who thought he had greatness in him, who felt it in his gut. The gym had only one ring for sparring, its walls were decorated with fight posters of everyone from Ali to Little Red Lopez, and, just past the heavy bags, there was a sign on the door to Lupo's office that said "You Got to Have Balls to Conquer the World." Nick's were big and brass, and the day he walked into the gym you could practically hear them clanging.

But they ceased to matter after Alonzo Burgess. Something else was at work in Nick then, something that had no place in the fighting life. Cecil tried everything he could think of to get Nick back to where he'd been, bitching at him, sweet-talking him, even sparring with him before his first cable fight, ten rounds on ESPN. Cecil wanted to take him out of town, maybe someplace like Portland, far from the cameras and the Vegas vultures, but Frank Delzell wouldn't hear of it. He smelled money, which is what managers are supposed to do. Nick had become a draw, his stature enhanced by his unwanted reputation as a killer, and Delzell intended to capitalize on it. Nick, thinking there was no other way to get rid of the ghost that followed him into his dreams, came down on Delzell's side.

He knew he'd hurt Cecil when he did it, but Cecil stuck with him anyway, as though he could see what was coming. It happened in the fifth round, Nick pinning his man in a corner, freezing him with a body shot, then moving to throw the right hand that would shatter him. But the right hand lost its menace in midflight and missed by six inches because Nick found himself punching Alonzo Burgess, and Alonzo Burgess had suffered enough.

Delzell erupted at ringside, screaming that Nick should have the cocksucker wearing an oxygen mask. The crowd turned hostile, its booing punctuated by mutterings of a fix. Only Cecil understood. "It's the man in front of you," Cecil told Nick between rounds. "He the one you got to beat." Cecil demanded more punches and an attack to the body—"Crowd this mutha-fucka"—and Nick had every intention of doing what Cecil said. But when he went back out there, he knew he couldn't win. He was fighting two men.

If Cecil hadn't felt so bad for Nick, he would have told Delzell that was what he deserved for being such a greedy prick. The kid came first, though. Cecil wanted him to take some time off, maybe find a girl and a beach and forget he was a fighter for a while. But Delzell wanted him back in the ring right away to start rebuilding his reputation, and once again Delzell got his way.

Nick swore he saw black lights in his next fight, the lights he had always heard about from other men who had been hit on the chin just so. Everybody else talked about how the lights transported them to a mall or a car wash. What Nick saw in those lights when he got nailed was Alonzo Burgess, and this time Alonzo Burgess had no eyes. It was then that Nick discovered what he thought was the truth about himself, the truth that wouldn't become evident to anybody else until he had been dismantled by an opponent who should have been there for the taking. Nick's nose went first, hammered onto his right cheek, but it was the cuts he remembered most, under and over both eyes, blinding him with his own blood. His tongue got sliced up too—more blood, choking him, making him think he'd puke. But he willed himself to stay upright for all eight rounds, accepting the punishment as if it were his due, never forgetting that it still wasn't as bad as what he had delivered.

It looked like there were tears in Cecil's eyes afterward, but he had the strength to keep them from falling. He put a hand on Nick's blood-smeared shoulder while a doctor patched him up for the trip to the hospital. "Don't do this no more," Cecil said.

Nick nodded. Somewhere in the background Delzell was shouting, "What? What the fuck are you telling this piece of shit?"

Cecil was still looking at Nick when he told Delzell, very softly, "One more word, muthafucka, I'm a send you to the hospital with him."

Nick and Cecil heard the door slam behind Delzell. Out in the hall it sounded like something had been knocked over. Before Nick could say anything to Cecil, the doctor told them it was time to go.

✣ ✣ ✣

They were back on the sidewalk outside the Pantry now, nothing much of consequence having been said while they tucked into their steaks. Cecil had paid—he'd always been good that way—but when Nick saw him reach for his wallet again, he said, "Oh no, man, don't. I'm not looking for a handout."

"Ain't offering you one," Cecil said, and pulled out a scrap of paper. "Here. My neighbor asked me to give you this."

Nick took it and read a name and phone number written in an elegant male hand.

"Got nice handwriting, your neighbor."

"From autographs, most likely. Played for the Dodgers before your time. Onus DuPree."

"It says Scott Crandall here."

"On account of my neighbor's passing the message along for him. DuPree there said the man read the story in the paper. Might have some work for you."

The look in Nick's eyes turned suspicious. "What kind of work?"

"You gonna have to find that out on your own."

"I don't know," Nick said.

"Shit," Cecil said. "Someone throw me a rope when I'm drownin', you think I splash around askin' a bunch of damn questions?"

Nick wanted to argue the point, but Cecil silenced him with the look he used between rounds, the look that said the bullshit was over.

"Just make sure you call that fella Crandall, hear?"

Nick started to say thanks, but Cecil cut him short with a mumbled "uh-huh" and headed for the parking lot on the other side of ninth Street. He'd never been much for goodbyes, and when Nick called out his name and hurried to catch up with him, it was obvious he didn't appreciate it.

"Now what?"

"Make sure his wife gets this," Nick said. "For their kids."

Cecil couldn't hide his surprise when he saw what Nick had tucked in his hand: a hundred dollar bill.

"Thought you didn't have no money."

"I don't now. But if there really is a job in that number you gave me, maybe I can get back to sending a little something every month."

"He'll still be dead."

"Yeah," Nick said. "But I got to do something."

9

The desk looked as big as a playground to Jenny, although a playground was a pretty weird thing to think of in a lawyer's office. It was walnut, polished until it gleamed, and there wasn't anything on it except a telephone, a pewter pen set, and a notepad. She'd read somewhere that a clean desk went hand in hand with power, but she'd never understood the concept until now.

Truman J. Beiser, Esquire, sat behind the desk with his elbows propped on the arms of a large carved wooden chair, his fingers making a steeple in front of his expressionless face. He was bald on top, but his gray hair was long enough on the sides to be swept back into a ponytail. Sometimes he nodded, most of the time he stared at Jenny. He spoke only when she paused to wonder if she was making any sense. It was a pretty complicated story she was trying to tell the man she hoped would save her from getting her ass sued off.

"Go on," Beiser told her at every lull, his voice as blank as his face, and she would resume the story that had begun eight months earlier on a narrow street in Los Feliz. She and another driver had tried to squeeze past each other, and failed. Suddenly her first good car, a used 1998 Celica that she had bought with massage money, bore a creased fender that looked a lot worse than the nicks its doors had picked up in parking lots. It was, she supposed, the price she paid for being late for dinner at Farfalla with a couple of girls from work she really wasn't all that crazy about. At least the guy she had traded paint with was cute, and he seemed nice when he looked at the damage to his car and said it wasn't worth yelling about. They exchanged information—his name was Craig, he was a mortgage broker—and he promised not to get in touch unless there was a problem with the repair. When he didn't call, Jenny assumed everything was fine, although she wouldn't have minded going out with him.

Then she'd had a second accident just before Christmas. Totally her fault. In stop-and-go traffic on the 405—when wasn't the traffic there stop and go?—she had been digging around in her purse for a phone number when she should have been paying attention to the car in front of her. She plowed into it, of course. Nobody got hurt, but what was it with her driving lately?

When she opened the letter from the DMV, she discovered she wasn't the only one asking that question. The litany of sins it contained had led her to Beiser's desk. She hadn't filed paperwork for her first accident, prompting the DMV to suspend her license. But she hadn't found out about the suspension until the paperwork for her second accident began making its way through proper channels. And now the other driver—male, middle-aged, and uptight in the way that only the Bible-thumping religious could be—was making loud noises about a lawsuit.

"He straight up called me a little tramp," Jenny said.

"For driving with a suspended license," Beiser said, without enough inflection to make it a question.

"Yes. Do you believe that? He made it sound like I was naked." Jenny looked for a flicker of reaction, found none, and decided to play it safe. "I wasn't, by the way."

"Best to keep emotions out of this, Ms. Yee," the attorney said.

"I know. I mean I understand what you're saying. What I'm trying to find out is if you can help me. My friend said you're really good."

"I've only lost one case." For the first time, Beiser sounded like his engine ran on something besides soymilk.

"She told me that, too," Jenny said.

Maria, Jenny's best friend in massage, had recommended Beiser without telling her whether he was one of her clients. All she said was that he had saved her ass when she'd gotten in trouble with the DMV, but Jenny suspected the connection between them went beyond lawyer-client. Maria ran a place in a Chinatown high-rise that catered to professionals from downtown, mostly lawyers and stockbrokers. Beiser's office, on Wilshire near La Brea, wasn't so far away that he couldn't slip down there during lunch. On the outside, he didn't appear to be Maria's type—she was a magnet for freaks—but who knew what went on behind closed doors? And what did Jenny care, especially now? She had a more important question to ask.

"This is going to cost a lot of money, isn't it?"

"I'm afraid so," Beiser said.

"Can you give me an idea how much?"

"Off the top of my head, I'd say your DMV fine will run in the neighborhood of three thousand dollars."

"Even when they never notified me by mail?"

"They notify everybody by mail, Ms. Yee."

"But I never got it."

"Which is your problem, not theirs."

The unfairness of life washed over Jenny like acid rain. She could feel herself starting to pout, and she didn't like it. But she liked what was happening with the DMV even less.

"Look at the bright side," Beiser said. "You'll have your license back, and you'll have taken a major step toward avoiding a lawsuit."

"I just hope a cop doesn't stop me when I'm driving home," she said, trying to laugh.

"Should be an incentive to drive safely," he said, without a glimmer of a smile. "But before you go, there's one other subject we should discuss. My fee."

"Oh, right," Jenny said. "That."

"It will run between three and four thousand dollars." He waited for Jenny to say something, but she had lost the power of speech. "Does that sound like an amount you're capable of handling?"

Another ten or fifteen seconds passed before Jenny could offer up a tiny yes.

"Good," Beiser said, letting just enough enthusiasm creep into his voice to prove that he liked money. "I'll need a small retainer, say a thousand dollars, and once your check clears, I'll get to work."

Jenny told him she would write a check and put it in the mail as soon as she got home. It was a perfect time for him to suggest that they could take money out of the equation and trade his services for hers. To her relief, he didn't. There was enough shady stuff in her life already, and now there would have to be more. She was already picturing how empty her safe-deposit boxes were going to look. She only knew one way to fill them back up in a hurry.

✤ ✤ ✤

Asian girls were always in demand, even the snotty princesses who didn't want to get all the way naked, acted like they were afraid to touch guys and, when they did, accused clients of making them break a nail. Guys put up with it, Jenny supposed, because they wanted something different from what they were getting at home, and since most of them were white, it didn't take a genius to figure out the rest. So Jenny, driving west on Wilshire with her suspended license and wishing she could just read Robert Lowell's poetry now that her Vietnam paper was finished, knew she wouldn't have a problem finding a job. Where the job was would be the problem, because everywhere she had worked was a place she never wanted to see again.

Her journey through the netherworld of massage had begun in East Hollywood, in an apartment that was worse than the neighborhood, as hard as that was to believe. The girls thought they were too hot to change the sheets, and her boss was a cokehead who never bathed and slapped his wife around when she was seven months pregnant. Two weeks and Jenny was out of there. She was gone even faster from her next stop, a flea-infested apartment on Laurel Canyon run by a Russian couple who just grunted when the masseuses complained about bites all over their feet, ankles, legs, and asses. Then it was Woodland Hills, where she met Rosie and ate mushrooms while a big orange cat named George sniffed the 'shroom dust off the floor and ricocheted around the room like a furry pinball.

When she and Rosie stopped laughing, they went to work for a black woman who had set up shop in the North Hollywood condo where she lived with her husband and daughter. Jenny and Rosie passed themselves off as Japanese sisters, and even though they kept it to hand jobs, they were making two thousand dollars each, sometimes more, for a four-day week, in by eleven, out by five. And that was on a dead-end street so creepy that clients were always saying they didn't want to park their Porsches there. But the worst thing about the condo was when they had clients at the same time and one of them had to use the little girl's bedroom. It was pink and lacy and Jenny noticed how it unnerved some guys, probably because it reminded them of the children they had at home. The ones it excited, she jerked off as quickly as possible.

North Hollywood ended when the black woman got crazy greedy and doubled what Jenny and Rosie each had to pay her to two hundred dollars a day. A couple of months later they stopped working together. Too much jealousy, even though Jenny was glad Rosie had taught her how to use blush: all over your face, not just on your nose. They just partied together now, and Rosie still thought she was prettier, and Jenny still felt queasy whenever that little girl's bedroom crossed her mind.

Every stop she made, she seemed to lose a little more of whatever innocence she'd possessed when she started. But she didn't begin to notice it until she had gone through the phony bust on Beverly Glen and started working downtown with Maria. This was before Maria got her own place; the boss was a music producer who always fell in love with the girls he had working in a fancy condo. Maria was one of those smart people who never thought about going to college because nobody in her family ever had. Like why bother, you know? She was seven or eight years older than Jenny, and she knew how to play the game.

She was also the first person Jenny had ever watched have sex. They were in a two-girl session—another first for Jenny—when the client said he would pay an extra hundred for full service. Maria had seen him before, so maybe that was why she said yes. Afterward, she tried to give Jenny half of the extra hundred he had paid, but Jenny told her it wasn't necessary, she'd just take what she earned for the massage; the rest was Maria's. They had been friends ever since.

They worked together until Jenny couldn't stand their boss hitting on her any longer, probably four months, which was an eternity in the business. By the time she left she had slept with a client for the first time. He was so good-looking, she blushed when he walked in the door, but they didn't do anything serious until he was back for his sixth visit in a month—and then all she let him pay her for was the massage. But after they went out a few times—real dates, to a movie, to dinner and dancing—he stopped calling. It was what happened with every regular eventually, but she still felt bad. The second client she slept with, an older guy this time, was a lawyer with a wife and three kids and a plan to pay Jenny's rent and tuition. Jenny took him up on his offer and left the business. But after three months of his obsessive behavior and phone calls from his wife telling her she was stealing the children's private school tuition, Jenny bailed.

"I'm too young to have so much baggage," she told Maria, and Maria responded by asking Jenny to work for her at the place she'd opened in Chinatown. She said clients from downtown still asked about Mika, which was the name Jenny had used there. But Jenny wanted to work on her own. More and more girls were going independent now that they could advertise on the Internet and get a classier clientele than they did from ads in in *L.A. Weekly* or the *L.A. Xpress*. But a funny thing happened once she started working out of her own place. She got lazy, and she had never been like that in her entire life. Too much easy money, she decided. She made almost twenty thousand dollars in her first month and a half on her own, and after that, she couldn't be bothered to book more than two or three clients a week, one of them being the guy who became her deadbeat cell phone boyfriend. Finally, when her cash reserves barely covered her rent, she decided she would be better off working for someone else, someone who would give her a place to be and a time to be there. And Sherman Oaks had been perfect, right up to Barry with his nice ass and his convertible top that didn't work.

The thought of what had happened after he dropped her off that fine January afternoon still made her shiver, the way she was shivering now as she pulled into her apartment building's underground garage. It was one of those things her memory would never turn loose of, and it would only get worse as the business beckoned again. She had made so many stops, even if they were all really the same, right down to the girls and the clients. One big treadmill, and where could she go on one of those? Sometimes she wished she could get off it. But that scared her too.

10

It must have been the wee small hours of the morning when the apartment manager slid a note under Nick's front door. Nick pictured the poor guy staying up past his bedtime to make sure the lights were off, then carrying out the landlord's orders on tiptoe. The apartment manager looked like a mouse, even had a rodent mustache, and he had probably been ready to scurry away if he got caught in the act.

Nick didn't want anyone to be afraid of him any more than he wanted to be reminded that rent for April was due in two weeks and he still hadn't paid for March. Worst of all, he didn't want to think Coyle was his last best hope before he dialed the number Cecil had given him, but that was what Coyle was.

"I was hoping you'd heard something," Nick said on the phone that morning. "You know, about the job you said might open up."

"Right," Coyle said. "There was a driver supposed to be moving back to Oklahoma, but every month he's got some new reason he's still here. This time I heard it's his old lady. Says she don't want to go somewhere there ain't a beach, like anybody would want to see her fat ass in a bikini."

"So what do you think? Should I try chasing down something else?"

"You got something?"

There was no mistaking the hopefulness in Coyle's voice. He was looking for a way to get off the hook.

"Maybe," Nick said.

"Maybe's better than nothing."

"Yeah, I haven't even talked to your boss yet."

"Oh, it'll happen, trust me," Coyle said. "Just hang in there a couple more months."

"I'll do that," Nick said.

But when he hung up, he marked Coyle off as one more bullshit artist, one more source of empty promises. Everybody lies, Coyle had said so himself, and now he had proved it.

✢ ✢ ✢

Scott could tell the fighter didn't want to call. Okay, ex-fighter if that's what he insisted on, like these animals ever really changed no matter what happened to them. Anyway, this guy Pafko's voice gave away his reluctance and uncertainty, maybe even his embarrassment at having to phone a stranger about a job, particularly when he didn't know what the job was.

Scott felt good about how he picked up on all that. It was his acting classes paying off again, keeping him alert to human behavior whether it was with his eyes or his ears. He remembered how he had tried for the same qualities in his own voice when he was doing a scene from Chekhov or Arthur Miller, somebody like that. It had been years ago, before his rise and fall on TV, and he kept meaning to take classes again to see if he could tap back into whatever it was he'd had in the beginning. Something always came up, though, like the indie feature his agent mentioned yesterday—a long shot, but what wasn't in Hollywood?—and, well, like the call from this guy Pafko.

About time, Scott thought. The girls had been on his ass to crank up security since they started hearing there was at least one rape and robbery every week lately. Then again, it wasn't like they were getting their news on TV or in the newspaper. The attacks were the kind of cheap shit that never turned up anywhere except the blogs and chatrooms the girls flocked to. They took it as stone fact that these motherfuckers had decided they preferred pussy and money to time off. Scott did his best to tune out the growing hysteria until Sierra showed up one morning saying the animals had attacked jack shacks in Santa Monica and Mid-Wilshire. Sierra was his best earner, and she believed that fucking the boss was part of her job. Attention had to be paid.

The way it normally worked, Scott watched over his flock himself, but only on Thursdays and Fridays, when business was off the hook. The other days, he'd drop in every three or four hours, just enough to let the girls know he cared. To tell the truth he couldn't stand being around them all the time. They were worse than actresses—too needy, too neurotic, too nuts.

Scott had hoped that DuPree would lend him some muscle. Of course the girls would have shit if DuPree had. No matter what their race, they weren't crazy about black guys to start with. But DuPree was in a category all his own: he was butt-puckering scary. He swung by maybe once a month to check out the new talent—and there was always new talent, stability being no more necessary than sanity for a hand-job queen. He never paid or left a tip, and if the girls who saw him had horror stories, they either kept it to themselves or never came back to work. Scott let it all slide. He figured knowing DuPree had its advantages.

He was enjoying one of them now, in fact. DuPree's old man—drunk most of the time, DuPree said—had found a way to get his number to this guy Pafko. Next thing he knew, Pafko was on the phone, listening to Scott refuse to get into specifics about the job until they met in person. Reluctant, uncertain, embarrassed, or whatever else he might have been, the fighter still wound up saying yes. *Holy shit,* Scott thought after he hung up, *this guy might actually be desperate.* Scott liked that possibility a lot.

✠ ✠ ✠

They were supposed to meet at two-thirty and it was almost three now. Nick found himself wishing he had picked up a paper before walking into Junior's Deli, then remembered all over again how pissed off he would have been if he had seen Andy Rigby's name in it. The only thing that interrupted his boredom was visits by a waitress with a bright red dye job. Every five minutes she wanted to freshen his coffee, or maybe get him something to eat—she was pushing the Reuben hard. Nick kept telling her he'd wait until the guy he was meeting got there. "You sure it's not a girl that stood you up?" the waitress said at last, walking away with a wink and a laugh. Nick shook his head and resumed looking out the window onto Westwood Boulevard. Only problem was he didn't know who he was looking for. Fifteen minutes later he stopped caring.

He was sliding out of the booth, thinking it could use new vinyl, when someone behind him said, "Nick, right?"

He turned and saw a guy who would have looked like a lot of other handsome guys in L.A. if he lost his second chin and started running and doing crunches. Even the blue V-neck sweater the guy was wearing over a white T-shirt couldn't conceal how thick he was through the middle. But he had the kind of sandy brown hair that probably always looked right, he was fashionably unshaven, and there was mischief in his brown eyes that must have raised hell with the ladies.

"I thought it was you," the guy said. "From your picture in the paper."

"I guess that makes you Scott," Nick said.

"Yeah. Sorry I'm late."

Nick thought the guy looked too pleased with himself to be sorry.

"Sit down," Scott said, already doing so himself, not bothering to shake hands. "You're gonna have some lunch, aren't you?"

"Already ate," Nick said.

"Well, I didn't." Scott waved the waitress over, probably winning her undying affection by saying, "Hey, good-lookin'." He ordered a Reuben with potato salad and a cream soda while Nick sat there wondering why everybody in this town gave you a first name and let it go at that.

"So, Scott," he said when the waitress was gone, "you always have people you never met deliver messages for you?"

"You talking about anyone in particular?"

"Cecil Givens."

It took a moment before Scott said, "Oh yeah, right. He lives next door to a buddy of mine's pops." Scott gave Nick a strange look. "What's the matter, you don't trust me?"

"Not really, no. And by the way, you were forty-five minutes late."

Nick was surprised to see the guy smile and nod like some wise old professor.

"I like it," Scott said. "You really don't give a shit."

"What's there to give a shit about?"

"A job."

"The one you wouldn't talk about on the phone? I don't think so."

"Relax, we're going to talk about it. What's the rush?"

"I don't want to waste my time."

"Okay, I can appreciate that. But I'm a people person. I like to find out what makes them tick before I invite them into my world. You were a boxer, right? A good one, I heard."

"For a while."

"Yeah, I heard about that, too."

Nick didn't say anything.

"I wonder if I ever saw you fight," Scott said. "I used to cabaret in Vegas a lot."

"Never fought there. Just trained."

"Too bad. The fights were totally cool for getting the night started. Women loved them. Ever notice that? All that shit going on in the ring, blood and sweat, broken noses, broken ribs, and you could practically smell the bitches in heat. I'm not talking about skanks either, pal. This was big-league pussy."

Scott was savoring the memory when the waitress came with his food. Nick wondered how much longer he could make himself sit across from this shithead.

Scott took a bite of his Reuben and licked the Russian dressing off his fingers lasciviously. While he was chewing, he said, "Ever do any security work?"

"Like bounce at a club?" Nick said.

"Along those lines, uh-huh."

"A couple times, when I was a kid. But not after I turned pro, no. I tried to do all my fighting in the ring. Didn't always work out that way, but—"

Scott took a slug of cream soda. "Yeah, I read how you clocked that fucker that tried to rob you."

"He didn't give me a choice." Nick could feel the same tension he had felt then creeping back into his face, jaw clenching, eyes narrowing.

It was obvious that Scott noticed. He hadn't taken another bite of his sandwich. "I got this job I think you could handle," he said.

Nick nodded.

Scott leaned across the table and said, dropping his voice down low, "Some girls that work for me need looking after."

"Let me guess: they're not Girl Scouts."

"See, what I got is a therapeutic massage salon," Scott said. "It's a sideline for me, but I enjoy the business, you know, making people happy."

"Horny guys," Nick said.

"When you get down to it, yeah. But it's not like they're rolling into a strip mall, doughnut shop on one side, dry cleaners on the other with autographed movie-star pictures all over the walls. The place I got is very classy, an apartment in Westwood. And the clientele is very classy too. Lots of names you might recognize. So everything's real discreet, just like you working for me would be. With me so far?"

"Yeah," Nick said. "You're a pimp."

"No," Scott said, breaking out his smile again, "but I play one on TV."

"That's where I've seen you," Nick said. "On TV. Scott Crandall, huh? I couldn't put your name with your face."

"Don't tell me that. The last thing an actor wants to be is anonymous."

"But if he's running a string of girls—"

"Then anonymity is everything. Just don't go thinking I'm the Happy Hooker. I'm strictly a businessman who deals in pleasure for his fellow man, and the girls that work for me aren't hookers per se. A couple of them are actually certified massage therapists. The others just say they are. It's a good rubdown for everybody who pays, and what happens behind closed doors is up to the girl and the client."

"And if the clients get out of hand, that's where I'd come in," Nick said.

"Right," Scott said. "But you can't get too heavy, no Wild West shit, at least most of the time."

"You mean I'd get one day a week to go nuts?"

"Not even. Just special occasions."

"I didn't know there was a holiday for people who liked getting their asses kicked."

"There isn't. But there's a couple guys running around town, robbing massage girls, raping them. Real animals."

"You don't need me, you need the cops."

"Yeah, but the girls break out in a rash when it's anything to do with the law. These motherfuckers would have to disembowel one of them before they'd call the cops."

"So they come knocking, it's open season on their asses."

"You got a gun, Nick?"

"No."

"Just your fists, huh?"

"I can always pick up something hard and hit 'em on the head."

Scott nodded approvingly. "A master of improvisation."

"I'm not anything until you tell me what the job pays," Nick said.

He watched Scott pretend to do the math in his head, as if he didn't know exactly how little he thought he could get away with offering. Nick, meanwhile, was trying to balance his instinctive distrust of this asshole with his need for money.

"Five hundred bucks a week," Scott said. "Cash."

"Monday through Friday?"

"Plus half days on Saturday. Never on Sunday, though."

"Those Saturdays ought to be worth an extra fifty."

Scott grinned. "What are you, the fucking Teamsters?"

"Hey, I had to ask."

"Ask me something else," Scott said.

Nick wanted to ask if this fading pretty boy had any idea how far down the ladder guarding a bunch of hand whores was from throwing bags at LAX. But what he said was this: "When do I start?"

11

Not even noon and the old man was deep in the Courvoisier. A half-empty bottle sat on the wobbly wooden coffee table in front of him. He was staring into the distance from his base of operations on a floral sofa covered with the plastic his late wife had insisted on. When his son walked through the front door, he acknowledged his arrival with a fart. Only then did the old man cast his yellow eyes on DuPree's look of disgust and grunt in satisfaction.

"Better go easy on the rice and beans," DuPree said.

"Man's gotta eat."

"Then eat something else when you know I'm stopping by."

"Stop by more often and I will."

The old man had him there. DuPree was a stranger in the house where he grew up. When he visited he did so reluctantly and without an ounce of guilt. If there had been a guilty moment in his life, DuPree had long ago forgotten it. He was only there out of obligation, as if putting up with the old man for a few minutes were no different from throwing pocket change in a beggar's cup. He made no secret of his feelings either: As soon as he arrived, he was ready to leave.

"Got to take care of business," he said. "I don't grab the money when it's there, someone else will."

"Business, huh?" The old man sipped his Courvoisier. "Don't wind up with your ass back in jail."

"What you mean by that?"

"Shit, boy . . . "

The old man didn't need to say more. It was as if those eyes of his, the color of infection, could look into the soul that DuPree himself knew was diseased.

His best defense was to stare back at sixty-two years of wasted promise. Onus DuPree Sr. had been the greatest high school athlete L.A. ever saw, the Dodgers' center fielder before he was twenty, and now look at him sliding his hand inside those sorry-assed sweats and scratching his nuts.

DuPree knew the old motherfucker still cursed Bob Gibson for breaking his shoulder blade with a fastball in '62—wasn't any damn accident either, not like his knee the next year, the one that surgery never fixed. He could talk for hours about Gibson and never once mention all the boozing he'd done, reefer he'd smoked, pussy he'd chased. Big a mess as Onus Sr. was, it was a wonder he had lasted nine seasons. Only a truly great athlete could have done it. Even DuPree had to admit that.

"Whoa, whoa, whoa," he said. "Let's back this up, start all over."

"You think it'll get better?" the old man said.

"Can't get worse."

"Better not."

The old man chuckled, something rattling in his chest until it came loose and he spit it into a handkerchief that looked like it had never seen a washing machine. He examined what he had coughed up with a lab tech's lack of emotion before he looked back at DuPree.

"Why you here anyway?"

"On my way to El Monte."

"Shit, all they got there is tacos and stolen cars."

"Dogs, too."

The old man eyed him curiously. "What you want with dogs?"

"A pet."

"Goddamn, boy, you never liked no dog when you was com- ing up. Beg like a bitch for one, and then I'd have to take care of the motherfucker. How many times that happen? And what about that little shit, he barked so much, you put his damn eye out?"

"Fuck you talking about?" DuPree said. "That was an accident."

"You was the meanest child I ever saw," the old man said.

DuPree knew it was true. His mother had known it too, right from the jump. There'd been nights when he lay in bed listen- ing to her telling the old man their only child was all the way wrong, that the innocence in him rotted when he took his first breath. The old man didn't want to hear it, but once his Ruthie was gone, killed on the freeway, and they both were running free, father and son, nothing could hold back the truth. Didn't matter that DuPree was a football star with a full ride to USC and all that shit. He was still hurting people in fights, hurting them bad, and robbing them when the alumni couldn't get him money fast enough. When he was finally arrested, it cost him his scholar- ship and fourteen months at Terminal Island. Now, a dozen years later, it was the only thing the old man judged him by. That and what his wife whispered from her grave.

"What fool gonna give you a dog?" the old man said.

"I'm on my way to find out," DuPree said.

"Then it ain't for certain."

"Damn right it is. I got a friend set it up."

"You got a friend thinks you fit for a dog? A motherfucker that dumb, you should be askin' him for money."

"You didn't have such a nasty mouth, I might bring him around."

"Shit."

"All right then," DuPree said. "Let me just thank you. It's what I came for, anyway."

"Thank me for what?" the old man said.

"Passing along that phone number. The one you gave your neighbor."

The old man brightened for the first time. "Oh yeah. Givens. Good fella. Stops by for a drink when he's in from Vegas."

"Works with fighters, right?"

"Yeah."

"Anybody I ever heard of?"

"Geronimo Byrd. John-John Causion. Too Sweet Jimmy Gonzales."

DuPree shook his head. "No champions, huh?"

"No, I guess not." The light disappeared from the old man's face.

"Don't look so sad, you still a winner." DuPree dipped into the left front pocket of slacks softer than the inside of a woman's thigh and pulled out a portion of the money he had taken from the dealer he'd robbed. "Here, to help you keep it together."

He held the bills out to the old man. After a moment of internal debate, the old man took them, then did his best to make a sizzling sound and dropped them on the floor.

"Too hot to handle," he said.

"Well, goddamn," DuPree said, doing everything in his power to suppress the urge to yank the old man off the sofa and choke the yellow out of his eyes.

As soon as the old man saw that, he burst into laughter, coughing and spilling the last of his Courvoisier onto the sleeve of a ragged white cardigan already splotched with stains. "Got your ass, didn't I?" he cackled.

And he had, without witnesses, which meant DuPree could laugh too, cutting loose the way he never did on the street. When he regained control of himself, it was for just long enough to say, "You old motherfucker," as if it were a benediction.

✤ ✤ ✤

He checked his cell for messages, erasing the latest one from Scott, figuring he knew what the white boy wanted. He'd be saying they should get together for a drink, or maybe hit 4Play, where they served lap dances instead of alcohol. It had been too long since they hung out—that's how Scottie was probably seeing it. He was one hanging-out motherfucker. But as it neared midnight, DuPree needed him like he needed the clap.

He wasn't sure he'd ever been this far east, getting off the 10 on Rosemead Boulevard and heading into a neighborhood he was certain wouldn't open its arms for a brother in a Beemer. It was heavy Latino around here, from the bars and burrito shacks to the names on the storefront businesses. He didn't need daylight to know what the houses and apartments looked like, the paint on their stucco bleached by the sun, the front lawns as worn and tired as the blue collars that hung in the closets inside. The way L.A. was going, the whole city would look like this pretty soon, a Gonzalez on every mailbox and La Eme or Los Norteños calling the shots.

DuPree wouldn't have come here if Artie Franco hadn't made some calls to cool out everything in advance. Artie had that way about him. The only time DuPree had ever seen him get ugly was after Slape pumped two rounds into the wall of the last bank they'd taken down. Slape said it was to get everybody's attention. And Artie said yeah, the cops included. DuPree had thought Artie was going to shoot Slape right there. But now the two of them were asshole buddies as far as wanting to do an armored car next, and DuPree was the holdout, arguing that there had to be a better way to make a big score. Slape accused him of being unprofessional, but Artie was still trying to make nice. That was why he stepped up when DuPree said he was thinking about getting a dog. Artie knew just the place.

DuPree nosed his car down a street lined with warehouses and garages. Trucks and tractors without their trailers were parked here and there, not a human in sight. Artie had told him there wouldn't be, so DuPree kept driving until he found an alley just past a shipping company. No lights, not much room for a car coming from the other direction to get by, a bad place for a brother to get stuck. DuPree headed down it anyway thinking, *Fuck 'em, let 'em try.*

He found the garage where Artie had told him it would be, a flat-roofed building behind a chainlink fence topped with razor wire. Security lights shined down on a loading area cluttered with thirty or forty unremarkable cars, vans, and pickups. As he started to drive through the gate, a hard-looking kid stepped in front of his car—shaved head, tattoos curling up from under his flannel shirt's collar, probably strapped. DuPree stopped, his right hand automatically going to the Glock wedged under his thigh.

Sizing up the BMW with a jacker's eye, the kid walked to the driver's side and waited for DuPree to power down his window. "You got business here?" the kid asked.

"Yeah, if Ynez is around," DuPree said.

The kid thought about it for a moment before pointing to a dimly lit corner inside the fence. "Park over there," he said.

DuPree ignored the instructions and parked out where the kid at the gate wouldn't have any excuses if something happened to the car. Then he tucked his gun in the rear of his waistband, climbed out and waited for the kid to complain. When he didn't, DuPree started toward the garage, the sporadic noise from the crowd inside growing louder with every step. At the far end of the building, a heavyset guy was taking a leak against the wall and talking to a buddy who stood nearby with a bottle of beer in each hand: "He say, 'Wednesday, you s'posed to call me Wednesday,' and I tell him, 'Oh, I been drinking then. When I drinking, I forgot everything.'"

The guy's buddy was more interested in eyeballing DuPree, but DuPree kept walking. The centerpiece of the garage was a sliding overhead door that had been lowered and probably locked. Beside it was a door DuPree opened by turning a knob. He stepped inside as the crowd let loose a primitive noise. An instant later, his breath was taken away by a smell that was a mixture of sweat, cigarettes, pot, beer, grilling meat, piss, shit, and blood. Same as Compton, DuPree thought. Doesn't matter if the crowd is black, brown, or whatever. Put a pit-bull fight indoors and it always got funky.

Maybe a hundred people—men, women, even children—were gathered around the wire-enclosed fighting ring where a black dog and a red one were chewing each other up. Judging by their gore-covered heads and chests, the dogs had been at it for a while, and it didn't look like there was any quit in either of them. Some of these fuckers would fight for hours, forty-five pounds of muscle and bone never making a sound while they sent arcs of blood into the air. It was like they were out to prove they were better than the people who bet hundreds, even thousands, of dollars on them and laughed at their pain when they won, cursed their weakness when they lost.

The red dog was down now, his chest torn open so wide it looked like you could reach in and pull out his heart. But even with his blood spilling onto the ring's industrial carpet, he refused to give up his hold on the black dog's rear leg. The black dog fought back by chewing on the red one's head, finally locking on the bone above the eye. The crowd, juiced by the sight of pain and the prospect of money changing hands, got louder, drowning out the noise of combat. But DuPree had watched enough of these fights up close to know the sound the black dog was making, like chewing on a knucklebone.

He stood at the rear of the crowd for a moment longer and then moved on. He hadn't come for entertainment, and if he had, he was in the wrong place. Too many gang kids were scattered around what was once a garage or a chop shop. Maybe they were promoting the fights. Or maybe it was their fathers, the *veteranos* who had more time for this kind of shit.

One of the gang kids spotted DuPree and nudged a buddy, the two of them giving him a look that said they'd blow his black ass away if they didn't have dogs to root for. For L.A. Mexicans, it was a superiority thing that went back to the fifties, when a black gang from Compton traveled to the east side to fight and got carved up by switchblade *pachucos* who ambushed them from the rooftops. The brothers ran, and the spics were still bragging about it, especially the old fuckers who dated back to the Sixth Street and White Fence gangs. DuPree had heard it all in prison. He didn't need to renew the discussion with a couple of assholes whose great-grandfathers might have been there that night.

So he kept moving, not too fast, not too slow, sending a message to anyone who noticed that he wasn't someone to be fucked with. Wasn't here to fight, wasn't here to buy chronic or coke or roofies. This was a business trip. The only other people he saw with a similar demeanor were two middle-aged women at a tired wooden stand against one wall, selling beer and Pepsi, grilling beef and chicken, and tossing around tortillas that looked handmade. It was the lone good smell in the pit-bull funk.

When he was in front of the stand, one of the women looked up and said, "DuPree?"

"You see any other brothers in here?" he asked.

The woman was short and thick, wearing jeans and a gray Old Navy sweatshirt. Her hairline dipped almost to eyebrows that needed weeding, the roundness of her face was undone by a double chin, and there was a gap between her two front teeth. All that and she wasn't long on personality, either. She didn't answer DuPree, didn't smile at him, didn't do anything except wipe her hands on a towel and mutter a few words in Spanish to the other woman. Then she looked back at DuPree.

"You got the money?" she asked.

He hated the lazy menace in her Spanglish accent. "You got the dog?" he said.

"You don't trust me?" The possibility made her smile.

"I don't even know who you are. I assume you're Ynez, but you could be anybody."

"I tell you I'm Ynez, that make you feel better?"

"It's a start. But I still want to see the dog."

Leaving his words hanging in the air, Ynez fished a box of Kools out of her jeans, shook one loose, parked it in a corner of her mouth, and fired it up with a Zippo. Not until the Kools were back in her pocket did she let DuPree know she had heard him. She gestured with her head that he should follow, and started walking.

DuPree, coming up behind her wide ass, resisted the urge to ask if they served pit-bull tacos. A question like that, she might get all righteous on him. Besides, he already had a damn good idea what happened out back, where they kept the dogs that were getting ready to fight and killed the ones that came out of fights too ruined to go on living. They doused the poor fuckers with gasoline and set them on fire. DuPree had already had enough stink for one night.

Ynez stepped through a door next to an unlit window at the rear of the garage. A fluorescent light went on overhead as DuPree followed her into what turned out to be a bare-bones office. Just a dented metal desk with no paperwork on it, a cheap rolling chair, and an old-fashioned girlie calendar, not even a nude, like it wasn't 2003 yet at the transmission shop that had sent it out.

"The dog's in here?" DuPree asked, suspicious.

"Close the door," Ynez said.

He wanted to beat this bitch until she answered his fucking question. But this was her turf, and he hadn't forgotten about her homeboys out front. He knew she hadn't either. Better to close the door and keep an eye on her.

She flicked the ash from her cigarette and stuck it back in her mouth before she stepped behind the desk. That was when

DuPree heard a dog bark. Ynez bent at the waist and started pulling on something. DuPree heard scraping on the concrete floor to go along with the barking, and then he saw a wooden crate come into view. Inside, looking like it was searching for a way out, was a white pit bull.

Ynez jerked a thumb back at DuPree and said, "This man want to be your new daddy, Blanco."

"He's some kind of champion, right?" DuPree said.

"Kicked ass every time he fought. Shit, I made *mucho dinero* with this bad boy."

"You gonna take him out of that thing? It's not like he's going to chew my ass up, is he?"

"You scare, maybe you not the right daddy for him."

"Only one way to find out."

Ynez opened the hatch at one end of the cage, reached inside, and came back out with a firm grip on the dog's collar.

Goddamn, DuPree thought, *Blanco is one ugly motherfucker.* His face was wreathed in wrinkles, and the rims of his eyes were the same inflamed pink as the tongue that dangled from his mouth like a dishrag. It looked like somebody had trimmed his ears with garden shears and left them all ragged and nasty. And there were scars on his head and neck, and scars upon the scars.

"You sure he never lost?" DuPree asked.

"Shit, don't you know nothing?" Ynez said. "A pit gets scarred up like that, it means he never let no dog get on top of him."

She took her hand from the dog's collar, and for a moment the dog seemed content to stay beside her. Then she picked him up, turned him around, placed her hands on his haunches, and shoved him toward DuPree, who wondered if he could get his Glock out in time to shoot it before it did much damage—and shoot Ynez too. But the dog was smiling and his stump of a tail was wagging as he made his way toward DuPree with a thick-chested swagger.

"Moves like Mike Tyson," DuPree said.

Ynez, busy lighting a fresh smoke off her old one, arched a brow in agreement.

DuPree dropped to one knee and petted Blanco, tentatively at first, and then, once he was sure the dog wasn't going to tear his hand off, with more enthusiasm. The dog's smile got wider. "Well, shit," DuPree said, "look at your happy ass."

"Five hundred," Ynez said.

DuPree looked up at her, the dog forgotten. "Artie said a hundred fifty."

The woman's hairy brows slammed together indignantly. "Fuck you talkin' about? For a champion?"

"You said yourself there's no more fights in him. He's just a tired old motherfucker wants to curl up by my feet."

"He can still make babies."

"I don't think so."

"Who tell you that?"

"Artie."

"That lying motherfucker."

"Where's his babies? They out there fighting now?"

Ynez glared through the smoke from her cigarette.

"So," DuPree said, standing to make sure she knew just how much bigger he was than her, "a hundred and fifty?"

"Four hundred," she said.

"A hundred and fifty."

"I don't got to sell him, you know. Maybe I keep him for my own."

"Bullshit. All you're going to do is kill him."

"Bullshit on you, *pendejo*. I love that fucking dog." Ynez dropped her cigarette on the floor and ground it out with the toe of her cut-rate sneaker. "Three hundred."

From beyond the closed door, DuPree could hear the crowd getting loud. The fight must have been heating up; one of the pits might even be dying. Blanco growled and started toward the door, probably remembering the urge that had been built into him by all those hours on a treadmill, all those hours learning to kill cats and dogs, all those hours in the ring when the pain paid off in adulation. DuPree strained to keep the dog where he was. Motherfucker was as strong as he was ugly.

"In a minute, man," DuPree told the dog. Then he looked at Ynez. "You got a leash to go with his collar?"

"Around here someplace, yeah," she said. "But we ain't made a deal."

"Just give me the damn leash," DuPree said.

Muttering and frowning, Ynez rummaged through one desk drawer after another until she found it. "See?" she said.

He snatched the leash from her hand and examined it. "It'll do," he said. When he looked up again, Ynez was standing in front of the door, blocking the way out. She was holding a knife.

"I think he cost five hundred after all," she said.

"Yeah, I can see how you would," DuPree said.

He reached over and pulled Blanco's wooden carrier toward him. Then he used his grip on the dog's collar to maneuver him toward the crate, expecting a struggle, but Blanco went in without a fuss.

DuPree lowered the hatch, secured it, and stood again. "Five hundred, huh?" he said. He started to reach in the right pocket of his leather jacket, then stopped. "Be cool now," he said. "I got money in here, not a gun, okay?" Ynez nodded and clutched her knife a little tighter while DuPree carefully extracted a wad of bills. Shifting it to his left hand and making sure to put it on display for her, he started peeling off Franklins. "One, two—"

Ynez was leaning forward to get a closer look when DuPree hit her with a short right uppercut that slammed her teeth together hard enough to crack them. If she wasn't out on contact, she was after she flew backward, the knife falling from her hand and her head bouncing off the door with a concussive thud that made Blanco bark.

Good thing the crowd was still screaming for doggie blood. They hadn't heard a thing, and they weren't going to notice DuPree getting the fuck out of there either, as long as he moved fast. He'd have to make this right with Artie Franco, of course, tell him about the knife and the five-hundred-dollar bullshit, but that was for later.

DuPree flicked off the overhead light and pulled Ynez away from the door. He liked the way the bitch had slid down it like a fucking bird dropping. He liked the idea that he had a pet even better. He opened the door a crack and checked outside to make sure all the noise meant the crowd was still looking the other way. There was a steak bone in the car, and he didn't want to make his man Blanco wait for it any longer.

12

A goddamned jack shack, Nick kept thinking on the drive over that first day. Of all the places he thought he'd never work, this had to be number one. Amazing, the things you do when money is tight. But he told himself the job was just for a couple of months—and then he found himself smiling at the thought of sitting around with the women he'd been hired to protect. Hell, how tough could that be?

The tough part looked like it would be finding a parking place. It was almost ten-thirty when he finally ignored a sign that said he needed a special sticker and squeezed his pickup between a new Lexus SUV and one of those little Benzes. That's the kind of neighborhood it was, people living in high-rises that weren't quite as fancy as the ones on Wilshire but still driving cars that made them look like money. They would probably think Nick was working on a nearby renovation project when they saw what he was leaving on the street. That was fine with him. He just didn't want any tickets. Didn't want any record that he was in the neighborhood either.

He walked a block and a half to the address Scott Crandall had given him, wondering how long the remaining duplexes and single-family homes would survive before they were torn down for more high-rises. The place where Crandall did business looked new and exclusive: ten stories, circular drive, lots of ferns and plants that flowered even in winter, and glass double doors that wouldn't open until Nick found the intercom and got whoever was waiting upstairs to buzz him in.

He took the elevator to the eighth floor, exited and turned left, then saw the faux-gold apartment numbers on the wall and went the other way. Eight-twenty-four was a corner apartment. Before he could press the doorbell, a guy burst out of the apartment across the hall to confront him.

"Tell that bitch Ling to leave Eddie alone," the guy said, anger in his voice but tears in his eyes.

"Ling?" Nick asked. "Male or female?"

"You think you're funny?"

"I'm asking a question, that's all."

"Female, she's a female, the little twat," the guy said. "Like there isn't a world full of straight men for her to sink her claws into." He brushed at the tears that were starting to spill down his cheeks. "Just tell Ling I suck cock better than she does, and Eddie knows it."

He spun on his heel and went back through his door as fast as he'd come out of it.

Nick was wondering what the hell that had been about when the door to 824 opened and a woman peeked out at him, her eyes heavy with mascara.

"Nick?" she said.

"Yeah."

"Hurry up, get in here."

Nick shrugged and stepped inside. The woman closed the door so quickly that it clipped his heel. The light in the entryway was dim, but up ahead it looked like the late morning sun was doing its job.

"What was all that about?" Nick asked.

"Not here," the woman said. "Come on."

She kept her distance as she led him into the apartment. Nick guessed she was twenty-five or maybe a little older if she scraped off her makeup. Her hair was dyed strawberry blonde, and he thought it looked good on her even if it did come out of a bottle.

She was wearing something he would have called a robe if it wasn't black silk, frilled with lace, and left unbuttoned to reveal tits so perfect he didn't want to know if they were fake. He couldn't help staring, and when she caught him, she gave him a frown that must have poleaxed unwanted admirers in settings where the play wasn't for pay.

There were Japanese dividers up in the living room, and from the other side of them, a second woman's voice could be heard: "One-sixty for a half-hour, two hundred for the hour . . . Just me and my girlfriend in a high-rise, very luxurious . . . That's right, completely nude."

She was hanging up when Nick walked around the divider and saw her sitting on a tired sofa, staring at him blankly, the outline of her nipples obvious under her red teddy. Good luck guessing what nationality she was. Maybe Asian, maybe Latin, maybe something he'd never heard of—anything was possible in L.A. All Nick knew was that she was so exotically beautiful she probably could turn that gay guy straight.

"Are you Ling?" he asked.

She laughed. "What makes you think that?"

"Well, there was this guy out in the hall—"

"Neal," said the woman who had met him at the door, as if that explained everything. Maybe it did, because the woman on the sofa laughed again.

"That's not Ling, incidentally," the first woman told Nick. "She's Kianna. I'm Sierra."

"Okay," he said, nodding, trying to file the names in his memory. "Does somebody named Ling work here?"

"Sometimes she does," Kianna said, ignoring one of the two phones on the teak coffee table as it rang. "When she's not, like, stoned or crashing her car or begging Mommy and Daddy in the Palisades for more money."

"Shut up, Kianna," Sierra said.

"It's true."

"It's not anybody's business but ours, okay?"

"Whatever," Kianna said, and picked up the phone.

Her conversation became background music as Nick turned his attention to Sierra. It was obvious she was the one in charge, and that she liked it that way.

"I guess Scott told you your job," she said.

"Yeah, make sure you and her"—Nick nodded at Kianna—"don't have any problems."

"But no rough stuff. Unless things get really scary."

"I'm not here to hurt anybody."

"You better not be. The last thing we need is you beating up some guy or whatever when he just needs to be put on the elevator. We don't want the neighbors calling the cops. That would be fucked."

"You're not worried about what's-his-name out there?"

"Neal? No way. Eddie would have a shit fit. Just be cool, all right?"

Nick nodded. No sense in speaking to someone who wasn't interested in hearing the sound of his voice.

"You'll be opening up mornings," Sierra said. "I'll give you the key before I take off today. Appointments start at eleven, and the girls should show up a half-hour before so they can book appointments for lunch. That means you've got to be here by ten-fifteen. Not like today, in other words."

"I didn't think parking would—"

"I'm not saying girls won't be late. Some of them, I swear to God, you're lucky if they get here at all."

"Got it," Nick said. "Any place to park that's better than the street?"

"There's two spaces in the garage, but the girls get them. For safety reasons. In case any crazies they meet here start waiting outside. It happens, you know."

"Maybe I can look around if I run out every couple hours to move my car."

"Whatever, as long as there's no clients on the way up."

With the ground rules laid out, there was nothing left for Nick and Sierra to talk about. The only voice heard belonged to Kianna as she worked the two phones, most callers apparently seeking nothing more than titillating conversation as they tried to start their hearts with a morning tug. Every once in a while, she cast an annoyed glance at Sierra, but Sierra ignored her. Typical queen bee.

She kept it up until the intercom buzzed. "Must be my eleven o'clock," she said. She hurried toward a speaker next to the front door and asked who it was. When a voice said it was Phil, she buzzed him up without telling him the apartment number. "Comes every Wednesday," she told Nick, giggling, expecting him to acknowledge the double entendre. He forced a smile and hoped for her sake that her skills in bed were better than her sense of humor.

"You want me to open the door for this guy?" he asked.

"I'm trying to get him in here, not chase him away," she said.

Behind them Kianna laughed. Nick felt his ears burning, but he kept his eyes on Sierra. "So," he said, "what do I do?"

"In there," she said, pointing toward a side room. "And shut the door behind you."

"You want me hiding?" The idea was strange, even insulting.

"Yes, hiding. Now do it before he gets here."

Nick started to ask her, What the fuck? Then he thought better of it and stepped into what looked like a second bedroom, telling himself to take it slow and easy, get a handle on the situation, the way Cecil taught him to. He flipped a switch and an overhead light came on, revealing three pieces of fifth-rate erotic art on the walls and taupe carpet in serious need of vacuuming. A futon covered by a multicolored comforter had been pushed up against one wall. Beside it were fancy plastic bottles filled with oil and lotion.

Something was spilling from a bottle that hadn't been closed and was now lying on its side, next to a puffball of carpet fabric, a box of tissue, and a CD without a case.

He kneeled to see what these girls listened to, only to be distracted by the mess on the floor. The unvacuumed carpet was stained with whatever the girls used on their clients, and maybe human fluids as well. There were tall candles on both sides of the futon, and wax from them had spilled onto the carpet. What surprised him most was how much hair there was everywhere, on the pillows and the comforter, in the wax deposits, even on the CD player. The long hair was obviously female, but the short, curly hair had to be pubic and was most likely male. He made a mental note to be careful where he put his hands before he finally got around to picking up the forlorn CD. He'd never heard of a band called Enigma. Shrugging, he searched for the CD's case. When he couldn't find it among the half-dozen others that were safe in their cases, he laid it atop a CD player stained by oily fingers.

A half-open door beckoned from a few feet away, so he rose and stepped through it just far enough to turn on the light. It was a bathroom, and one look told him not to venture any farther. The faucets in the sink and shower were dripping, staining the porcelain with rust in shapes that might inspire visions both sacred and profane. The wastebasket overflowed with tissue, paper towels, tampons, and God knows what else.

The presumably clean towels stacked behind the toilet suggested a touch of order that was quickly belied by a wet towel hanging on a rack and another on the floor. Good thing the lid on the toilet seat was down. He didn't want to think about what might be under it.

But when the candles were burning, the overhead light was off, and the curtains were closed, a guy whose only concern was his hard-on wouldn't notice any of it. Nick smiled as he remembered the times he had been blinded by horniness, and he wondered at the temptation he would face in the days and weeks ahead. Those were good-looking women out there, especially Kianna. She was enough to make him wonder if employees got discounts. Then again, it had never been his style to pay for it.

He stood and moved toward the only significant piece of furniture in the room besides the futon, a padded chair that looked like it belonged at a dining table. Before he reached it, he saw a door that had to be to a closet. What the hell, he'd checked out everything else. He opened it and saw the flimsy things the girls wore dangling from wire hangers. An instant later he was hit by an overpowering smell that had nothing to do with lingerie. It was pure stink.

The source was a pile of sheets and towels that had been thrown in the rear of the closet as soon as whatever happened on them happened, probably yesterday, although a smell like that could have been a week in the making. There was a vacuum cleaner tucked in a rear corner, too. As Nick wondered if it had ever been used, the bedroom door opened and Kianna stood there staring at him accusingly.

"Oh, shit," she said, "You're not a pervert, are you?"

"No, I'm . . . " He was searching for words and not finding them. It was Kianna's fault. Her boobs were right there ready to be stared at, and he didn't want her busting him for it. The look he'd gotten from Sierra had been embarrassing enough. But Kianna's boobs were still interfering with his ability to form an explanation, and it didn't seem like the time to bring up the general filth in the bedroom or the stench in the closet. Finally, against these impossible odds, he summoned a complete thought: "I'm looking for a vacuum. Thought I'd clean the place up."

"I don't think so," Kianna said.

"I'm serious."

"Are you sure?"

"Yes."

"Really?"

She kept staring at him, suspicion narrowing her eyes while a smile tugged at the corners of her mouth. She was beautiful even when confused.

"Hey," Nick said, "I found the vacuum, didn't I?"

She thought about that for a moment. "Okay," she said, letting her smile seize control of her face. "I was just going to ask if you wanted to come out. You really don't have to hide. Sierra was being a bitch. Just make sure you stay behind the dividers when there's clients, okay?"

"Will do," Nick said.

She turned and walked back to the living room. He followed, enjoying the view despite his suspicions about her hygiene. There was no TV—Scott had said he didn't want his girls wrapped up in *The Bold and the Beautiful* when they should be taking care of business—so Nick watched Kianna carefully pour oils and lotions she'd purchased at a ninety-nine-cent store into fancy unmarked bottles. "All the girls do it," she said. "Clients don't know the difference."

Sierra glared at Nick when she stepped out of the master bedroom to say her regular was getting dressed, but that was all. Maybe it was because she was preoccupied by the complaints she registered as soon as the poor goof was gone. She said he had the hairiest back she'd ever seen, and today he'd had toilet paper stuck to his ass, too. Kianna said she thought TP ass was cute.

A little before two, after Kianna had seen two clients and Sierra her second and third, Scott came by, fussing over the girls before he pulled Nick aside and shoved a notepad and a pen at him. They were for keeping track of how many clients the girls saw and how long the sessions lasted. Each girl, at the end of her shift, had to stop by a metal security box under the kitchen sink and deposit an envelope bearing the number she'd been assigned and containing the house's share of her daily earnings. "These fucking women would steal my goddamn lungs if I let 'em," Scott said. "And do not let them talk you into any kickbacks, man. Do not." Then he grabbed Sierra by the arm and steered her into the master bedroom for a massage, playfully slapping her on the rump and telling her she looked hot.

What Scott wanted, Scott got. Nick understood that. But it still bothered him more than he'd imagined it would. It must have showed, because he could see Kianna subtly shaking her head, reminding him to stay cool. "Scott always fucks her," she said. "I mean, it's what you've got to do to work here. But, like, once is enough, you know?"

Nick nodded and let it go at that. Kianna was soon back on the phone, lying on the sofa, acting like he wasn't there when she rubbed and scratched and picked at the remnants of the Thai lunch she and Sierra had had delivered. They hadn't offered him any, and he wasn't going to ask, even though his stomach was growling and Kianna seemed like the type to share. Until he got some money in his pocket, he'd have to remember to bring something from home, a sandwich or at least an apple. Plus, a newspaper to read so he wouldn't go nuts from boredom.

Sierra emerged from her romp with the boss looking flushed and messy. Five minutes later, Nick heard Scott before he saw him: "Christ, only one clean towel in the fucking bathroom." He finished his point when he stepped into view. "You damn well know I always use two. What the fuck is going on here, you want to tell me?"

The girls looked too frightened to speak. Once again Nick felt as though he'd been rendered invisible.

"This goddamn place costs me twenty-five hundred bucks a month and you've got it looking like a fucking pigsty." Scott turned his glare toward the other bedroom. "I don't even want to go in there, do I? Probably some kind of toxic waste site."

Nick fought back a smile.

"Get off your lazy asses and clean everything the fuck up. Jesus, how you going to make any goddamn money if it looks like a shithole in here?"

He slammed the door when he left. Nick couldn't help thinking the guy's performance was a rerun of something he'd done on TV. But it was too early in the game for Nick to be running his mouth about the boss, so he sat back and watched how the girls handled it.

"Get off your lazy fucking ass, Kianna," Sierra said, turning anger to petulance by mimicking Scott.

Kianna wrinkled her nose and said, "It's a fucking what kind of waste thingy did he say?"

"Toxic."

"It's a fucking toxic waste . . . "

"Site."

"Waste site. Yeah."

When they finished bitching and laughing, they began to clean up. Kianna, carrying a load of sheets and towels to the laundry room, looked like she wanted to ask Nick for help. "Uh-uh," Sierra told her, leaving unspoken the warning that he would rat them out to Scott.

The girls' shift was supposed to be over at three, but one of their replacements, a slender, waif-like Latina calling herself Riki, didn't show up until half past. Kianna seized the moment and split, saying she had to pick up a friend at LAX. With the phones ringing infrequently—Wednesdays were always slow, the girls said—Sierra devoted most of the next half-hour to muttering about how Ling always screwed her over like this. Ling was the AWOL masseuse, and the longer she was out there ignoring Sierra's messages and pages, the more interested Nick was in getting a look at her.

The big moment arrived at five-thirty, a good hour after Sierra had finally stormed off while Riki was telling her latest telephone

suitor, "There's no full service but I do allow mutual touching."
As Nick tried to break the code, Ling swept through the door like
royalty, carrying three bags from Bath & Body Works and not
bothering to apologize for being late.

When she noticed Nick, she looked down her elegant nose at
him and said, "Are you waiting for Riki?"

"No, I'm waiting for you," he said. "Been here all day."

"Is that a joke?"

"Afraid not."

"Well, like, clients aren't allowed in until it's time for their
appointment. Besides, I don't even know you."

Riki hung up and filled in the blanks for Ling: "This is Nick.
He's the security guy Scott got for us."

"He thinks he's funny," Ling said.

"I'm just trying to tell you I bumped into the guy across the
hall this morning," Nick said, blanking on the name and getting
no help from Riki. "Probably be a good idea to stay away from his
boyfriend. He was pretty upset."

"That little faggot Neal," Ling said, as if that explained everything. "Tell him he can go fuck himself."

"I'm not sure I'll see him again," Nick said.

"Whatever," Ling said, and she began taking oils and lotions
out of her bags, telling Riki how much they cost. Riki smiled
a ninety-nine-cent-store smile, as if to say Ling didn't know the
joke was on her, and Nick studied Riki's hair, which had been
bleached blonde and enhanced with braided extensions that went
to her waist. When she caught him looking—these girls were aces
at doing that—she gave him a little smile.

Ling booked only one appointment, a regular she polished off
in twenty minutes. Then she rushed to see Eddie, her lover with
the shifting sexual preference.

"You're not worried about the other guy?" Nick said.

"Neal? He's at work by now," Ling said. "Like a good little boy."

When she was gone, Nick felt a weight descend on him. He was more than physically tired, he was sapped in a way that made him wonder how many more days of this he would have to endure. It must have shown on his face, because Riki tottered over on five-inch heels after buzzing up her seven o'clock and deposited herself beside him on the sofa, pushing her braids off her shoulders so he could see her tiny breasts under a sheer negligee. "Want to hide in the closet and peek when I do my next client?" she asked. "I'm a squirter."

The warmth of her smile confused him at first. He wanted to think he had misunderstood this girl who must have been in high school only a year or two before, but he knew he hadn't. There was no other kindness she was equipped to offer. Just the same, he told her, "I better hang around out here." Her smile collapsed, and the day weighed more than ever.

13

It had been sunny, but the temperature hadn't climbed out of the sixties, so like any self-respecting Cali girl, Jenny spent the day freezing and wishing April was over. Now, as night fell, she was bundled in an XL fleece hoodie she had borrowed from an old boyfriend and never returned. It made her hips look enormous, but she didn't care. Fresh from work, Maria and one of the girls from her Chinatown place, a blonde who called herself Twyla, were making sure there was plenty to look at. They both had on camisoles that showed off their boobs and low-rise Juicy sweatpants so every man in the grocery store could see the tops of their thongs and the tailbone tattoos they called tramp stamps without a trace of irony.

Jenny couldn't resist glancing at the men and categorizing them—*Client . . . Not a client . . . Client*—the way she and Rosie used to when they goofed on everyone who ogled them at the Sherman Oaks Galleria. *Ogled.* Jenny loved that word. But she wondered if it really applied here at the Ralphs on La Brea and Third Street, where some of the oglers had to be Orthodox Jews. The neighborhood was loaded with them, guys who spent their Sabbath walking around in black suits and hats, looking very somber and holy. She used to see them on her way to work at Maria's place downtown, and even then she had wondered how many of them got massages. She knew it wasn't like being religious meant you never got horny. One of the girls she had worked with even had a rabbi for a client. Jenny tried not to imagine what it was like to jerk him off. Too bizarre, you know?

But Maria wouldn't have thought twice about it if she had the pope in her hand. She was oblivious to everything except money and finding ways to spend it. Her primary luxury, it seemed, was useless boyfriends. The first one Jenny knew about was a fat black drug dealer named Mookie who lived in his mother's guesthouse in Leimert Park and wouldn't sleep with Maria if she hadn't seen enough clients. For the last year she'd been supporting a photographer whose work was so bad that everyone except Maria realized it. He wasn't even cute, just a skinny white guy about forty who acted like his chin stubble made up for the hair he was losing. Maria bragged that he was a great artist, and the photographer was always trying to get the girls to pose nude for him. Some actually did, the really stupid ones.

It was the easiest thing in the world for Jenny to tell Maria's picture-taking boyfriend to fuck off, but Maria was another story. She was acting like she'd never heard Jenny's horror story from the Valley or processed her need to do massage only in a place that had security. Maria, in her blissful, willful way, had decided she would make dinner for Jenny and convince her to work in Chinatown. Why Twyla was included, Jenny still hadn't figured out. But there the three of them were in Ralphs, bending over the poultry case and laughing as the chill tweaked Maria's and Twyla's nipples.

Not ten feet away, an elderly man stared until Twyla gave him a nasty look. Then she turned back to Jenny and Maria and said, "What are we doing here anyway?" Her words sounded fuzzy enough to make Jenny think she was stoned.

"I'm going to cook chicken," Maria said.

Twyla looked down at the contents of the case. "Wow, is this chicken?" she said.

"Yeah, this is chicken," Maria said. "See on the package? It says right there."

Twyla stared at the words as if they were written in Sanskrit. Finally she said, "What if they're lying?"

"They can't do that," Maria said. "It's against the law."

"I don't know," Twyla said. "I've never seen chicken when it looks like this. I mean not, like, cooked. How can you be sure this is chicken?"

"I just can, all right?" Maria said. "And I'm going to cook it, and then it will look more, you know, like chicken."

Jenny listened to them for as long as she could stand it before wandering off in search of Top Ramen. Peeking down one aisle after another, she wondered just how weird her day was going to be after it had started so wonderfully. She had handed in a paper on Elizabeth Bishop's influence on Robert Lowell, hoping it would convince her teacher that Bishop was more important artistically and politically than the nutcase the class wasted so much time studying. Even if her plan didn't work, Jenny had learned more about Bishop—her twenty years in Brazil, her love affair with a female architect there, her dying too young at Harvard. Only now were Brazilians paying tribute to Bishop by reading her poetry and turning her life into a biography, a play, and a movie. It had taken so long because they had considered her scandalous for dressing in men's clothes and speaking in curses and just generally being Bishop. *Scandalous* was another word Jenny liked.

She wondered if it applied to the special on Top Ramen she found. Ten for a dollar—do the math and you were getting a whole dinner for ten cents. Definitely scandalous. But she wouldn't say so to Maria and Twyla. They weren't big on vocabulary, or anything else to do with words. Like reading, for instance. *Cosmo* was as deep as they got. And Jenny, finding them in the checkout line, could tell Twyla was a *Cosmo* girl just by the way she was ending a conversation on her cell, flirty and oblivious.

"It's black, very short, and very revealing," Twyla was saying. She smiled at what she heard next. "Okay, nothing underneath. See you in an hour."

She clicked off and turned to Maria, who was emptying her basket of chicken, frozen peas, white wine, and Ben & Jerry's Chunky Monkey. "Sor-reee," she said. "My favorite client."

"You've still got to eat," Maria told her.

Twyla grabbed a bag of Skittles off the candy rack. "Dinner," she said. Then she smiled as if struck by divine inspiration and grabbed a second bag.

Jenny, watching, saying nothing, decided that Twyla was one of those crack babies who are never hungry. All they crave is the energy to do more drugs. For them, Skittles was the perfect food, no fat, just sugar. Of course the sugar eventually turned to fat, but they never thought that far ahead. And if you suggested chocolate, which Jenny usually did to anyone who was hungry, they'd inevitably say, "My God, how can you eat chocolate?" *Right,* she thought, *like it's healthier for you to smoke a gram of ice every two days.*

It turned out that the chicken was no healthier than crack or chocolate after Maria broiled it beyond recognition. Good thing they could open the kitchen window in her frayed Silver Lake apartment or the smoke would have forced them to evacuate. For a moment they debated moving straight to the Chunky Monkey, but Jenny insisted that they needed to eat something at least a little bit healthy first. "Like Top Ramen?" Maria asked tentatively. Jenny screamed with delight. Dinner was served ten minutes later.

She was washing away the salty aftertaste with some Two-Buck Chuck when Maria said, "You didn't like Twyla, did you?"

"Did it show?"

"Yes. You bitch."

Maria laughed, and Jenny did too.

"I'm sorry. She just really annoyed me, you know? Who talks to a client about not wearing panties when they're in the checkout line at Ralphs? Plus she's a drug addict, right? Living on Skittles? Come on."

"At least Twyla never noticed you passing judgment on her. She was too busy being—"

"A skank?"

"Whatever."

"I'll probably never see her again anyway," Jenny said.

Maria nodded. "I can make sure you guys work different shifts at least. Hey, don't look so surprised. You're coming to work for me, Jenny. No way you're not."

Jenny's mother was the last woman to speak to her with such authority. Sometimes in dreams, sometimes when she was just stuck in traffic, Jenny could still hear her mother's voice scolding, nagging, pleading. It was a voice strained by the responsibility that came with not having a man around to share the load. Most of them split or were so brutish and unfaithful that pretty little Eun-Chu Yee did the splitting first, always certain the next one would be the right one. But when she finally found the right one, he died almost as soon as she wrapped her loving arms around him. She spent the next six years trying to kill her pain with drink, and then she died too, leaving Jenny, at sixteen, to either find another mother figure or fend for herself.

Maybe it was the extended time alone, with no guidance beyond instinct, that made Jenny respond to Maria the way she had. More than simply being older, Maria possessed the kind of wisdom that wasn't available in a classroom. As clueless as she was about romance, she was shrewd and clear-eyed when it came to separating clients from their money. Jenny didn't always approve of her methods—too cruel, she decided—but she recognized a survivor when she saw one. And at the moment, with her finances drained by the DMV and her lawyer, surviving seemed like the most she could hope for. But she still found herself resisting Maria's edict. She thought it must be a daughter thing.

"You don't have security," Jenny told her.

"You can work eleven to two, whatever days you want," Maria said. "Nobody gets robbed then."

"Did you take a survey?"

"I just know, okay? I've been in the business forever and . . . Look, two or three clients on whatever days you want, and then you go home. What could be safer?"

"A place with security," Jenny said. She wanted to add that she needed to see more than two or three clients a day, but she kept it to herself.

"You keep sixty percent," Maria said.

Jenny smiled. "I was going to keep sixty anyway."

"So you'll come?" Maria said. "Is that what you're telling me?"

"Is it me you want in particular," Jenny said, "or are you just, like, really hard up for an Asian girl?"

"I want a girl that's totally responsible, all right?" Maria said. "Not a flake, shows up on time, doesn't lie about how many clients she sees. And does her share of the laundry."

They both laughed. Jenny was compulsive about the laundry.

"If she's Asian too, that would be so cool," Maria said. "And you're, like, the only girl I know that's all those things."

This, Jenny knew, was as close to begging as Maria was going to get. And she liked Maria, she honestly did. There wasn't another girl in the business she trusted, respected, and enjoyed hanging around with as much. But Jenny still said, "I'm sorry, I can't do it. Not if you don't have security."

"You fucking hate security," Maria said. "Ever since that guy at my old place jacked off in your towel."

"He saw me in the shower, I think," Jenny said. "I guess he didn't know how to handle it."

"He handled it too much if you ask me," Maria said.

More laughter and then Jenny said, "That was before what happened in Sherman Oaks. Maria, I saw how those girls looked. I don't want to be like that, ever. And besides, that idiot who jerked off isn't exactly what I've got in mind now. You know, for security. It's got to be somebody, like, legitimately scary."

Maria responded with what Jenny thought of as her Mona Lisa smile, not that Maria knew what the Mona Lisa was, not that Jenny should have been thinking that way about a friend. "I've got something better," Maria said.

"Are you paying off the police?" Jenny asked, thinking for the first time that the job offer might work out after all. And wouldn't that be cool, working with Maria again.

"There's two or three that are clients," Maria said, "but no, that's not it."

"So what is it?"

"Can you keep a secret?"

"Maria, how many times have you asked me that since we met each other?"

"I don't know."

"Like hundreds, all right? Maybe millions. And have I ever told your secrets to anybody? Never. So quit playing games and either tell me or don't tell me."

Jenny startled herself with her boldness, feeling the shifting of power in their curious relationship. She wondered if Maria felt it too. Probably not, because Maria was lowering her voice as though she were afraid the apartment was bugged.

"I got a gun," Maria said.

Jenny's new sense of empowerment vanished. She could barely make herself say, "A gun?" It sounded lame and predictable, stupid even, but with the bottom dropping out of her stomach, it was the best she could do.

Maria said a lot more about what kind it was, and how many bullets it fired, and the damage it could do to a human being. She talked about taking lessons and going target shooting with her boyfriend and keeping it in her purse at work. She might even have mentioned how she could loan it to Jenny for protection if she was at the apartment by herself. But by that point, Maria's sales pitch had turned into a drone that threatened to drive Jenny out of her mind.

"I don't like guns," she said.

"You don't have to," Maria said. "Just pretend it's, I don't know, like your favorite blanket when you were a kid. Your security blanket. Come on, Jenny, you know you loved your blankie."

Maria manufactured a laugh, and Jenny wondered if she was overreacting. It wasn't like Maria had shot somebody with the gun she was talking about. She was trying to get Jenny to come to work for her, and this was how she thought she could close the deal. But even sugarcoating the idea couldn't settle Jenny's stomach.

"I'm not feeling very good," she said. "I think I better go home."

"But we've still got ice cream to eat," Maria said.

14

Coyle kept sniffing around like he could smell perfume on Nick the way you can smell cigarettes on a guy who hangs around smokers all day. Of course the girls didn't wear perfume, or use scented lotion and oil for that matter—clients were paranoid about anything that might tip off their wives and girlfriends. But Coyle's smile still made Nick uneasy every time the subject was the job he never talked about.

The last thing Nick needed was to have Coyle bugging him for an address and, once he got it, angling for a discount. There was an element of embarrassment in Nick's silence, too. What kind of job was guarding the girls in apartment 824? Hell, he wasn't even the piano player in the whorehouse.

He told Coyle he was doing a little maintenance work at an apartment complex. As vague as that was, there was an element of truth to it; he was always picking up after the girls who seemed to make a bigger mess than ever once they recognized how hung up he was on cleanliness. Typical Coyle, all he wanted to know was how the women in the complex looked. He even threatened to swing by some day and check them out. "Place got a pool?" he asked, as though he could wear down their resistance simply by slathering them with sun block. "No, no pool," Nick said. It was a lie, but Scott didn't allow the girls to go swimming in the rooftop pool, so the lie was close to true, and it turned out to serve a purpose. After Nick told it, Coyle didn't seem as interested.

It would have been a different story if Nick had talked about the slow stretches when the girls—except Sierra, of course—decided to have some fun with their bodyguard. They'd be tired of calling friends and chattering about everything from shoe sales to yeast infections, and there was Nick, the perfect cure for their boredom: a guy. They'd get wicked grins, the way Heather and Brandi did one drowsy Thursday when they tried to convince him to strip for them. "Come on," Brandi said in her Spanglish purr, "you see us naked all the time."

She and Heather flashed their tits at him while they tried to guess how big he was and how long he could go for. "If I told you," Nick said, "you'd never leave me alone." Which got all of them laughing until the phone started ringing again. Every once in a while after that, he saw them looking at him as if they wouldn't mind finding out how good he really was in bed.

He would have needed his plumbing checked if he didn't regularly get hard enough to cut diamonds. The girl he found himself thinking about most often was Kianna, who seemed available some days and as far away as the moon on others. Nick guessed she'd gone to the moon one afternoon when she came back from the bathroom sniffling and making a face. *Cocaine drip,* he thought. Riki had called in sick, so Kianna was the only one working. She seized the moment by perching on the arm of the sofa where Nick had parked himself and caressing his cheek as her breasts spilled out of a lace teddy.

"I like your stubble," she told him.

"Forgot to shave," he said.

"Keep forgetting."

"Even if it makes me itch?"

Kianna caressed his cheek again. "Mmmmm. Doesn't feel so bad to me."

"Me either, as long as you're doing that."

"Anything else you'd like me to do?"

Damned right there was, but before he could let her know what he had in mind, Scott walked in, abusing his agent on the phone and acting like a bigger star than he'd ever been. Nick wondered later why he hadn't just gone ahead and taken his best shot at Kianna because Scott was so wrapped up in himself that he never would have noticed. But Nick hadn't, and after that, all he got from Kianna was an occasional wink or a finger wagged at him like he was a naughty boy. And that, he thought, was as far as his chances went for getting a piece of ass on the job.

So he went back to being invisible and listened to the stories the girls told about the lawyer who came back to L.A. from a Supreme Court case wanting to be peed on and the late-night TV car salesman who dressed like a little girl and took a dildo up the ass. Sometimes all a client had to do to inspire ridicule was take his pants off.

"Curlicue dick," a pixie named Bambi announced one day after seeing a tiny, hatchet-faced movie producer. "It looked like a pig's tail."

"Oh, I've had guys like that," Sierra said.

Trust her to turn any conversation into a competition, Nick thought.

"No, worse than a pig's tail actually," Bambi said. "You could open a bottle of wine with it."

"Like a corkscrew, you mean?" Sierra asked.

"Uh-huh, uh-huh."

"So did he corkscrew you?"

The girls shrieked with laughter.

The parade through the front door never ended, men with money and sex drive to burn, some barely out of their teens, some way past retirement, almost all of them as ordinary-looking as a speed bump. Once the door closed behind them, though, they had a license to get weird.

One evening a bleached blonde named Tiffany emerged from the master bedroom wiping a gooey chocolate confection off the ample body she hadn't bothered to cover with a robe. Her client, so meek-looking he seemed almost prim, had shown up with two chocolate cream pies from Marie Callender's that she had automatically assumed were for the girls. But no, he carried them into the bedroom, removed them from their boxes, placed them on the floor at the foot of the bed and then took enough plastic wrap from his briefcase to cover the bed. He didn't want a massage, he just wanted Tiffany to walk back and forth in the nude while he sat on the bed and masturbated. "When he came," Tiffany said, "he stomped both his feet in the pies and—sploosh!—all over the place."

Nick shook his head in disbelief.

"What?" Tiffany asked.

"You girls are crazier than any fighters I ever met."

✣ ✣ ✣

Tiffany stuck around long enough to tell her story three more times, and then she was gone to wherever massage girls went when they went *poof*. By Nick's fifth week, that seemed to be happening a lot, the girls coming and going almost as fast as the clients. Kianna found out she was pregnant and headed north to San Jose to stay with her mother. Sweet little Riki loved the money, but the coke she bought with it rendered her so unstable that Scott fired her.

Only Sierra acted as if she were in for the long haul. She was a schemer and an angle player, cut from the same cloth as some of the managers and trainers Nick remembered from the fight game. Scott hadn't appointed her second in command, but that was the role she assumed when he wasn't around. "Don't fuck with me," Sierra warned more than one girl. But Nick knew there would be one who wouldn't take her at her word. It was a redhead named Tracy who was meeting clients away from the apartment and not kicking back 50 percent to Scott. When Sierra found out, the girl was gone before her shift was over.

"Fucking thief," Scott said.

"Didn't realize how good she had it here," Sierra said.

"Where's the appreciation, you know? I hate people like that."

"Me too."

"Damn, I need to unwind."

As if on cue, Sierra began to massage Scott's shoulders. "How's that?" she asked.

He turned to look at her. "Don't know what I'd do without you."

"Yeah?"

He responded by steering her to the master bedroom without another word. *What a piece of work,* Nick thought. Sierra was operating under the impression that she had something special with Scott, and Scott was enough of a businessman not to let her suspect otherwise.

If Sierra was easy for Nick to figure, Ling was borderline impossible. She showed up just a couple of days a week and usually saw only one regular. Any other business she got was by accident. Sierra said the only reason Scott kept Ling around was because she was Asian. Sometimes just saying an Asian girl was working would attract clients. Once they were in the door, they would be given the bad news that Ling had been called away because of a family emergency. But Heather, a redhead, was available. Or how about Carmen, the new Latina? There were other new girls as well, their phony names blurring together until Nick decided not to worry about remembering them all. He'd be polite and let it go at that. It wasn't like they noticed him anyway.

The clients turned out to be less trouble than the girls. Nothing more than a couple of drunks, a deadbeat who tried to skip out on Carmen without paying, and a guy who somehow got past the security door in the lobby and came upstairs saying he had an appointment with Ling. She hadn't worked in nearly a week at that point, so Nick hustled the guy to the elevator, telling him to stop the bullshit and squeezing his bicep just hard enough to let him know the pain could get worse.

Nick didn't mention it to Scott. Sierra did. But most of what she told him was intended to make Ling look bad, not compliment Nick for snuffing out a situation that could have brought the apartment manager down on them. "That bitch causes trouble even when she's not here," Sierra said.

"So get me a kinder, gentler dragon lady and I'll give Ling the boot," Scott said. "Otherwise, we need her. You know we do."

"Okay, I'll find another girl," Sierra said.

"Asian," Scott said. "Not some East L.A. *chiquita* that calls herself Hawaiian."

"I know the difference," Sierra said.

Nick couldn't tell what bothered her more, Scott's being so specific about his requirements for Ling's replacement or the thought of doing business without an Asian masseuse. Nick wondered about it himself until the afternoon Scott buzzed up a friend of his. A guy named DuPree.

Right away Scott started talking like he was from South-Central and gave the guy what Nick guessed was the latest soul shake. Nick had never kept up with the grips even when he'd been in a gym with black guys every day. All he knew was that this guy kept staring at him the whole time Scott was fronting. When Scott finished, DuPree had a question for Nick.

"Who the fuck are you?"

Scott answered before Nick could: "That's Nick, my security guy. I told you about him."

"Oh, yeah, the killer," DuPree said, still eye-fucking Nick.

"Left your manners in jail, huh?" Nick said, pissed off that Scott was using him like some kind of a show dog.

"Who you think you're talking to?" DuPree asked.

"I don't know, you delivering pizza?"

"Say what?"

"I'd like a ten-inch pepperoni."

"You a funny motherfucker, ain't you?"

DuPree gave Nick a look that was supposed to shrivel his balls, but Nick just stood there and sized him up. DuPree had to be three inches taller than he was, broad at the shoulders, narrow at the waist, with elevator shaft eyes that went all the way to the basement. But Nick had fought bigger men, beaten them and left them hurt and bleeding on the streets he once ran.

"Guys?" Scott said tentatively.

DuPree ignored him. Nick did too as he imagined what DuPree was thinking: how he'd like to cancel Nick's ticket, piss on his body and leave him for the worms. It wasn't because DuPree wanted anything Nick had or even because Nick had stood up to him. It was just who DuPree was.

"Come on, guys." Scott was trying again. "You gotta chill out."

It was the same shit as always, with or without the ghost of Alonzo Burgess. Nick wondered what it was about him that kept drawing him back to confrontation and violence. Maybe it was no more complicated than his having an instinct for recognizing an asshole who needed a beating. But Nick wished that just once a fight would be about something more than that. That was all. Just once.

"Want to see one of the girls, bro?" Scott said.

Nick saw a little of the badass in DuPree go away.

"Come on, man," Scott said. "Make you feel better."

"You got a problem with that?" DuPree asked Nick.

"Knock yourself out," Nick said.

It was the end of the day, and Sierra and yet another new masseuse, this one calling herself Hanna—she had a Swedish accent to go with her blonde hair and blue eyes—were ready to leave. They'd both seen five clients, and they were tired. "Jerk-off fatigue," Sierra called it. But being tired didn't explain the expression on her face when he proposed a massage for DuPree. She was scared.

Nick saw the look and thought it might be on with DuPree after all. He was here to protect the girls, and Sierra looked like she wanted protecting. Maybe it was innocence that made Hanna volunteer, or maybe she needed the money, or maybe she just liked black guys. It might have been all three, Nick thought, as he watched her take DuPree's hand and lead him to the guest bedroom, smiling as if he were her dream come true.

Sierra, her expression shifting from fright to disapproval, held her tongue until the door closed. Then she wheeled on Scott, saying, "Why do you bring that animal around here?"

"You don't get a fucking vote," Scott told her.

"You know—"

"Shut the fuck up. Whatever the man wants, the man gets, and whoever trots her sweet ass into that room with him damn well better provide. Are we clear on that?"

Sierra stared at him defiantly. It was obvious she wanted to say no, that she wanted to tell Scott to go to hell. Even Scott, usually so self-involved that he noticed nothing else, must have picked up on it. But there was something in his anger that took the backbone out of her, something that made Nick wonder what had happened the last time she stood up to Scott.

"I'm still waiting for an answer," he said.

"Yes," she said.

Her voice was almost inaudible; that should have been a concession in itself. But Scott wasn't going to let her off easy.

"What?" he said.

"I said yes," Sierra told him, her voice getting louder as her shoulders sagged. "DuPree gets whatever he wants. We'll treat him like the king of, I don't know, fucking Africa."

Scott worked up a big smile and wrapped an arm around her. "Come on," he said. "Let's do some lines."

He guided her toward the master bedroom. As she disappeared through the door, he looked back at Nick with a grin and pumped his fist like he was jerking off.

Even when he wants to be a good guy, Nick thought, *he's an asshole.*

✥ ✥ ✥

While Scott and Sierra broke the house rule against drugs, Nick sat in the kitchen, savoring the solitude, not bothering to turn on the lights as night fell. His thoughts were about leaving as soon as possible, just getting the hell away from this fucked-up business even if he'd have to come back to it in the morning. The strong were always feeding on the weak. It had been that way in boxing, and it was the same in this world of see-through blouses and pumped-up tits. Fucking wearying was what it was, Nick decided. Soon enough he was asleep.

When he woke, he made his way back to the living room, where the lone source of light was the lit end of Sierra's cigarette. She flinched when he turned on the floor lamp next to the sofa where she was camped out.

"They gone?" he asked

"Yeah." She stubbed out her smoke on the top of an empty Diet Coke can and dropped the butt inside.

Nick walked to the sliding door and opened it a crack to get some fresh air inside. One more edict from Scott: he didn't want the apartment smelling like an ashtray. Sierra knew it. But she had another cigarette lit by the time Nick turned around. She inhaled deeply, savoring the smoke as if it coated her nerves as well as her lungs. When she finally exhaled, she leaned back and the smoke formed a cloud over her head.

Nick looked closer at her then and saw Sierra as he never had before—worn to a nub, her vanity replaced by uncertainty and regret.

"What happened with Hanna?" he asked.

"Nothing."

"Bullshit."

"Hey, don't talk to me like—"

"I want to know what happened."

Sierra took a long drag on her smoke. "She didn't tell me."

"You saw her, though?"

"Yeah, when she was leaving."

"Did she look like all right? Did she say anything?"

Sierra paused to take another drag. "Goddammit," Nick said, knocking the cigarette out of her hand and grinding it out on the carpet with the sole of his shoe. "I want to know if Hanna was all right."

"You're never all right after you see DuPree," Sierra said.

"What do you mean?"

"Jesus Christ, use your fucking imagination."

Nick did, for just a moment. He didn't enjoy it.

"Was DuPree still around?" he asked.

"No, he'd taken off by then. Him and Scott both." Sierra shook her head. "I should have done him myself."

"It's a little late to volunteer."

"Fuck you," Sierra said, but her voice had none of its usual edge. "These girls come into this business just out of high school or maybe fresh off the boat, and they don't know shit about what they're getting into. They run into a guy like DuPree, they got no idea how rough it can get. That motherfucker, I wouldn't be surprised if he was, like, one of those psychos going around raping and robbing everybody."

"You serious?" Nick said.

"I don't know what the hell I am. I just know what's on the Internet. Plus I talked to some girls I used to work with."

"So tell me."

"You get off on this, is that what it is?"

"I want to know what I'll be up against if these assholes show up here."

"Yeah, right." Sierra chewed on a hangnail for a moment. "They found this girl that works alone, over by the Beverly Center, and after they finished with her, they fucked her in the ass with a gun. The barrel, you know? Over and over, taking turns, the sick motherfuckers. I heard she almost bled to death."

Sierra stared at Nick through hard eyes.

"Glad you asked?"

"Jesus," Nick said softly, and offered up a silent prayer for the girl in Sierra's story, and for Hanna, and for all the other soiled butterflies out there, whoever they were.

✥ ✥ ✥

Scott was already at the apartment when Nick showed up the next morning, proving there was a first time for everything. Scott was a late-afternoon, early-evening guy, so Nick figured he was going to get bitched at for his run-in with Scott's buddy. DuPree, that was his name. But Scott turned the conversation upside down by talking about the new TV series he was starting work on, as if Nick gave a damn.

"I really need to focus," Scott said. "Like, I know enough not to let myself get too high—Hollywood can crush your soul—but, man, this time I'm getting that old tingle."

"Throw yourself a party," Nick said.

"You got a bad attitude, you know that?"

"It's the only attitude I got."

"Well, cool it, all right?"

"I was going to tell you to do the same with that gangster you got for an asshole buddy. What the fuck were you thinking about, bringing him in here?"

Scott shook his head theatrically, the half-assed actor in him finally coming out as it did in almost every conversation he had. "You and that goddamned Sierra," he said. "I'm telling you . . . "

"It was Hanna I was thinking of," Nick said.

"Who?"

"You don't know?"

"How the hell am I supposed to keep track of—"

"Your buddy was with her last night."

"Okay, now I know who you're talking about. Miss Sweden, the blonde with the tits out to here. So what if DuPree saw her? He sees a girl every time he comes over."

"I think he hurt this one."

"Did she tell you that?"

"She didn't hang around to tell anybody anything."

"Then what makes you so sure she's hurt? For all you know, the little cunt took her money and ran off to see her fucking coke dealer."

Scott picked up his canvas script bag and started toward the door. Nick was right behind him, saying, "What if she didn't? What if she went to the ER instead?"

"Come on, lighten up. This is all because you've got a hard-on for DuPree. Let me tell you something: He stops by pretty regular, so you better get used to him."

"Does he tear up one of your girls every time?"

"We'll talk about it if the one you're so worried about ever shows up again, okay?" Scott paused before he opened the door. "Trust me, she was a flake."

"Hanna. Her name was Hanna."

"They're all flakes."

"Maybe so," Nick said, "but DuPree isn't going to hurt any more of them. You can tell him or I will. That shit's over."

15

Lay down the law to DuPree? Scott may have told Nick that was what he'd do, but fat fucking chance. Scott wasn't about to do anything that would get his head out of the place it was in. He told himself he was right where the Duke must have been for *Sands of Iwo Jima* and McQueen for *The Great Escape*. Sure, the money was shit, just seventeen-five an episode, but Scott's agent had promised they would renegotiate if the show got picked up for a second season. It was called *Mercs*, short for mercenaries, and Scott was playing Mac Alston, ex-Delta Force, now selling his killing skills wherever there was oil money, raghead motherfuckers, and slinky women with big tits.

"*Sergeant Rock* on steroids," his agent said.

"*Stormy Weathers* stranded in the fucking desert," Scott said.

It was more cheap-assed syndication, the kind of crap that would play in Des Moines at one in the morning. But Scott had been around long enough to know that miracles did happen— he'd been one himself, why couldn't he be one again? Besides, it wasn't like Hollywood was beating down his door. The trick was not to behave like this was his first job in a year. The trick was to act like a star.

Right away Scott started bitching about how his camos had to be just right, not simply torn and weathered so they looked like he had traipsed across the Sahara in them, but tricked up so they wouldn't show the vast expanse of his sea-bass white belly. And he told the head makeup girl he'd need vats of liquid tan to make sure he was the same color all over. When he winked, she made a face and started working on the young stud playing his sidekick. Scott admired the makeup girl's ass, showcased in cut-off jeans. Then he made a mental note to suggest that his sidekick die a horrible death in the pilot.

Bobby Jerome, the executive producer, might go for it as long as it didn't cost money. He and Scott went all the way back to *Stormy*, when Bobby didn't have his own sound stages, his own helicopter, or what seemed like all the money in the Santa Clarita Valley. In those days he'd been preoccupied with making people forget he'd started out in porn in the seventies, flashing his own hairy ass if it meant he didn't have to pay an actor. (Or, as his harshest critics suggested, pay to get laid.) The common wisdom was that Bobby cleaned up his act after his partner was shot to death while enjoying a poolside blowjob at his home in the Hollywood Hills. The killer had never been caught, and Bobby's career had taken off. As Bobby himself liked to say, always with what he considered an enigmatic smile, "Make of it what you will."

Scott still wondered where Bobby, who normally spoke in grunts and fucks, came up with that. It couldn't have been anything he'd read—Scott wasn't sure Bobby could read—and he was too passionately cheap to have paid a writer to put the words in his mouth. But at the moment Scott had more pressing concerns. His sidekick was one; the little prick could die in his arms, and then Scott, tears streaming down his face, could get revenge by mowing down a couple hundred Saddam Hussein–looking cocksuckers. Bobby loved that shit.

The problem was, he loved the director of the pilot, too, and the director was the other bug up Scott's ass, a preening jerkoff who waltzed around the set in the kind of cape only Superman and Batman should have been allowed to wear. It was bad enough that he hadn't shown up until the next to last day of preproduction, like his previous commitment to do an episode of fucking

JAG qualified as an excuse. But that was just the beginning. This dipshit who could barely cut it as a gofer on *Stormy Weathers* was now badgering the actors to say their lines faster and faster, and it wasn't like he was dealing with a cast of seasoned pros who could shrug off his bullshit. Only the unwanted and the unwary wound up doing claptrap like *Mercs*, and the unwary, Scott's sidekick included, were bewildered after the first day of shooting. The director never noticed, probably because he was gearing up for his next chance to bellow an "It's in the movie!" instead of a simple "Cut!" It was all Scott could do not to grab him by the throat and scream, "It's not a movie, you simple motherfucker, it's a fucking TV show!"

Scott thought he would mellow out that evening—a little wine, a little smoke, a five-hundred-dollar piece of ass—but it did no good. He couldn't sleep until he had assured himself he would go straight to Bobby in the morning and tell him to get rid of the shit-for-brains director. Or maybe he'd just let Bobby watch the dailies and decide for himself that the director was as useless as tits on a board. No sense in Scott flexing his star muscles if he didn't have to.

But he still got out of bed with tension knotting his neck and shoulders. He had an 8 A.M. call, which put him in makeup by 6:30, the head girl working on him again, looking pretty even when she frowned and told him to stop twisting around. He tried to obey and enjoy the view. The sun had streaked her short blonde hair, and there was a spray of freckles across her nose. She was wearing a sweatshirt from a surf shop in Huntington Beach, and Scott, wondering what she had on under it and hoping it was nothing, felt himself getting hard. When he shifted in his chair, he got the friction he hoped for.

"Would you please stop that?" the makeup girl said.

"Yeah, if you'll do me one favor," Scott said. "Just a little something to loosen me up."

The makeup girl paused from her work on his eyebrows and gave him a weary smile. "I'm not jerking you off, asshole."

"Forget that," Scott said. "I want you to put a lip lock on the spitting end of my fuck stick."

No woman had ever slapped Scott as hard as the makeup girl did, dropping everything in her hands and unloading with the palm of her right. His ears were ringing.

"What the fuck?" he said, sounding confused, even innocent.

And she slapped him again.

Two hours later, he was officially unemployed. Bobby didn't want to hear about all the times Scott had used the same line— and scored with it. "That day's fucking gone," Bobby said, the old porn king suddenly assuming the role of moral arbiter, the shining knight who wouldn't tolerate sexual harassment on any set of his. Scott, his head swimming, tried to defend himself by saying how much *Mercs* needed him, how he was the only star who could carry the show. Bobby just laughed. There were dozens out there like Scott, big apes who had played Hercules and Sinbad and were just as desperate as he was to become something besides the answer to a trivia question. "Every scene you did yesterday was shit," Bobby said. "Shit, shit, shit." When Scott finally slunk out the door, he was certain the director had poisoned Bobby's mind against him. Some day he might even track down the back-stabbing motherfucker and kick his ass. But when he checked his watch, he knew he had more immediate concerns. Not even ten, still plenty of time for more to go wrong in his world.

✤ ✤ ✤

At first Nick didn't connect Ling with the noise he heard in the hall, the muffled voices, the slamming doors, the thumping that could have come from a late furniture delivery. Sierra was busy with a client and Ling had slipped across the hall to do whatever she did with the gay guy in there. She seemed to spin a little more out of control every day: totaling her BMW, dropping out of Pepperdine, catching hell from Scott for bringing drugs to work, tying up the phone with screaming matches with her parents, and smirking when they bought her an even more expensive BMW.

It was obvious Ling didn't need massage to survive, but she couldn't walk away from it. Maybe she liked to hear clients telling her she was beautiful. Maybe the money financed the drug habit she kept secret from her parents. Who the hell knew? Certainly not Nick, who had felt her contempt from the first time they laid eyes on each other. And yet he couldn't keep his mind off the life she was turning into a train wreck, couldn't stop thinking she was kidding herself if she planned on putting it back on the tracks with a regal toss of her hair.

She was in his head again when the noise in the hall was punctuated by screams that could only have been hers. He threw aside the *Daily News* sports section he'd been reading and rolled off the sofa, running as soon as his feet hit the floor, bumping one of the room dividers in his rush past it and scarcely noticing. It was still wobbling when he yanked open the door and charged out, expecting to find Ling being gutted like a fish. Instead, she was scratching Neal with her long acrylic nails, leaving his cheek gashed and bloody.

Neal screeched with pain, clamping his left hand to his wound while he flailed at Ling with his right. "Bitch, cunt, twat!" he screamed.

"Faggot asshole!" Ling screamed back, and went for his eyes.

Neal, backpedaling frantically, got his feet tangled and fell on his ass in front of his open apartment door. An instant later, a man peeked out, beyond handsome, perfect in every respect—except for the terror that filled his blue eyes. *Got to be the Eddie that Ling's banging,* Nick thought.

But Eddie was the furthest thing from Ling's mind now. Moving as though she weren't wearing fuck-me shoes, she went after

Neal, and Neal, sitting there helplessly, burst into sobs that shook his frail body, a lamb ready for slaughter. Ling took one more step and started to kick only to have Nick grab her right arm and yank her backward. The kick just missed Neal's face. An inch closer and her five-inch heel might have taken out an eye.

She wheeled around to see who had grabbed her, shrieking, "Get your fucking hands off me!"

Nick started dragging her back to the apartment, trying to keep her moving without hurting her. She dug her heels into the carpet, and he thought he heard one of them snap.

"Goddammit, let me go!"

She wasn't looking at him when she screamed, though. Her focus was on the place she had just left against her will. He tried to keep her moving without hurting her. It wasn't easy.

"Eddie!" she shouted. "Eddie!"

That was when Nick saw what Ling did: her lover kneeling beside Neal, comforting him, kissing him and stroking his arm, both men crying.

"No," Ling said, her voice reduced to an anguished whisper.

She went limp in Nick's grasp. He had to hold tight to keep her from collapsing. Then she began crying too, and he felt his control of the situation evaporate. He could stand there propping her up until his arms fell off, but she was the one who would decide when they would move again. It would have been comical—the tough guy undone by a woman's tears—but when he looked down the hallway, he saw the first crowd he had drawn since he was fighting. From every door, tenants were staring out at him and the sideshow he had just been part of.

16

There was some fundamental law of economics at work, Jenny was sure of it. Well, yeah, she told herself: everything out and nothing in equals empty safe-deposit boxes. But it was more complicated than that because she'd had no way of knowing how quickly her problems would deplete her finances. It wasn't just her lawyer's retainer and the penalties from the DMV. It was her rent and, talk about ironic, her car insurance. Now next month's rent was coming up, plus she still had to pay the rest of what she owed her lawyer. Some nights she couldn't sleep because she was so pissed about all the money she had wasted on things she couldn't even remember. Some days she woke up pissed because she was being so picky about a massage job; she'd never been this picky about clients. Maybe she'd have to offer her lawyer a deal after all, her services for his. How tacky would that be?

Jenny was wrestling with the question when Sierra called. It was the same name she'd used when they worked together in Woodland Hills. Could it have been real? Jenny wondered. No, she probably kept it to make sure her clients followed her. The two of them had never been friends or anything. In fact Jenny thought Sierra was pretty much a bitch, beautiful but vain and bossy and, like so many girls, super catty. Sierra had never said much to her, or to Rosie either, which made Jenny wonder if she had a problem with Asians. But now Sierra was on the phone acting like she really cared what Jenny was doing.

"Going to school, mostly," Jenny said. She wondered how Sierra had gotten her number. Probably from Rosie.

"You working anywhere?" Sierra asked.

"No, I'm taking some time off to concentrate on my classes," Jenny said. "I want to maybe go to UCLA next year."

"Oh," Sierra said.

She sounded disappointed, like she was already giving up on the massage job Jenny hoped she was preparing to offer. Like, why else would she have called?

"But tuition keeps going up every year," Jenny said. "I've got to save lots of money."

"Yeah, I heard it was pretty expensive." Was that relief in Sierra's voice? "Maybe I can help you—if you, like, still want to do massage."

"I suppose," Jenny said, trying to find the right tone, not too eager, not too distant.

She leafed through Bishop's *Complete Poems: 1927–1979* while Sierra laid out the situation: upscale apartment on the Westside, two shifts a day Monday through Friday, one on Saturday, two girls per shift, the girls keep everything they make in tips but the boss gets 50 percent of the donation.

"I told him all about you," Sierra said, "but you've still got to meet him before you get hired."

"Right," Jenny said. "I can see if I like him then."

"And if he likes you," Sierra said.

Okay, she's still catty and she's definitely polishing the boss's knob, Jenny thought. But she said, "Can I ask one other thing?"

"What?" Sierra said as if she were suddenly weary of this conversation.

"Is there security?" Jenny said.

"For sure," Sierra said. "These days you'd have to be, like, totally insane not to have security, you know?"

Jenny knew.

✤ ✤ ✤

She walked into the Coffee Bean & Tea Leaf on Montana thinking that this Scott guy she was supposed to meet wouldn't win any points for originality. But everybody else came here—off-duty soccer moms, directors between movies, the idle rich down from Brentwood—so she guessed that a pimp could too. She just hoped she wouldn't run into someone from school or any old clients among the polished wood surfaces and the jars full of coffee beans. Not that old clients were much of a concern. For one thing, L.A. was so big that it seemed to swallow everybody. For another, at two on a Tuesday afternoon—okay, a quarter after—they were probably all at work, making money they could spend on girls they weren't married to or dating, girls like the one she would become again if this meeting went right.

She spotted a guy she thought was Scott at a corner table. Faded denim shirt outside his khakis, probably to cover his belly. *Yeah, definitely,* she thought once she got closer and saw his jowls. But he was still handsome in a scuffed-up way. She wondered what kind of problems he had that he would let himself go like that. She was sure he'd tell her. Guys always did, once they stopped wondering how she looked naked.

"Scott?" she said, stopping two steps away from the table.

"If you're Jenny," he said, "you're late."

"Sorry," she said. "Parking was, like, impossible." She was going to add that she was being extra careful because she was driving without a license, but then she thought better of it. Too much information.

When she sat down, she made a point of shaking his hand. It felt like a dead fish. There wasn't any light in his eyes either. He wasn't like the other guys who had interviewed her for massage jobs. They'd all tried to impress her, flirting and cracking jokes like they were on a first date or something. Maybe he was tired. No, that couldn't be it, not in a place where caffeine ruled. She decided that he'd just been shortchanged in the personality department. But she still said, "Nice to meet you," and tried to sound like she meant it. She needed the job. Or she thought she did until Scott said he wanted 60 percent of what she got for every massage.

Sierra had told her fifty and Jenny didn't even want to settle for that. "Sixty?" she said. "No way." And took a sip of green tea.

"That's what the other girls give me," Scott said.

Okay, Jenny thought, *he's a liar too.*

"You know you'll make a fortune doing extras," he said.

"I don't do extras."

"Right."

"I don't. Really." Okay, now she was lying. But she didn't do extras for many clients, usually just one guy she decided was special, maybe even started seeing away from work. In the massage business, that practically made her a vestal virgin.

Scott resumed looking at her straight on. Maybe he was starting to believe her. "You must not have any regulars," he said.

"Oh, I have lots of them."

"And you don't do extras. What do you do, hypnotize them?"

"Trade secret."

"I get it. Some Asian deal, right?"

"Maybe," Jenny said. What was it about the mysteries of the Orient that made douchebags like this guy so easy? She had no idea if there were any mysteries of the Orient at all. "But I thought we were talking about your cut," she told Scott. "I mean, like, sixty percent is pretty steep. Everywhere else I've worked, I was always able to make my own deal."

"What did you have in mind?" he said.

"Sixty percent for me," she said.

At last his eyes showed something: disbelief. "Now you're fucking with me," he said.

"No, I'm straight up telling you I'll still make lots of money for you even if you only take forty percent."

"And then you'll tell the other girls, and then they'll be bitching to me: 'How come Jenny—'"

"I always call myself something else," she said, wishing Sierra hadn't told him her real name.

"Whatever," he said. "They'll be bitching about how come you get sixty and they only get fifty."

"But you just told me they got forty."

Jenny made a point of smiling when she said it, like she'd caught him checking her out in a department store.

Scott smiled back and said, "Whoops."

"It's all right," Jenny said. "I understand."

"You do?"

"Sure. You're running a business and you want to make the best deal you possibly can. It's common sense."

"Right," Scott said, nodding, trying to look, wise although Jenny didn't think he had the face for it.

"So can you live with sixty-forty for me?" she said. "I don't think you'll be sorry."

"Oh yeah?"

The question hung in the air while Scott sized up as much of her as he could see, the face, the long hair, the pink sweater. Jenny imagined that he probably remembered the tight jeans she had on too.

"Okay," he said. "I guess I can live with that."

But when he cranked up his smile, experience told her what was coming next.

"Just to be on the safe side, though, I'm going to need you to give me a massage. You know, so I'll be sure you can handle the job."

It looked like he was trying not to leer. She had to give him credit for that. But she still said, "In your dreams."

✦ ✦ ✦

Coco or Koko? Jenny wrote both names on a legal pad in long-hand and stared at them. She didn't like her penmanship, never had. Why couldn't it be elegant and graceful? Maybe because she wasn't elegant and graceful, she thought. Then, laughing, she printed both names in block letters.

There, that was closer to the way her next massage name, whatever it turned out to be, would look on the IrubLA website and in the back pages of *L.A. Weekly*. The Internet ad would feature a photo of her, one breast seductively bared but her face blurred so if anybody from her real life saw it, they'd say, "Hey, that looks like . . . but no, she'd never do massage." That was all Jenny asked of the ad: plant the seed of doubt, give her plausible deniability, so she could move on unencumbered.

But with her face blurred, she needed to choose a massage name that would establish for even the densest horndog that she was Asian. Scott's first choice had been Asia, as though a million other girls, Asian and otherwise, hadn't already used it. The suggestion was, to Jenny's mind, further proof that the man was not a genius. Then again, he might have been trying to make nice with her after she had shot down his request for a freebie. It would have been a deal breaker if, after scowling, muttering, threatening, and pleading, he hadn't backed down. He would never tell anybody what happened, of course—he'd probably say just the opposite—but that would only put him in the same category as the other men she had worked for.

So Asia was out, and it had lots of company on Jenny's discard pile. Another girl had snapped up Suki in the short time since she'd abandoned the name, and she didn't want to go back to Kimmi, the only other name she liked. There were already two Jades working as well as a Mei, a Mai, and a Mai Tai. Kiannas and Briannas came and went with great frequency; Mikas and Mikos did too. The barrage of exotic pseudonyms had Jenny on the verge of a headache. Then *Ling, Ming, Ping, Pong* raced through her mind and she burst into laughter. Good thing she wasn't doing this at the library; people would have thought she was crazy. It would be hilarious to call herself Ping-Pong except she wasn't trying to scare clients away or, as would inevitably happen, inspire one of them to show up with two paddles and a ball in an attempt to charm her. Ming was too close to Ling, and there was already a Ling working for Scott, although he didn't seem to be overjoyed with her.

Back to Coco and Koko. Jenny knew that both names had wear and tear on them. But they hadn't been used in—she was guessing now—at least six months, and in the massage business, that was the equivalent of mummies in a tomb in Egypt. So it all came down to two letters, C and K, and when she made her decision, it was based purely on aesthetics. Koko with a K struck her as too harsh, and she wasn't that kind of a girl. She was Coco with a C because C looked softer.

17

It was almost quitting time when Sierra told Nick to stay put. He was surprised she was still around. She had seen her last client of the day half an hour before, and it wasn't like her to wait for Ling, who was polishing off a regular she would start bitching about the moment he was gone. Nick wondered what the poor son of a bitch's sin would be. An unwashed butt? Fingernails bitten until they were bloody? A flare-up of psoriasis?

Nick never found out. As soon as Ling rushed her client out the door and tottered back into the living room on red stilettos, Sierra pounced.

"Scott's hiring a new girl," she said. "Asian."

"Oh?" Ling said, unfazed. "Who is she?"

"I think I used to work with her," Sierra said.

"You think?" Ling said. "Like, do you have amnesia or something?"

"No," Sierra said, drawing the word out, annoyed.

"When does she start?"

"Tomorrow."

Nick saw Ling's head snap back, like she'd been hit with a stiff jab.

"Tomorrow?" she said. "That's cool, I guess. I was going to take tomorrow off anyway."

"You didn't tell me," Sierra said.

"Well, I would have."

"Right."

Ling didn't seem to notice Sierra's sarcastic tone or the glare that accompanied it. "I'll bet I'm prettier than your friend, aren't I?" she said.

"She's not my friend," Sierra said. "But no, you're not prettier."

Nick watched Ling's eyes burn with the first signs of anger and frustration. He found himself wishing she'd shut up, but knew she couldn't.

"Then she's probably stupid," Ling said.

"I don't think so," Sierra said, relishing another chance to sink her claws into Ling. "She goes to college."

"Like, beauty college?"

"UCLA."

"Well, I go to college too."

"You told me you dropped out."

"Just for the semester. I'm going back in the fall."

"Great. You guys will have lots in common."

Sierra smiled triumphantly while Ling stood there searching for words with which she could fight back. When she couldn't find them, she dropped to her knees and burst into tears. "I hate her!" she wailed, pounding the floor with her tiny fists. "I hate her, I hate her, I hate her!"

A wave of sorrow swept over Nick, catching him by surprise. How could he possibly feel sorry for Ling? She was arrogant, unreliable, uninterested in getting along with anyone whether it was a client, another masseuse, or Nick. He knew this upscale jack shack would be better off without her, and yet seeing her humiliated, stripped of pride and dignity, went far beyond any payback he had imagined. It was like watching an execution. He wished he hadn't been a witness to it, just as he wished he hadn't watched Holmes beat Ali. When he glanced at Sierra, hoping she would show a little compassion, he saw her giving Ling the finger even though Ling wasn't looking at her. It was apparently the thought that counted.

Sierra never noticed when Nick eased toward the guest bedroom. He stayed there until he was sure both girls were gone without a goodbye. His gut told him Ling wouldn't be back. It happened all the time, some girls crying, some pissed off, some just screwed up, but he still wasn't right with it.

✤ ✤ ✤

He parked on the freeway side of Beloit, where he could always find a space next to the rusting wire fence. Maybe the people who left the spaces empty were afraid the branches that fell off the eucalyptus trees would hit their cars. It was the kind of thing Nick didn't worry about. His pickup was so dinged up that a few more dents wouldn't hurt it.

As he started toward his apartment, he saw two of the Mexicans from next door trying to lift something large and ungainly into the back of their rattletrap truck. It looked like a contraption for aerating lawns; he'd driven one the summer after he dropped out of high school, working on a golf course and getting the roughest ride he'd ever had. The damned thing felt like it weighed a ton back then, and it didn't appear to have gotten any lighter. The Mexicans, just skinny kids really, didn't have a prayer in hell of getting it up where they wanted it to go.

Nick thought of the kids' two bosses already inside kicking back with cold *cerveza* and walked over to see if he could help. "You need a couple boards," he told the kids. "Then you can run that thing up in there easy."

They looked at him, uncomprehending, and dropped the machine, laughing self-consciously when its handle banged into the grill of the dirty Ford Taurus behind them. Okay, so there wouldn't have been room for the boards even if they had them.

After that, Nick didn't bother asking if they *se habla*'d English, he just grabbed hold of the aerator and waited for them to realize he was willing to lend some muscle. The kids looked at each other, grinning and chattering in Spanish. One of the few words he understood was *pendejo*. Okay, they thought he was a sucker. But he didn't let go of the aerator, and soon enough the kids got the message: three was better than two when it came to wrestling this big son of a bitch.

The kids stepped up to the aerator, Nick counted off—"*Uno, dos, tres*"—and they lifted. Nick could hear them grunt with effort, and he felt them wobble, but when they saw the gringo doing his share and more minus the bullshit, they found the little extra it took to get the aerator onto the truck bed. The kids clambered after it to tie it down while Nick savored the blood surging through his muscles. It reminded him of the way he used to feel after sparring.

"*Gracias*," one of the kids said. He and his buddy were back on the street now, still smiling, and his buddy was offering Nick a can of Tecate.

It was warm, but Nick accepted it with a *gracias* of his own, then gave them a little salute with the can and headed down the narrow, overgrown walk to his apartment. He would damned sure drink the beer once it had spent some time in his fridge and he had taken a shower. But his plans went on hold when he opened his door to the sound of a ringing phone.

He answered it before he turned on a light, and heard Cecil saying, "About damn time. Where you been? I keep leavin' messages you never answer."

"My answering machine's been screwed up," Nick said.

"Bullshit. You been duckin' me."

Cecil had heard Nick lie before, about how he felt between rounds, about whether he was doing his roadwork, about all the things fighters lie about. The lies hadn't worked then either.

Nick couldn't help laughing. "Come on, Cecil, let me get away with something, would you?"

"Too late to start that shit."

Nick knew Cecil well enough to know he was smiling. Not a big smile, just this little thing he did with the right side of his mouth.

"How you been?" Nick asked. "You doing all right?"

"Gettin' old, that's how I'm doing," Cecil said. "You wanna hear me complain, I'll buy you another dinner next time I'm in town. I like an audience."

"All you got to do is call."

"Now you startin' with the bullshit again."

"Give me a break, would you? I been busy."

"Doin' what?"

"I found a job," Nick said. "Maintenance. In an apartment building."

"That right?" Cecil asked. "Who you working for?"

"You know the guy. You gave me his number."

"Maintenance, huh?"

"They didn't have an opening for president," Nick said, worried that Cecil's radar had picked up another lie.

"My neighbor's boy working with you?" Cecil asked.

"Someone from Vegas? Not that I know of."

"My neighbor in the 'Shaw." Cecil sounded agitated, the way he used to get when Nick didn't stick and move. "DuPree."

It took a moment for Nick to realize Cecil was talking about the guy Scott had brought around the apartment, the one who had mad-dogged him and maybe hurt that girl Hanna. The hard-on with the ex-con stare.

"Oh, yeah, I met the guy," Nick said. "Hangs out with my boss. But he's not working there."

"Don't be bullshittin' me," Cecil said, surprising Nick with the sharpness of his tone.

"What the hell, Cecil? You pissed off because I didn't call and say thanks, I got a job because of you? Then I'm sorry, all right? I apologize. I'm grateful for the help, you know I am. But jump back, would you?"

Cecil wouldn't. "Been botherin' my ass since I give you that number," he said. "I don't want you havin' nothing to do with that boy DuPree. You hear me? Nothing."

"What's the problem?"

"He's evil."

"How about we split the difference and call him an asshole?"

"You ain't hearin' me," Cecil said. "This muthafucka's a criminal. You give him half a reason and he will put you in the ground."

"If he tries," Nick said, "he better bring a big shovel."

18

The morning of her first shift, hours before she had to make the short drive to Ashton Avenue, Jenny kept wondering if there was a genetic explanation for the life she was going back to. Her mother had used her body as a means of survival too, although the circumstances in her case had been far more extreme, maybe even life threatening. She had nothing else at her disposal, poor Eun-Chu Yee, abandoned in Seoul by the farm boy who got her pregnant with Jenny and beaten by the sweet-faced GI who took her for a wife and brought her to America.

He beat her there as well, on the ragged lawn of an apartment complex in Downey, a blue-collar refuge obscured by the glare of L.A.'s glamour. Her screams cut through the hum of traffic on the 605, but not until years later did Jenny learn about the miscarriage and the little sister who was never born.

Eun-Chu Yee was brave to talk about such things, brave in a way Jenny couldn't be about the GI who had sneaked into her bed to touch her and make her touch him. Jenny had always imagined that he went straight from one of their forlorn assignations to the strip club where he found her mother a job. He was leaving for a post in Germany, and he wanted to make sure the two of them could get by without any help from him. What he didn't count on Eun-Chu finding in that cinderblock fleshpot was the power she held over men.

Maybe the source of it lay in her sculpted cheekbones and sumptuous breasts, or the shimmering hair that flowed to her waist until she decided it was boring and chopped it off. Even then, shorn to the ears, eyes gleaming at the shock she inspired, that self-made gamine looked better, sexier, more intriguing than any woman Jenny had ever seen. But there was more to her mother's impact on men than the desire she stirred in them, and it was written in her impetuousness.

Eun-Chu Yee was a creature of impulse, forever embracing a new enthusiasm and then dropping it in a heartbeat for the next one. Jenny suspected it was that way with men, too. She had seen the parade through the tumbledown places where they lived, the broken-walled apartments and converted garages where she learned to hate the smell of kimchi and picked up the physical mess in her mother's wake. The psychological mess was for Eun-Chu Yee to handle on her own, no matter how limited her resources.

The only break she got was named Dailey Watkins. Jenny thought her mother had met him in the club where she danced, as if that mattered, as if you think less of an oak tree because it grows in a junkyard. Dailey's black skin scared Jenny at first. It was, she thought, an understandable reaction after the way black GI brats had bullied her in Korea and black school kids had welcomed her to the States by mocking her slanted eyes. But if Dailey sensed her fear, he said nothing, preferring to win her with his laughter and the offer of his hand to hold. "You one more princess, ain't you?" he said. "Just like your mama." And he won her heart, just like he'd won her mother's.

They lived in Long Beach, in the house on Obispo Avenue where he had taken them, its flower beds perfectly tended, its stucco walls painted just so. He never complained about the kimchi and he said he loved Korean barbecue as much as he did the ribs he brought home from Compton. Jenny believed every word because she had watched him in the yard with her mother, cutting roses to put in a vase, and she had seen how he stroked her mother's hair. There was something approaching reverence in that simple gesture, something that crystallized the love Eun-Chu Yee had done without for so long.

She had a year to treasure it, and then it was gone, stolen from her by the accident that killed Dailey on the construction site where he was working. "He was the man God sent me to love," she told Jenny. And what was there to say after that except good-bye to the security he had given them? They were princesses no more, thrust back into a life of drifting and jobs that Eun-Chu Yee never discussed. Jobs in hostess bars, Jenny guessed. More jobs stripping. And with them came men introduced by only their first names, men who craved her mother's beauty and mocked her broken English, men with beer and liquor and Polaroid cameras who would take her mother into the bedroom after she had posed for them wearing nothing but a stunned smile, her legs spread wide.

It should have been a relief when she found religion, but the transformation only produced another kind of madness. Every mundane act, every conversation, every breath seemed to evoke a burst of praise for the Holy Trinity that Jenny's mother had somehow reduced to two, "the God and the Jesus." Jenny couldn't bring friends home for fear they would be sermonized, proselytized, anesthetized. She was hardly able to bear the thought of going home herself until her mother backslid into more booze and rump shaking.

Saturday night had triumphed over Sunday morning, and Jenny felt like celebrating until the police woke her with the news that Eun-Chu Yee had died in a one-car crash with only a bottle of cheap Scotch for company. Jenny was sixteen when she was thrown into the survival test called life, and now it was six years later and she was wiping away tears she hadn't expected to cry. They were all she had to offer the memory of her mother, unless she wanted to include her new job. Her mother might not have approved of it, but she certainly would have understood. Maybe it really was genetics.

✣✣✣

Okay, a little lipstick, a little blush. Forget about Elizabeth Bishop and prepare to get naked. *La-la-la-la, la-la, la*: just like that, she was Coco. It was easy for Jenny to make the transformation because life became so uncomplicated when she turned herself into this fantasy creature who existed solely for sex. All she had to do was laugh and be pretty and she was insulated from real life.

When she showed up for her first day in Scott's harem, she would have sworn she could feel a change, but maybe it was the new thong she was wearing. She rang the apartment from downstairs and a man answered. *Must be the security guy,* she told herself, and didn't give him another thought until he opened the door to 824 for her.

"You're early," he said.

"I'm kind of obsessive-compulsive," she said.

"Me too," he said. "Just don't expect to find anybody else like us here."

"Why am I not surprised?" she said, smiling and getting a crooked, almost boyish grin in return. She liked it. All she'd been hoping for was someone who wasn't drooling, and here was a guy she wouldn't have minded hitting on her in a club. And yet he was different from the lawyers and software designers who usually took a run at her. They didn't flow when they walked, and he did. Their eyebrows and cheekbones weren't riven with scars, and his were. She didn't need to look at his fists to know she was in the presence of a tough man, but that was cool. She'd never met one before. Her only real question was, what would she talk about with him? She would figure it out soon enough. At the moment there was something else she needed to know: "Is Scott around?"

"He's not exactly a morning person," the security guy said.

"Oh." For a moment, she thought about explaining what had happened when Scott interviewed her, how she had been late and that really wasn't like her at all, hence her arrival at 10:23 A.M. Instead, she reminded herself of who she was supposed to be and said, "I'm Coco," and offered him her hand.

"They told me you'd be here," he said as he took it. "I'm Nick. Any problems, I'll take care of them for you."

His grip was comforting, like he was saying she could trust him. His eyes said the same thing. But she saw sadness in them, too, and she got the feeling that the sadness was there to stay.

Jenny was wondering what that was all about when she realized she hadn't let go of Nick's hand. When she did, she tried to hide her embarrassment by glancing around the apartment. "Nice place," she said. It was better than saying it was just like every other upscale massage operation she'd seen. She wondered if they all got their room dividers from the same store.

"You want to hang up your stuff, the master bedroom's that way," Nick said.

"Thanks," Jenny said, grateful he had looked at her face and not her boobs.

She had everything in a tan canvas tote: a pink teddy and a white one, a black slip dress, a short red-and-gold robe, a bunch of thongs all jumbled together, two pair of heels, cheap oil and lotion, the fancy unmarked bottles she would put it in, and her music. There were the CDs she'd bought on her own—Sade and Enigma—and CDs she'd learned about from older men she had dated, Miles Davis's *Kind of Blue* and Chet Baker's *Chet*. Plus Mazzy Star, of course. She hadn't listened to them since she'd fled the Valley, but she knew one thing: Her first client would hear Mazzy Star whether he liked it or not.

When she came out of the bedroom, everything put away neatly, Jenny wanted to ask Nick why the place was so clean, but Sierra was already there answering the phone so she kept her mouth shut. Didn't want to sound like she expected to work with a bunch of slobs even though she did.

"Hi," Sierra said when she hung up.

"Hi," Jenny said. "Your hair looks great."

It was dyed a champagne color and cut in a way that reminded Jenny of Jane Fonda in an old movie she'd seen. Jane Fonda as a hooker. She wondered if Sierra realized it.

"Thanks," Sierra said, flashing a real smile. "I thought I'd try it, you know? Like, it'll grow out if it's a disaster."

Jenny decided she didn't know about the Jane Fonda movie.

"They're calling already," Sierra said. "I booked an eleven-thirty for you."

"Thanks. Was it, like, anybody you know?"

"I don't think so. Said his name was"—Sierra checked her steno pad—"Greg. All I can tell you is, he sounded like a guy that needs to get off with a hot Asian."

"Rice chasers," Jenny said, laughing. "The story of my life."

And so it began again, in that high-rise a block south of Wilshire: Jenny opening the door for a stranger who would be seeing her naked inside of ten minutes, and letting her instincts dictate what happened after that. They were in the guest bedroom; no amount of flattery would have convinced Sierra to give up the master when they had appointments at the same time.

Greg turned out to be slender and darkly handsome, with a hundred-dollar haircut and teeth so white they looked like they had been dipped in high-gloss paint instead of merely capped. When she heard his voice, a baritone oiled with sincerity, Jenny started thinking she had seen him before. It took a couple of minutes before she realized where it had been: on the TV news. Not one of the big stations, one of the others. She thought the news was propaganda—why didn't those people just come out and say that George Bush wanted to blow up the world?—and she was tempted to tell him so. Yeah, and his name wasn't Greg, either. But first things first.

"Ready to turn over?" she asked.

"Do me a favor?" he said.

Uh-oh, she thought. "What kind of favor?" she said.

He reached into the briefcase he had been careful to set beside the futon. He pulled out a toothbrush.

"Would you stick this up my ass?"

"No," Jenny said with seen-it-all-before calm even though she hadn't seen this before.

"Coco, come on," he said. "If you do that with the toothbrush, I'll come like Vesuvius."

"I'm sure you'll do that anyway," she said.

"Please, Coco." His baritone was reduced to an unbecoming whimper.

"I told you no," she said. "Now please turn over."

"You're sure, huh?"

"Yes, I'm sure."

"Okay." Rolling onto his back, he looked like a little boy who'd been cut off on seconds at dessert. "You won't tell anybody, will you?"

Like who am I going to tell? Jenny thought.

✤ ✤ ✤

The phones had stopped ringing, the way they usually did after lunch, and Sierra was in the master with a regular who walked in apologizing for canceling the day before. It was the only quiet time Nick was likely to have until evening. He was reading the sports section from a *USA Today* he'd found abandoned in a coffee shop, the rest of the paper lying at his feet. The new girl was curled on the other sofa, lost in a hardback book she had pulled from her tote and not noticing when Nick glanced over at her. He liked what he saw.

As soon as she had walked through the door, he'd wondered what she'd be like in bed. He'd wondered about the other girls too, but this one—*What the hell is her name?* he asked himself—this one made him think the sex would be fun even if it was for pay. There would be laughter afterward, not an anxious glance at the clock, and maybe if you got her laughing long enough, she'd want to go again. Or maybe she'd just want to talk, and it wouldn't be about her rotten ex-boyfriend or whether you liked her eye shadow. For all Nick knew, it might be about the book she was reading.

He could see old-time soldiers on its dust jacket, guys riding horses and swinging swords, but he had to squint to make out its title. *The Charterhouse of Parma* had just registered on his brain when the new girl looked up. Right away she made sure her robe covered her boobs, as though he hadn't already seen them when she came out of her second session. The gesture told him she thought he'd been trying to sneak a peek, that she'd probably decided then and there he was a creep.

He asked the question that was on his mind anyway: "What's a charterhouse?"

"A monastery," she said, sounding like she expected to have to explain what a monastery was.

"Some Catholic I am," he said. "I should have known that."

She didn't say anything, but she did smile.

"Parma's got to have something to do with Parmesan cheese, am I right?" he said.

"Yeah, they make it there."

"There where?"

"In Northern Italy. Toward the French border."

"You been there?"

"No, I just read about it."

Nick was right. She liked to laugh. She was doing it now. But he still couldn't think of her name, and it was driving him nuts.

"So your book," he said. "True story or made up?"

"A novel," she said.

"You like it?"

"Great so far. I mean I'm only on page two-thirty-seven, but there's all these rich people scheming back in the nineteenth century, and a nobleman getting thrown in prison, and an aunt loving him enough to break him out."

"He the good guy?"

"I'm not sure there are any good guys, not like Americans expect anyway. The writer, Stendhal, he's French, and the way he saw it, everybody's pretty spoiled and corrupt. And they're all, like, I don't know, in love with themselves."

"But you keep reading anyway?"

"Of course. It's way better than modern novels."

Nick shook his head. "Keep looking. There's got to be a good guy in there somewhere."

"Why?" the girl asked, smiling as she closed the book, using a finger to mark her place.

"Well, it's a story, and stories always have good guys."

"Not necessarily."

"Okay, maybe if it's a true story, there isn't one. But you said your book is made up. So why would the writer waste his time on a bunch of—"

"Corrupt narcissists?"

"College girl, huh?"

"Sorry," she said, a guilty look on her face.

It stayed there until Nick said, "Why be sorry? If I was smart, I'd talk that way too. Corrupt whatevers, huh? I would have just called them scumbags."

"Me too," the girl said, "but we just met."

They both laughed. Then Nick said, "So you're positive there's not gonna be a hero?"

"The book's not about that, I don't think."

"What's it about then?"

"Happiness. They're all searching for it."

"They going to find it?"

"I don't think so."

"You don't?"

"I'm not sure anybody ever finds it," the girl said. "Not all the time anyway. If you're happy all the time, you're an idiot. Of course, you don't want to be unhappy all the time either. I used to be like that. Unhappy, I mean. And then I told myself I was going to change and be happy every single minute. But that's impossible. So now I'm just, like, trying to balance things out."

"You were unhappy all the time?" Nick asked.

"Yeah."

"What was wrong?"

"I'd rather not talk about it."

She gave Nick an apologetic smile and started reading again, leaving him to do whatever he wanted, go back to his sports section or keep wondering what her great unhappiness was. Her problems certainly didn't show on her. Nick guessed that was part of her appeal to clients. He had felt it himself, the two of them talking the way they might have over lunch or maybe even on a date. She was the first of the massage girls who made him feel good about his sleazy, off-the-grid job. But he couldn't remember her name until Sierra came back and called her Coco.

Nick was trying to embed it in his memory when Scott showed up with far different concerns about Coco. "New girl doing all right?" he asked Sierra.

"Four clients already," she said. She looked at Nick. "Or is it five?"

"I'll check the book," he said.

"Whatever," Sierra said. "She looks like a good producer."

"Figured she would be," Scott said.

"Asshole," Sierra said.

Scott wiggled his eyebrows. "Hey, power has its privileges."

Nick knew it shouldn't have come as a surprise, Scott banging the girls who worked for him. This wasn't a piano recital. The girls got hired because they looked good and didn't hesitate when it came to sex with strangers. But he still felt, well, not bad exactly—let down was more accurate—to hear Coco lumped with the others. The only question Nick had about her after that was how long she'd last.

❖ ❖ ❖

The girls for the evening shift flaked. Or maybe it was just Ling, who didn't bother to call. "I knew we'd never see that bitch again," Sierra said, not sounding the least bit unhappy. The other girl, Heather, had gotten on her cell to say she had car trouble and was stuck in Culver City. No way Sierra could complain about that. Massage girls seemed to have cornered the market on cars that broke down every other week. Jenny sat there hoping hers wouldn't be next.

She and Nick were the only audience Sierra had for her masseuse updates and excoriations. Scott had already split and Sierra was eager to get going. She kept talking about a doctor's appointment she couldn't miss. But if Jenny took off too, the way she already should have—her shift was supposed to be over at four—that would leave no one to take care of business, and the phones were starting to ring again. Scott would go out of his mind.

"I can stay," Jenny said. "If you want me to."

"You mean it?" Sierra asked.

Jenny considered the question for a moment. She had been doing massage long enough to know the favor wouldn't be returned. But she needed the money, and her need outweighed her well-advised reluctance. "Yeah," she said. "I guess."

Sierra acted like she didn't hear the qualifier. "That is so cool," she said. "I owe you big time, I mean really. Just let me know what I can do for you, okay?"

"Okay," Jenny said. But as she started to wonder whether Sierra had a date or an appointment with a drug dealer, a bolt of fear jerked her gaze toward Nick. "You're sticking around aren't you?" she asked.

"Yeah," Nick said. "First in, last out—that's me."

Jenny was too relieved to make her laugh sound sincere, but she didn't care. She had her peace of mind, and it couldn't be disrupted even when her five-thirty didn't show. He'd sounded like a jerk on the phone anyway. Her seven o'clock, on the other hand, was so sweet he made her teeth ache, extra polite and full of compliments. *Come on,* she thought, *even I know I'm not beautiful— why don't you just settle for cute?* The client said he was a lawyer, so maybe he couldn't help running off at the mouth. But how successful a lawyer could he possibly be? Jenny wondered. He was so pale she thought she'd be able to see through him if she held him up to the light. Fair skin, blond hair, invisible eyebrows, eyes with most of the blue wrung out of them. Good grief, the translucent man.

By the time she came back with a hot towel to clean him up, he was asking if she ever did outcall. The answer was no, for the moment anyway. She knew what would come next: maybe they could get together for dinner, not a date really, just a chance for them to talk in a more relaxed atmosphere. She wanted to ask if the hand job she'd just given him hadn't been relaxing, but resisted the impulse. He looked like a pretty sensitive guy. Now that she'd spent an hour—okay, more like forty-three minutes—with him, she even believed that his name was what he said it was, Mark. And Mark, the translucent man, was infatuated.

Infatuation meant repeat business, but he gave her a fifty-dollar tip too, which was something the vast majority of the infatuated usually managed to forget. As soon as he was gone, though, Jenny put her mind on other things. For one, she was exhausted; her hands, arms, and back ached, making her wonder how real massage therapists, the ones with licenses and strict rules of conduct, could stand it. And then there was the apartment; if it wasn't clean when she walked out the door, she wouldn't be able to sleep no matter how tired she was. *The curse of OCD*, she thought.

When she heard the vacuum cleaner start up, she couldn't have been more surprised if Spider-Man had flown through the window. She walked to the guest bedroom door and looked inside. Nick was hard at work, and he stayed at it until he realized she was watching.

"Hey," he said, turning off the vacuum.

"Do you do this every day?" she asked.

"Somebody's got to."

"Everywhere else I've worked, it's always been me."

"You want to take over, be my guest."

"No, that's okay. I'll wash a load of towels."

"Yeah, I noticed you use a lot more than Sierra."

"I hope that's a compliment."

"It is. Means you're not asking these guys to lie down in whatever the guy before them left behind. Just because the towel gets turned over doesn't mean it's not still there, you know."

"Gross," Jenny said, wrinkling her nose.

"But true, right?" Nick said, and he started to laugh.

Then she laughed too, harder than she had before, hard enough for her to think he would make her laugh again. The security guy. She couldn't believe it.

19

Scott kept telling himself he should have shaken off the bad karma from that makeup bitch by now. He'd assumed the new Asian girl would get him started, but all she'd done was outsmart him. Lots of brainpower, those Asians. Of course he'd never seen any evidence of it in the others he'd hired. They were all nuts. But this Coco, aka Jenny—what the fuck kind of Korean name was Jenny anyway?—wouldn't let him get away with scamming her on the split, and she wouldn't let him get in her pants, either. If he hadn't been so hot to dump Ling, he would have told Jenny to pay for her own green tea and split. Oh, fuck it, she was in the starting lineup until she pissed him off, as she inevitably would, and that freed Scott up to contemplate how his world was shrinking.

There were no meetings with producers, no invitations to parties that were worth a damn. He'd been three weeks without an agent and it looked like the Rock or Dwayne Johnson or whatever the hell he was calling himself would sprout tits before he got another one. Even DuPree was playing games, going days before he returned Scott's calls, and that was the last thing Scott needed. He needed a score, something that gave him a rush, that made him think of himself as anything besides another Hollywood reject who ought to be back in acting class, polishing his craft, as though he'd had any craft to start with. Until his second act came along, it would be all he could do to drag his ass out of bed before noon and stare at a life circumscribed by two overpriced apartments, the one where he lived with his decaying dreams and the one where girls peddled their asses to provide his only source of income.

Just two days ago he had fired Heather after she called to say her car had broken down again. Fucking idiot bitch should have learned about cabs. Other than Coco, it wasn't likely the new girls he'd hired would be any better equipped in the brains department. One was a brunette named Brianna, the other a black chick calling herself Cookie. He wondered if DuPree liked black chicks. And then, as he picked up the phone and hit speed dial, he thought, *fuck DuPree*. And fuck black chicks and white chicks and every other kind of chick. What made any of them so fucking special anyway? The ad he kept in *L.A. Weekly* must have generated a million calls from girls who were hot to make a living on their backs. What a fucking town. Shake a tree and whores fell out of it. Whores and actors, like there was any difference between the two.

✛ ✛ ✛

It was a weak moment, DuPree saying yes when Scott called about lunch. DuPree had been surprised to hear from him, what with that lame-assed TV series he was supposed to be shooting and all. But then Scott said the thing had blown up on him. "Creative differences," like DuPree knew what that meant. But he felt sorry for his pet white boy, so they headed to a Eurotrash hangout on the Strip where he'd eaten a dozen times and still couldn't remember the name, just the blue awning out front.

Scott was plowing through a T-bone and *pommes frites* while DuPree picked at his *salade niçoise* and smiled to himself when that phrase creative differences came back to him. In his world, differences got settled with guns. He wondered how that would play in Hollywood, a bunch of slick fuckers who made a fortune with pretend violence, running for their Range Rovers when he walked in the door slinging honest-to-God lead. With guns every place he looked, it wasn't all that imaginative, but he would sure as hell establish the fact that he was righteously indignant.

"Okay, I told you my sad story," Scott said, taking a break from chewing. "What you been up to?"

"This and that," DuPree said. "Nothing to get erect about. Just looking for my next business opportunity."

"You still haven't told me exactly what your business is."

"Imagine that."

"It's not illegal, is it?"

DuPree scowled. The white boy was all the time asking about things he didn't have a right to know. Maybe he felt entitled, seeing as how he'd pulled DuPree's ass out of the fire that night in front of the Standard. DuPree had just taken apart a pumped-up bouncer who had dissed him once too often, collapsed his face with a right hand and kicked him until he was bleeding all over Sunset Boulevard. Women were screaming and paparazzi were snapping pictures and two more weightlifter-bouncers were bearing down on DuPree when Scott rolled up in his raggedy Porsche, shouting, "Get in!" DuPree had no idea who he was, but he knew a getaway car when he saw one. Off the two of them went, Scott chattering about how he'd wanted to fuck that bouncer up himself.

That was more than a year and a half ago, before 9/11, and the motherfucker hadn't shut up since, talking about coming up hard in foster homes and detention centers, just like Steve McQueen. Most of the time DuPree let his bullshit slide—he was just a punk-assed white boy who was pretending when he acted and pretending when he wasn't. But sometimes, like now, DuPree enjoyed fucking with him.

"What you saying, Scottie?"

That stopped the white boy in mid-chew.

"You saying I got to be a criminal on account of what's any African-American male if he don't work in the motherfuckin' entertainment industry and he still got him some fine clothes and a phat ride and acts like, damn, I'm as good as any white man?"

At least the white boy had the presence of mind to swallow his steak before he said something. "It's just a question, dude. You don't have to get all Quentin Tarantino on me."

"You ask the same question every fucking time I see you," DuPree said.

"Because I'm interested in what you're up to," Scott said. "Sincerely, man."

"Told you before," DuPree said. "Not much."

It was the truth. Artie Franco, going to pick up his old lady in Whittier, had been blindsided by two kids in a stolen car. He landed in the hospital with a broken leg, broken ribs, bad face cuts, and a back screaming for surgery. All of which meant Artie was in no shape to get in DuPree's face about clocking that tortilla queen with the pit bull, never mind convincing him to rob an armored car.

"But," DuPree said, "as I think I also told you, I am exploring opportunities."

"For business," Scott said, leaning across the table, his voice dropping conspiratorially, his T-bone forgotten.

"That's right."

"You ever work with a partner?"

"Sometimes."

Now DuPree knew where this was going. He should have seen it coming, all the hints Scott had given him, more and more of them as his acting career went down the toilet, and now bringing it home with this:

"I want in."

"Scottie," DuPree said, "there's nothing to be into."

"Yeah, I understand. But when there is."

"Just like that? Without knowing anything about anything?"

"Man, I know, all right? You think I'm just some dumb fucking actor, but I've seen a lot of shit. I can handle myself. Fuck, I saved your ass, didn't I?"

"Yeah, you did," DuPree said, wishing he had jumped into any car except Scott's.

"Okay, then," Scott said. "You find something you think I can help you with, call me."

DuPree nodded and said, "All right, I hear you." Then he pointed at Scott's plate. "Mind if I take that bone home for my dog?"

20

That guy Mark kept coming back to see Coco. It seemed like he was there every day she worked, and she worked almost every day. Nick couldn't help thinking Mark's business must be going to hell, as much time as he was spending away from it. He was some kind of lawyer, but not necessarily a dream date. "He's starting to make me uncomfortable," Coco told Nick one afternoon. "Like way too possessive, you know?" She didn't stop seeing him, though.

Have it your way, babe, Nick thought as he watched her guide Mark into the master bedroom, his eighth visit in the few weeks she'd worked there. Or was it the tenth? Whatever the number, it fed a feeling that Nick couldn't deny. He was jealous. A little bit anyway. It was probably why he had such an easy time remembering Mark's name. Mark was the competition, even if Nick was the only one who knew it.

He wanted Coco for his own, the way he had her in his imagination. At first he wrote it off to physical attraction: the shimmering black hair that hung down her back, the chimes that rang in her laughter, the eyes that made him think of teardrops. But Sierra was probably prettier than Coco, and Kianna definitely had been. They were the kind of women he'd met in bars when he was young and on the prowl. He'd had his pick of them when it looked like he had a future. Now that he didn't, he realized what they lacked and what Coco had. She was funny enough to make him laugh and smart enough to make him wish he'd stayed in school. Maybe best of all, she wasn't mean in the small-minded, scorn-your-sister way that made so many massage girls act like they had venom in their lipstick. At this stage of his life, a little kindness went a long way with him.

He hadn't been with a woman in more than a year, so long ago he could scarcely remember. The last one had lived upstairs. She'd come home from her job at Nordstrom, he'd come home from throwing bags at LAX, and they'd make the walls shake. It was never about dinner or a movie, just sex. And then she split for Portland to live with her sister and seek a man less haunted than Nick, a man she wouldn't find staring into the distance when she woke in the middle of the night. "I can't touch you in the place that needs touching most of all," she told him. "I can't touch your heart."

Her words echoed those of the women who had shared Nick's bed before her. Good women mostly, but none equipped to get him out from under the shadow that robbed him of whatever sunshine found its way into his life, not just once or twice but every time he tried to let it in. No wonder he had all but given up on the idea that he could find a way for the past to coexist with the present.

The present was where Coco entered the equation, not that she'd ever know it or even think about it. Christ, she looked young, while Nick couldn't get past the age in his eyes and the scars surrounding them. He wondered if the scars scared her, though she never gave that impression. She seemed to trust him from the day they bonded over their mutual need for cleanliness. She might even like him, but only the way she liked a neighbor who always said good morning or someone who cut her hair the way she wanted it. Yeah, that was it, Nick told himself. She had to like him—he was the guy who would save her if things got scary.

He found himself feeling mellow whenever she was on his mind. She took the rough edges off his thoughts and freed his imagination to go places it hadn't been since his career, his life, everything went off the tracks in Oakland. One oddly quiet night in his apartment, his thoughts of Coco were easing him toward reverie again when the phone rang.

"Hey, buddy, you up?" It was Coyle. "I figured if I didn't talk to you now, I'd never get any sleep."

Nick knew instantly that Coyle was calling to tell him there would be no job driving a truck. He knew why Coyle was calling, too. Coyle was afraid Nick would kick the shit out of him. Nick had no such intention, but there was a measure of payback in hearing Coyle chatter nervously, sounding like he'd needed a few drinks to get his courage up, but probably just playing for sympathy when he said his own job was in danger. Something about new management, Coyle's brother-in-law out on the street, everything upside down. By the time Coyle finished, Nick hated more than ever the desperation that had made him listen to the son of a bitch in the first place.

"Tell me one thing," Nick said. "Was there ever really a job?"

"Jesus Christ, how can you ask me something like that?" Coyle said. "Of course there was a job. Shit, my brother-in-law was telling me just yesterday it looked like May first for you for sure."

Nick knew the truth then. It had all been bullshit. Maybe Coyle had hoped it would somehow come true, but it hadn't, so the hell with him. It wasn't as though Nick had been looking for anything after that beef in the parking lot. He didn't want to be called a hero, didn't want empty promises, just wanted to make enough to pay his rent. But when he tried to ask why Coyle couldn't have let it go at that, the words wouldn't come.

"Hey, look, I gotta get some sleep," he said. "Work in the morning."

"Then you got something," Coyle said.

"Same as before."

"Maintenance, right? You'll probably be happier doing that than driving a truck anyway."

Nick didn't say goodbye before he hung up and Coyle didn't call back saying they'd been cut off. He'd been found out and he knew it, but if that should have pleased Nick in some way, it didn't. His escape route had been closed. When he stared off into the distance in the hours after hearing the news, his vision of Coco was gone. All he could see was more dirty towels and sloppy women.

✤ ✤ ✤

Jenny put on her makeup and a fishnet dress as soon as she got to work, and when she walked out of the bathroom, there was Nick holding a vase with a dozen red roses in it. Beautiful, picture-book roses, in the hands of a guy who looked like he would have been more comfortable holding a spare tire.

"For me?" Jenny said. "Nick, that's so sweet of you."

She was trying to get a blush out of him, but all he did was wince.

"You got the wrong guy," he said. "They were out in the hall when I opened the door."

Jenny knew instantly they were from Mark.

"Okay if I put them on the coffee table?" Nick asked.

"Yeah, sure," Jenny said.

She could picture how Mark had gotten the roses up here, standing by the front door to the building, wearing a suit and tie and looking like he was waiting for a tenant to buzz him in, then darting inside as soon as someone stepped out and left him an opening. It was something other clients had done at other places, most of them content to leave their tokens of affection, a few ringing the bell or pounding on the door and claiming they had appointments. Those scenes at the door were never pleasant, spooking clients who were already inside, sometimes rousing the neighbors' suspicions. Mark was capable of the same thing, Jenny was sure of it.

"I'll tell him he can't do that again," she said.

"Good idea," Nick said. He produced a small white envelope from his shirt pocket and held it out to her. "Here, this was with them."

"If you'd thrown it away, you could have told me the roses were from you," Jenny said.

"Next time."

"Guys always say that."

She looked at the envelope and saw how carefully Mark had written "Coco" on the front of it, as if to signal his good intentions. She supposed she could have predicted what would be written on the card inside, the confession that in the short time he had known her, Mark had come to love her like no other woman in his life. *But you don't know me,* Jenny thought. *You don't even know my real name.*

And yet she felt herself blush the way she hadn't been able to get Nick to. Nick didn't notice because he was reading the sports page the way he always did, but Brianna did when she came back from showing a client to the door.

"Cool roses," she said. "I bet Nick gave them to you, didn't he?" She flashed a wicked smile in his direction. "Is that what you did, Nick? Gave them to your number one?"

"No," he said. "It was—"

"I think he's embarrassed. Wouldn't you say so, Coco?"

"A guy left them for her," Nick said.

But Jenny ignored him and told Brianna, "I've always heard it's the quiet ones you've got to watch out for."

"Nick's got a girlfriend," Brianna said.

"Come on, would you?" Nick said.

He was smiling, though, and Jenny couldn't help thinking he was enjoying the teasing. Then the phone rang and Brianna picked up and everything went back to normal. Nick headed for the kitchen to get a drink of water while Jenny resumed thinking about the dilemma called Mark.

He had brought her chocolates the second time he saw her, the fancy kind, from a place in Beverly Hills—Krohns, Kroners, something like that. And she'd gotten a black lace teddy from him just a couple days ago, not a cheap one either; it was straight from La Perla. But Mark had delivered those gifts in person, handing them to her like a high-school senior bringing his prom date a corsage. Now he was sneaking around, making himself a presence in her life even when he wasn't there in person.

He probably thought he was being romantic by dropping off the roses before he went to a meeting in Orange County, but Jenny knew he would be back soon enough, and the thought of it—the threat of it—stayed with her through two appointments, both with guys she had never seen before and likely never would again. Each of them asked for full service, but they were pretty nice about it when Jenny said no. No tips but no trouble—it was a fair exchange. Just pump and go, like a gas station.

Everything changed when Scott came by with DuPree not long after Jenny had shown her second appointment to the door. It was her first look at DuPree, but she'd heard about how he'd tried to pick a fight with Nick. Sierra said Nick had been totally cool about it, funny in a quiet way but not the least bit afraid, and Sierra hardly ever said anything nice about anyone. Jenny wished Sierra were with her now. Instead it was Brianna, who would be no help at all if things went sideways. That was hardly a reassuring thought as Jenny checked out DuPree standing there silently, looking very gangster as he stared at Nick through his sunglasses.

Nick didn't seem to notice. He was too busy listening to Scott give him a hard time about a girl named Heather. "You positive that cunt turned over every penny she was supposed to?" Scott asked.

Cunt was Jenny's least favorite word, at least when it was being used as an assault weapon. It struck her as hostile and angry, the polar opposite of pussy. Pussy sounded friendly. Lovers could always talk about her pussy. Since she'd been doing massage, she didn't mind if strangers did too. The nice ones, anyway.

"Yeah, I got it written down right here," Nick said, reaching for the notepad where he kept track of the girls' appointments.

"I find out different, I'm taking it out of your fucking pay," Scott said.

"You won't."

"Won't what?"

Scott bristled, and when he did, Jenny saw DuPree instinctively clench his fists, the muscles in his forearms bulging. Nick saw it too, just a flick of his eyes, and then he was back meeting Scott's angry stare.

"Won't find out different," Nick said. "Everything's written down the way you wanted—date, time, how long the session lasted, plus the money you got coming."

"Aw, fuck it," Scott said. "I believe you." He rolled his shoulders and made a face that got worse when he tried to loosen his neck. "Jesus fucking Christ, I'm all knotted up. Too much tension."

Jenny shot a glance at Brianna. They all knew what was next.

"Brianna, you got time for me, darlin'?"

"Sure, Scott." What else could she say?

He was following her into the master bedroom when he looked at DuPree. "Hey, don't just stand there," he said. "Coco's all yours."

Jenny saw a frown form on Nick's face and something different going on in his eyes. She'd never seen it before, but she imagined it was how he looked before a fight. When he glanced at her as if he was seeking her approval to go after DuPree, she shook her head discreetly. It was the closest she could come to telling him it would be cool, that she could handle everything. Of course it would have helped if she believed it herself.

✤ ✤ ✤

DuPree hadn't had any Oriental pussy since that dancer from Star Strip, over on La Cienega. Turned out to be a freak, and those big titties of hers were real. He hadn't known you could get more than a mouthful out of Japan or China, wherever the fuck she came from. But right away he could see there wouldn't be any of that with this girl Coco, in her little black dress, looking all cute and shit, just not loaded in the tit department. She might be a freak, though. There was always that.

"Make yourself comfortable," she said. "I need to get a new bottle of lotion." But as she started to leave, DuPree said, "Don't go rushing off," and he grabbed her by the arm and pulled her to him. Not too hard or anything—didn't want to bruise the girl—just letting her know she was with a man, making it clear this was his party.

He didn't say anything as he slowly turned her around and pressed himself against her ass, making sure she felt his stiff cock, then slowly grinding it against her. Not the crack of her ass, where he would have liked it—even heels weren't going to get her up that high—but somewhere close as long as he bent his knees. Now he wanted to hear something from her, a murmur or maybe a few words about how she couldn't wait—the only time that Oriental freak had stopped jibber-jabbering was when she was sucking his dick. But this one stayed quiet. He couldn't even hear her breathing get heavy.

He kept his grind going and leaned close. Damn, the girl smelled good. His mind was right as he eased down the top of her dress so her right tittie was bare and he could play with the nipple, teasing it with his forefinger and smiling when it stood up proud. Then he pushed the hair away from her ear and whispered, "You gonna give it up nice for me?"

She said something back, but he couldn't hear it. Or maybe he didn't believe it.

"What's that you sayin'?" he asked.

"I said no," she said.

DuPree turned her around to face him, not caring that he was rough about it, still enjoying the sight of her bare tittie.

"Not like you got a choice," he said.

"You didn't have one either, did you?" she said. "I mean, coming in here just because Scott told you to. That's not very flattering to me, you know."

She pulled the top of her dress back up without taking her eyes off him, and she smiled while she was doing it. Not snotty either. Making it friendly, like he'd stumbled upon her when she forgot to lower the shade.

But fuck friendly when the subject was pussy. "Scott got nothing to do with this," DuPree said. "I make my own damn decisions."

"Then that's something else we have in common," she said, still smiling. "We think for ourselves. So as far as, like, me giving it up, I don't think so."

"Got an attitude against black men, that it?"

"Black men are fine."

"Uh-huh," DuPree said. "Black men are fine, you just ain't giving it up for this one."

"Or anybody else."

"Black, you mean?"

"Black, white, whatever. I don't do that."

"Shit," he said. "What about those other bitches?"

"You'll have to ask them."

"I have. Answer's always yes."

He smiled back at her, cool, like they were in a bar, maybe along the water in Santa Monica, tall drinks in front of them, Alicia Keys on the sound system. No way this Coco girl could get around what he'd just put down.

"Maybe you should wait until Brianna's finished with Scott," she said.

And stick his business where that motherfucker just stuck his? Even with a rubber, DuPree wasn't about sharing pussy.

"Maybe I'll just bend you over and fuck you," he said. "What you gonna do about that, huh?"

She thought about it for a moment, her smile never changing, making him wonder if she was going to scream for the security guard. DuPree wouldn't have minded a bit, kick the man's ass and celebrate by getting his nut. Might even be better that way.

But she didn't scream. She just said, "You better make yourself comfortable so I can give you a massage. If we talk much longer, you won't have time for your happy ending."

✣ ✣ ✣

Nick couldn't stop himself from staring when she came out of the room. Didn't even try. Any sign of damage and he was ready to go in there and hold that asshole's head in the toilet until water came out of his ears. But there wasn't a hair on her head out of place. No tears in her eyes, no sign anywhere that she'd been roughed up. And then he saw her smiling at him.

Nick didn't smile back, not right away. He gave Coco a look that asked the question that was on his mind. She replied by heaving an exaggerated sigh of relief. That was when he smiled.

He did it again when DuPree emerged, looking like a guy who'd just had his pocket picked. DuPree glanced at the closed master bedroom door as if tempted to barge in and complain to Scott about what Coco hadn't done for him. Then he said, "Fuck it," and left without looking at either Coco, who was wrapped up listening to messages, or Nick, whose smile probably would have stirred up some drama.

At first Nick thought the thing with the messages was just an act, but no, Coco really was giving them her full attention. There was one in particular that she replayed three or four times.

He wondered what that was all about, but before he could ask her, Scott and Brianna were back in the living room and Scott wanted to know where DuPree had gone off to. "What the fuck?" Scott said to Coco. "You didn't do anything to piss him off, did you?" And Coco, smiling sweetly, said, "No way. It's like Tom Cruise says in that old movie. You know, the one where he's in high school and there's all these hookers and—"

"*Risky Business*," Scott said.

"Right, right," Coco said. "And Tom Cruise at the end says he deals in human fulfillment. Well, me too."

The amazing thing was she got away with it. Scott still wasn't happy, especially after he called DuPree on his cell and couldn't get him to pick up. But Coco had thrown him a bone straight out of Hollywood, and Scott was at least pacified. And then he was gone, off to wherever he went when he wasn't sleazing around the apartment. Brianna left fifteen minutes after that.

Then it was just Coco and Nick, with her finishing the last call she was going to take and sitting beside him on the sofa and saying, very softly, "Thank you."

"I didn't do anything," he said.

"But you would have," she said. "Wouldn't you?"

He shrugged. "Something like that, you don't know what's going to happen until it happens."

"I was so scared." She looked like she might cry. "I didn't know what I was doing. I just knew I couldn't let him . . . "

She shook her head, unable to make the words come out.

"It's all right, you got through it," Nick said. "You won."

"I don't feel like it."

"It's like that sometimes."

"Because you don't know what's going to happen, right?"

He was surprised to hear his words coming from her, surprised she'd been able to remember them when she was so shaken up.

"Was that how it was when you were a boxer?" she asked.

"After the bell rang, yeah, I suppose so," he said. "Every fight's different. It's like a story you make up as you go along."

It looked to him like she was thinking about that. At the same time she was studying his face, and he wondered what she was seeing.

"Did they hurt?" she said at last.

"What?"

"These."

She touched the scars over his eyes, first the left, then the right.

"Only afterward," he said.

"Even now?"

"Now it hurts to remember why they're there."

"I'm sorry," she said.

Her hand remained on his brow, cool and soothing. He didn't know why she was bestowing this balm on him. Was it for sport or was it out of kindness? He hoped it wasn't the first, didn't even want to consider the possibility. If kindness had inspired this gesture, he didn't think he deserved it, but he would accept it nonetheless.

21

Scott, his cell phone pressed to his ear, blinked in the late morning sunshine and uttered the closest thing he could think of to a prayer: "Come on, dammit, pick up." An instant later he heard the message on DuPree's cell again and slammed down the phone. "Son of a bitch."

Scott had called him until midnight without luck, and now that he'd hauled his ass out of bed, he was starting again. At least he wasn't feeding his pie hole as he wandered around his apartment in his boxers. Maybe he'd even lose a couple pounds before DuPree did him the honor of having an actual conversation. Then Scott caught a glimpse of his reflection in the living room mirror and realized he'd need more than twenty-four hours without double bacon cheeseburgers and chili fries. Twenty-four months was more like it.

He was about to hit redial when it occurred to him that DuPree was practically the only human being he spoke to regularly unless he was doing TV. There were the girls too, he supposed, though they weren't much more than hormone smoothies. Nick, on the other hand, looked at him like he was no better than a case of the crabs. Scott couldn't believe it—a fucking washed-up fighter who went all soft and gooey just because he killed some asshole who, given the chance, would have killed him. Who'd want to talk to a guy like that?

So Scott was down to DuPree in the friend department, and DuPree wasn't picking up. But maybe he would this time, Scott thought as he called again, hopeful and lonely, mostly lonely.

✥ ✥ ✥

Sometimes DuPree just needed to jack somebody. It was a feeling that came over him, nothing financial, more like the urge to eat or fuck. He didn't know who else was wired like that, probably every motherfucker in prison, but fuck them, he wasn't worried about anybody except himself. He'd get this jangling in his head, and the hash he'd smoked would only make it go away for a little while. Now it was there again, the signal that told him to go get some, whatever it was, and he was trying to hold it together long enough to weigh his options. It was what a motherfucker had to do.

He was heading north on the 101 with Blanco riding shotgun, ignoring Scott's calls, thinking he'd get off on Topanga and take it over to Malibu. The overcast would burn off by the time he got there, and he could inhale some of that ocean air and get his head right.

It was going on three months since the bank robbery, and the only thing he could see in his future was the armored car job Slape kept talking about. Except Artie still wasn't in any shape to watch his back and DuPree damn sure wasn't going to work with Slape and the Aryan psycho he wanted to bring in as Artie's replacement. A criminally inclined brother dumb enough to do that was bound to wind up dead in a ditch.

He glanced at Blanco, who had stopped slobbering out the open window and hopped onto the floorboard to gnaw on a steak bone. *Dog's got life whipped*, he thought. And he could feel himself getting angry about it, wondering did Blanco laugh at him, did he, in his little pit-bull head, want to hear DuPree calling him massah? "You white motherfucker," DuPree said, wanting to reach down and yank the bone away just to remind him who was boss. But uh-uh, not with Blanco. Damn dog's moods turned on a dime, and DuPree needed both his hands.

He just wasn't sure what for, was all. Any thoughts he'd had about taking down a bank solo had been forgotten when he heard the news out of Pasadena: same week, two jobs, two different robbers, two kills for the cops. He wasn't about that kind of a career move. Better to find him some more home-delivery drug dealers who needed robbing. But not Teddy George, who, if he was back in business, was guaranteed to have some crazy white boy with an Uzi beside him.

Motherfucker, DuPree thought, looking to change lanes as he neared the Topanga Canyon exit, not seeing some punk-ass kid on a rice-rocket motorcycle coming up hard on his right until he almost hit him. "Well, goddamn," DuPree said. The anger in his voice jerked Blanco out of his steak-bone reverie and sent him jumping back onto the seat to see what the cursing was about.

DuPree wanted to run the kid off the road and turn the dog loose on his bare legs. Him and all the other motorcycle fuckers weaving in and out of traffic on every damn freeway, riding the white lines in rush-hour gridlock, and most of the time looking like this bitch, in a T-shirt and shorts, as if that helmet on his head provided an invisible shield for the rest of him. But maybe DuPree wouldn't let the dog have all the fun, maybe he'd just drive right up over the kid himself, make him listen to the snap of his own spine.

Liking that idea a lot, DuPree stomped on the gas pedal, his speed going from eighty to ninety to . . . whoa, here came Topanga. What was he going to do, get off or kill the motherfucker? Another ten, fifteen seconds and he'd be past the exit, and the kid was already a speck in the distance. Damn, those rice rockets could move. And even if he caught the motherfucker, it was still the middle of the day, freeway crawling with witnesses. Fuck it, he'd rather be in Malibu.

On the drive through the canyon DuPree started thinking about how poor dim Scottie talked shit about wanting to walk on the wild side, play outlaw and wave a gun around. DuPree didn't think the man could rob a 7-Eleven without fucking up. But then DuPree thought something else: Maybe he could jack Scottie's massage setup. Just walk right in like those raping, robbing motherfuckers Scottie said his bitches were so afraid of, the ones that made him hire the punching bag he had for security. Scottie would never expect his dawg DuPree to fuck him over like that.

There was some planning to do, of course, no matter how bad DuPree's itch needed scratching. He'd check the place out next time he dropped by, talk to Scottie about how the business worked, what the big days were, which girls were the best earners. DuPree hoped that Oriental bitch was one of them. He'd kick the punching bag's ass, flat out devastate the motherfucker, and he'd take everybody's money, and then he'd bind and gag the other girls while he ripped Miss Saigon up good. Just thinking about it made his dick hard.

✢ ✢ ✢

For the first time he could remember, Nick slept through the Mexican gardeners' wake-up routine. He hadn't expected that, as pissed off as he was about Coyle's broken promise, false promise, whatever the hell it was. But there was no tossing and turning, no lying there staring into the darkness, not even any Alonzo Burgess flashbacks. It was as if the cool of Coco's hand the day before had banked the fire in Nick's mind.

The next thing he knew, he had fallen asleep again, and when he awoke this time, he was already late for work. He didn't bother checking the messages stacked up on his cell phone, and he didn't call to say he'd be there as soon as possible. For one day at least, he was on his own damned clock.

Sierra and Coco were waiting in the lobby when he got to the apartment, Sierra in a short skirt that made her look like she wore a price tag even off duty, Coco curled up against the wall with her nose in a book. "Jesus Christ," Sierra said, getting loud about it. "Where the fuck have you been?"

"Pipe down," Nick said.

The surprised look on Sierra's face nearly cracked her makeup. It was all she could do to paste her scowl back on when they got upstairs and he held the door for her. From Coco he expected something else, a little smile and a shrug at the very least. Instead she gathered up her book and her backpack and hurried after Sierra without looking at him.

Nick tried not to be obvious as he watched Coco check her messages. She put on a little performance for her own amusement more than anyone else's, frowning at the hang-ups and empty promises to call back, smiling broadly at the clients who asked her to get back to them. She said, "Oh, Mark, Mark," too, and shook her head wearily at her most devoted admirer's bullshit. There was one message, however, that appeared to mean more to her than all the others. It threw her into another gear as she hurried around the apartment, making sure Sierra didn't have a session scheduled so she could use the master bedroom and spending more time than usual fixing herself up for her noon appointment.

After the guy called from the lobby, Nick and Coco walked to the door together and waited for the doorbell to ring so Nick could check him out through the peephole. *A little on the slick side*, Nick thought; *certainly nothing to set off alarms*. He nodded his approval to Coco, expecting her to respond with the usual signs that this was all just a game, a roll of the eyes or a wiggle of the eyebrows. Instead, she looked eager to see the guy.

Nick retreated behind the room dividers and discovered that Sierra must have gone off to the second bathroom; she spent a lot of time there, doing her makeup or coke. He used her absence to pause just out of sight and listen as Coco opened the door, imagining how she was staying behind it so no neighbor would catch a glimpse of her in her sheer black slip dress. Then he heard the door click shut and her noon appointment said, "I thought I recognized your voice on the phone."

"I missed you," Coco told him.

✤ ✤ ✤

He was as handsome as ever. The corners of his eyes crinkled when he smiled and everything about his clothes was just so: black knit shirt, olive slacks, and a houndstooth sport coat that pulled it all together. It had never crossed Jenny's mind before, but he seemed distinguished. In a low-key way, of course. Maybe it was how he carried himself, or maybe it was the black leather briefcase he always had with him. It told anybody who noticed it that he was important. And important was a nice fit with distinguished, right? Maybe the Rolls really was his.

"You look great," Barry said.

"So do you," Jenny said.

"In case you're wondering, I haven't had any problems with my convertible top."

"I'm glad we got that out of the way."

And then, laughing, she did something she never did with clients, even her favorites. She hugged him before the massage, right there by the door. Didn't wait until they were in the privacy of the bedroom and didn't care if Sierra and Nick saw her. If Barry was surprised, it didn't show. He hugged her back with the kind of sincerity she never felt from clients, no matter how smitten they were with her. Come to think of it, she never felt it from most of her boyfriends, either. It made her want to kiss him, but she pulled away before she did, saying, "Come on," and taking him by the hand and leading him into the master.

It wasn't until they were inside that she realized she had forgotten to ask for his donation, the two hundred dollars he was supposed to leave on the counter so Nick could put it in the security box. She was trying to think of a clever way to ask for it when he handed her two crisp hundred-dollar bills. "Here," he said. "Better not get the boss upset." She liked him more than ever for that.

They had a lot of catching up to do once they were naked on the bed, Barry lying on his stomach while Jenny slathered him with lotion and tried her best to approximate a real massage. She maneuvered around him on her knees, and when she brushed up against him with a breast, he stirred with pleasure. What, she wondered, would happen when she straddled him to work on his back? One thing for sure: If she got close enough, he'd know exactly how excited she was.

"Mazzy Star, right?" Barry asked.

"What?"

"The music. Sounds like Mazzy Star's still your favorite."

"You remembered."

"I did better than that—I bought the CD." He raised his head and looked back at her. "I wasn't sure I'd see you again."

"Really?"

"Really." He lowered his head back onto his hands. "When I called to see you again over in Sherman Oaks, the phone was disconnected. Your ad was gone from the Internet, too."

"Things got a little bit crazy." It was as close to the truth as she dared go.

"You didn't get busted, did you?" he asked.

"No, there was, like, a problem with a couple of the girls, so I thought I'd take some time off. To concentrate on school."

"Is that what you're doing now? Going to school?"

"Pretty much. My last poetry paper is due next week, and then I've got a final in my Vietnam War class. After that, I'll try to decide what to do next."

"Any idea what it might be?"

"Well, I've been at a two-year school and I'd really like to go to UCLA."

"Sounds like a splendid idea to me."

"Me, too."

Jenny was ready to tell him she wanted to major in English when Barry said, "You know, I must have called every Asian masseuse in L.A. to see if you were working anywhere. Nobody ever keeps the same name, do they?"

"Not too often, no."

She hoped she didn't sound surprised by the change in the conversation's direction. And she wondered how many girls he had seen, and if he liked any of them as much as he seemed to like her. It was a dumb thing to think about, the kind of petty competitiveness she hated in other girls. She wanted to erase it from her mind right away.

"I'm glad you kept looking," she said.

He would have known how glad if he had seen her the day before. There was something savage about DuPree, and she realized how close she had come to experiencing the full force of it. If Nick hadn't been waiting when she walked out of the bedroom, she would have fallen apart. But she couldn't help wondering about Nick. Such a tough man but such a sad one, too.

And then Nick and DuPree ceased to matter when she heard the voice she thought was Barry's. He was calling about an Internet ad for Coco, and he left a number with a 310 area code. She wondered if it was the same number he had before—a cell phone, probably—and got mad at herself for not hanging onto it. No, wait a minute. She'd never done anything except scribble his number on a piece of paper even though she really liked the guy, and it was still there when she ran out the door on that horrible afternoon. She hoped it hadn't gotten him in trouble.

There had been no way to know on the phone. She had played it strictly as Coco when she returned his call, and he had gone along with the charade. He politely scheduled an appointment and left her to spend the night wondering if he had connected her voice to the Suki who used to work in Sherman Oaks.

Now he was here with her, and she wasn't going to bring up leaving his number at the other place unless he did. It didn't seem likely judging by the smile he was giving her.

"I really missed you," he said.

"You did?" she said.

He twisted around to look at her. "Yes. I wasn't lying when I told you I've been trying to find you."

"I'm glad."

"Glad I wasn't lying or glad I missed you?"

"Both."

"In that case, I'll gather my courage and ask if you ever go out with clients."

Jenny was surprised. Barry wasn't waiting until after what the more discreet girls called the release. In fact he was shifting to lie on his side, keeping his left leg bent to cover himself, and she wasn't massaging him anymore because it would have distracted her from the conversation.

"Not very often," she said. "Like almost never."

His smile disappeared. She hoped he'd made it go away to tease her.

"That's a pretty cautious answer," he said. "You're not under oath here, you know."

"I know," she said. "It's just that you live in Santa Barbara, I think you told me, and that doesn't seem very practical. For a date, I mean."

"I get it," he said. "You're one of those L.A. women who dates according to her area code. So what are you, a three-ten? A three-two-three? Certainly not an eight-one-eight—the Valley's so uncool even if we did meet there."

She couldn't help laughing. "Come on, do I really come across that shallow?"

"No," he said. "That's why I'd like to take you out."

"Oh. Well, thanks for the compliment. But there's still the fact that I'm here and you're in Santa Barbara."

"I don't live there all the time."

"Seriously?"

"Seriously. Right now I'm renting a house in the hills. Up by Appian Way."

"I kind of know where that is."

"Maybe you can visit sometime. It's not a castle, but it's got a pool and a nice view. I'll be there a lot for the next year, while I'm taking care of some business down here."

"Cool. I'd like that."

It was as close to a formal acceptance speech as she could offer, and she assumed that Barry got the message. She was about to cease being the fantasy he knew as Coco and Suki and start being Jenny Yee and all the good and bad that entailed. She would make the transformation expecting answers to the questions she had from the last time they were together. Was he married? (He didn't wear a ring and didn't have the marks left by one he had taken off, but that didn't mean anything.) If he was married, did he always go back to his wife when he was done fooling around? (Jenny was weary of guys like that.) Even if he was in a lousy marriage, were there kids involved? (Once was enough for that.) And what did he do for the business he was never specific about? (The answer had to be in his black leather briefcase.)

Still, if everything she heard from him was wrong, even if he refused to say anything at all, Jenny knew she was going to sleep with him. It wouldn't be during working hours, though, with people in the same apartment. It would be someplace she could enjoy the experience without embarrassment or the gossip it would generate. Someplace special. Okay, Barry's place. She was already thinking about it when she put some oil in her hand and told him to lie back and relax.

22

A blind man would have known something was going on between Coco and Barry. She sounded different when she talked to him on the phone, relaxed and funny, not mechanical and cautious, the way she was with most callers. When she caught herself enjoying the calls from Barry too much, she pulled back. But every time he walked through the door for an appointment, her smile came from someplace genuine.

The one time she noticed Nick looking at her, she shrugged helplessly. He took it as a good sign because it felt rooted in the moment they had shared. There was no such warmth when Sierra or Brianna or one of the ever-changing new girls was around. They'd been quick to tease her about Barry, calling him "your boyfriend," asking her if she'd fucked him in the backseat of his Rolls yet. "You'll have to wait until our sex tape comes out," Coco told them. Some actually believed her.

Sierra was the only one who didn't say much when Coco was around, but as soon as she was out of the room, the jack shack's queen bee let her venom flow. "Guess our little college girl doesn't have to worry about tuition anymore," she told an outrageously big-busted dunce named Melissa one day. "I wonder what she really has to do to keep him happy." The two girls rolled around in the possibilities like a couple of mud wrestlers, guessing everything from heroin smuggling to blowjobs for all the Bloods and Crips.

Nick had to leave before he called Sierra a cunt. He went out to the kitchen where all he could hear was the refrigerator humming, and stayed there until Coco came out of her session. She sensed the tension instantly.

"I don't want to hear about it," she said.

"Good," Nick said, "because I'm not telling you."

There he went again, protecting her. He knew she didn't always like it, but he couldn't help himself. He just had to make sure he didn't get stupid over her. His fantasies were one thing, reality far different. She was already hung up on another man, one who had a Rolls and what seemed to be truckloads of money and God knew what else. There was no sense in Nick beating his head against that wall.

And yet he didn't like Barry a damn bit. Barry was too much of a lounge lizard, one of those slick weasels who work the clubs every night and always seem to walk off with Cinderella. *Douchebag*, Nick told himself. And he wondered if someday he'd have to protect Jenny from Barry too, and if she would let him.

He felt a twinge of jealousy. How could she care about Barry so much? How could Barry get her to care? Fuck it, that's just the way it was. Nick was hired muscle, and for him to think he would ever be anything more was nuts.

He was staring out the trick pad's window at a city cleansed by spring rain. The haze that usually hung over L.A. had been washed away and replaced by a sky the color of blue you expect to see only in a movie. Out there somewhere, Coco was probably on her way over for another day of work, but Nick tried not to think about her. She wasn't his responsibility until she showed up. A responsibility, that was all she was.

✣ ✣ ✣

Jenny didn't mind that she hadn't been to Barry's house yet, or that they hadn't gone to dinner at Campanile or one of those other fancy restaurants he said he loved so much. It made what was going on between them seem like a courtship, as if they'd met at a club or a Starbucks and were letting things take their normal course. Of course, normalcy between a masseuse and a client with feelings for each other did have its privileges. The second time Barry came over and saw her as Coco, he went down on her. The time after that, she returned the favor.

Those intimacies kept intruding on her thoughts as she wrote her last poetry paper. The subject was Marianne Moore because the professor told her she'd devoted enough energy to Elizabeth Bishop. Like she knew anything about Marianne Moore. Like she cared. But now the paper had been handed in, and she was coming out of the final in her Vietnam War class. The whole time she'd been taking it, she kept hearing the voice of the last guest speaker the class had heard, a pretty middle-aged woman named Tan who had grown up as the daughter of the Vietcong chieftain in Cu Chi Province, where all the tunnels were. The woman recalled sneaking through the jungle with her father in the middle of the night when she was a child, and how they had stumbled into an American patrol. The woman laughed as she remembered fleeing in the darkness and the way she kept saying, "Run, Daddy, run!" That was the voice that stayed with Jenny, the one that called for daddy.

It didn't go away until she was driving to work, making the transition to Coco in her mind before she changed from her hoodie and jeans into something sheer and skimpy. She was think-ing about the viable candidates for romance she had encountered through massage—not the guys who had made it all the way into her life, but the ones who had fallen short. The funniest had been the easiest to dismiss, a surfer named Todd who was so blond he looked like a snowflake. Somehow Todd had wound up making a living in sales, a good one judging by the red Saab convertible he drove. His paycheck was probably the result of the same charm that got him in her bed before she was sure he deserved to be there. Or maybe she'd just been horny, because Todd seemed a lot less charming the next time he called. He was in a car with a bunch of guys from his office, and she could tell he was trying to show them how hot she was for him. "Come on, you had a good time last time, didn't you?" he'd asked. And she'd said, "Yeah, for a sport fuck." She could hear the guys in Todd's car laughing, but Todd didn't join them. He never called back.

Danny had been different, a sound editor from Warner Bros. who looked like he should have been an actor but was so shy that it was weeks before he even asked if he could kiss her breasts. He kept getting massages and telling her more and more about the wife who had walked out on him and his three-year-old daughter. The heartbreak in his life intensified Jenny's feelings for him, to the point where she was going to ask him out if he didn't hurry up and get around to it. And then—there always seemed to be an "and then" in her stories—Danny came to her one day and said he couldn't see her anymore. Didn't even take his clothes off for a final massage, just broke the news that he was getting married again, told her how much he was going to miss her, and left two hundred bucks on the table before he walked out the door. She didn't find the money until later, and didn't want it when she did. It only made her think of how bad she felt. The experience had been as painful as breaking up. She wished he had just stopped calling. That was what the guys she didn't give a damn about always did.

She was trying to erase Danny from her mind when she turned off Wilshire and started looking for a parking place. There were two in the underground garage that came with the apartment, but one was permanently reserved for Scott and Sierra always used the other. Jenny was telling herself she'd have to sneak down and grab it as soon as Sierra left when she saw Mark parked out front. *My very own stalker,* she thought.

It wasn't that he was dangerous or anything, as far as she could tell. Every masseuse who was the least bit cute had a Mark in her life, sometimes two or three of them, and they were always so predictable. After the flowers and the pledges of love, he wanted to catch Jenny as she walked in and maybe get a spur-of-the-moment appointment. Or ask her if they could go for a cup of coffee before she started work. There were worse things that could happen, and right now she didn't feel like dealing with any of them.

Hoping Mark didn't know what her car looked like, she drove past the apartment. As soon as she turned the corner, she grabbed her cell and called the apartment.

Sierra answered and right away said, "You're not calling in sick, are you?"

"No," Jenny said, thinking, *What a bitch.* "I just want to find out if I had any calls."

"Sorry, nothing from Barry," Sierra said.

Jenny hated her more than ever. "Okay. Anybody else?"

"A couple guys said they'd call back, but didn't leave their names." Sierra dropped her voice to a conspiratorial whisper. "Cookie talked another guy that called for you into seeing her. She's in with him now, in fact."

"That's all right," Jenny said. "Is that it?"

"No, fuck, how could I forget?" Sierra said. "I'm so stupid."

Jenny wanted to tell her she already knew that. Instead, she waited for the insincerity to subside.

"Mark called," Sierra said. "Like four or five times. Cookie talked to him last, right before—"

"He didn't leave a number, did he?" Jenny asked.

Once she had reassured Sierra that she really wasn't calling in sick—"Honest," she said—Sierra gave it to her. Jenny, making sure she stayed away from Mark's stakeout position, tried not to run into anybody as she drove and dialed. He picked up on the first ring.

"Hi, Mark," she said.

"Is this Coco?" he said.

"You mean you don't recognize my voice?"

Now she was the bitch. She couldn't help herself.

"Well, yes, sure I do," he said. "Of course."

"You've been calling, I hear," she said.

"Yeah, I'm, uh, I was hoping we could get together."

"Today?"

"They said you were working."

"I start at four."

"So is it all right if I come over? Can you fit me in?"

Okay, Jenny thought, *time to spring the trap.* "Are you close by?"

"No," Mark said, "I'm still at my office."

✢ ✢ ✢

This was a first for Nick: the call from Coco before she showed up, the client lurking outside, the request to chase him away. Nick knew the guy she was talking about instantly. Coco didn't make fun of many clients, but this one she did. Mark was the guy who wouldn't go away. Of course Nick thought of Barry the same way. But Barry wasn't the guy Nick was supposed to chase off. He would have enjoyed the hell out of that.

Mark was parked where Coco said he'd be, next to the circular drive on the left. Nick wondered why he never got a space that close. He made his way out to the sidewalk and looked around like he was expecting somebody. Mark lowered his head and pretended to be reading something. He looked like just another blond L.A. guy. No tan, though. And clear glasses. *Maybe that's what happens to lawyers,* Nick thought. *You're never out in the sun and your eyes go bad.*

Mark kept his head down as Nick stepped into the street and walked to the driver's window. Peering inside, he could see that Mark was zeroed in on some legal documents. He still didn't look up, even though Nick was sure he knew he had a visitor. There was nothing for Nick to do but rap on the window. Now

Mark was looking. But he kept the window up, his last line of defense.

Nick glanced around to make sure no one was watching. Then he said, "Roll it down."

"What?" Mark asked, acting like he hadn't heard.

"Your window," Nick said. He made a rolling motion with his right hand, wondering if Mark would notice how big it was and the way the knuckles had been flattened.

The window came down and Mark, trying to stay cool, said, "Can I help you?"

"Yeah," Nick said. "You can quit hanging around here."

"I don't know what you're talking about," Mark said. "My office called about some paperwork—I'm a lawyer—so I pulled over and—"

"Look, Mark . . . "

Mark blinked nervously.

"That's your name, right? Mark?" Nick didn't wait for an answer. "You're making a nuisance of yourself, and I'd like you to stop. Just start your car up and drive away."

"Did the manager send you out here?" Mark asked.

Nick shook his head. "No, I'm not sure the manager knows anything about me. I'm from upstairs. You know the place I'm talking about."

Mark looked toward the sidewalk for help of some kind. When Nick checked to see what was there, he spotted two women who had to be in their seventies walking up from the corner. Maybe that explained why Mark seemed so defenseless when Nick turned back to him.

"Does Coco know you're doing this?" Mark asked.

"She's the one that asked me to come down," Nick said.

It was hard for him to look at the wounded expression that came over Mark's face. Even if the guy was a pest and a creep and everything else Nick suspected he had it in him to be, he was devastated. It seemed like all he could do to drive away. Nick watched until he was out of sight, then headed back to the apartment, trying to forget the way the guy looked when his fantasy came undone.

✤ ✤ ✤

Nick wasn't all the way through the door before Jenny asked, "Is everything okay?"

"Well, he didn't seem too happy."

Jenny felt her stomach do a flip. "You mean you beat him up?"

"That was what you wanted, wasn't it?"

Nick looked so serious, Jenny thought she was going to have a heart attack.

"No, I just wanted you to, you know, like scare him, make him quit bothering me. I never said anything about—"

She stopped babbling when she saw Nick grin.

"Go ahead," she said. "I deserve it. But he is gone, right?"

"Yeah. To tell you the truth, he didn't seem like such a bad guy."

"He wasn't. He just got a little carried away."

Nick nodded. "I hadn't run into anyone like that before. Just a couple drunks or druggies, whatever they were, and a guy that didn't have an appointment. Otherwise, you hardly need me except for cleaning up."

"You've got no idea," Jenny told him. "The last place I worked, two girls got raped and robbed. I was the one who found them."

Nick let the silence settle around him and Jenny. "That's not gonna happen here," he said.

The job had taught Jenny not to believe men, but when she looked into the dark eyes beneath Nick's scarred brows, there was something besides sadness in them, and in that moment, she knew she could believe him.

✤ ✤ ✤

As soon as Scott arrived, he threw open the sliding doors to the terrace. The hell with how cold it was outside. Down in the fifties, he guessed. Like fucking Alaska. At ten at night, there wasn't anybody around to bitch and moan as he let fresh air in and the smells of perfume and potpourri spray out. *Jesus Christ! Somebody has been toking up.* Probably Cookie. A couple times he'd dropped by when she was working the early shift and her eyes were already red at noon. He'd have to tell Nick to stay on her ass. The last thing he needed was a neighbor getting a whiff of weed and calling the cops.

But the money was where it was supposed to be, in the security box, and Nick had left his accounting of the day's action. The guy never fucked up plus you could read his writing. Scott didn't understand how that could be, given all the times Nick had been hit in the head. Then he remembered it was Nick who had hit the other guy in the head too much. Now he was playing for Scott's team, making sure nobody cheated Scott out of his money.

Sierra was still raking it in, but Coco was the day's big earner, the way she was almost every day she worked. And tomorrow was Friday, always the busiest day of the week, guys needing to get off before they went home for a long weekend with the wives they were sick of and the girlfriends they didn't have the guts to dump. Scott shook his head, glad he hadn't turned the little bitch down for denying him his God-given freebie but still determined to get himself a piece. Who was the fucking boss anyway?

Then he resumed feeling sorry for himself. He'd been like this since *Mercs* blew up, assuming it was his privilege when he had to come up with the rent for two apartments, alimony for the ex he should have divorced before he knocked her up, and child support for kids he didn't care if he ever saw again. Now there was talk that the makeup cunt was going to sue him for sexual harassment. His monthly nut was already the size of Dolly Parton's knockers, and he had no idea how much longer he could handle it even without somebody new piling on.

There was no counting on Hollywood coming to his rescue again, and the only other real job he'd ever had was moving furniture back in Missouri. For a moment, he wondered if the massage business might be his salvation after all. Maybe he could branch out into escorts, big-ticket whores, and become a twenty-first-century version of Ben Gazzara in *Saint Jack*. (Or was it John Cassavetes? He always got them confused.) But *Saint Jack* was set in Thailand or Burma, one of those places where nobody called you a sinner for peddling pussy. Over here, even in L.A., it got your ass thrown in jail sooner or later. Just thinking about it sent Scott back into his tailspin. He was wondering if Cookie had left any of her dope around when DuPree called and asked, "What up, dawg?"

Dawg? Scott couldn't believe it. DuPree had gone such a long time without calling him dawg, the ultimate in street affection, that Scott had thought it would never happen again. Now that it had, though, he couldn't sound giddy about it.

"What," he said, "you call me up so I can listen to you talking to that pit bull of yours?"

"No, he's my white motherfucker," DuPree said. "You're my dawg."

It was then that Scott knew the tectonic plates in his life had shifted. Exactly how, he wasn't sure. But something was changing. DuPree would get around to it in his own time, on his own terms, cool as shit. Scott was ready for whatever it was, criminal or civil. It was like he'd always told himself: You want to survive in L.A., you got to be ready to reinvent yourself.

23

Typical Friday. Brianna bailed before her shift was over and Jenny was booked as soon as she got there. She barely had time to throw on her sheer red mini dress before her four o'clock buzzed from downstairs, five minutes early. He turned out to be a barrel-shaped guy who talked nonstop about a writer's need to find "the emotional center of dramatic situations." It sounded like he'd read some of the same books she had, and a lot more she intended to read now that she had some time away from school. When he was on the futon in the second bedroom, he shifted to a rambling monologue about his struggle to maintain his "artistic palette in the face of the corporate vultures." She wondered which studio he was talking about, but he didn't say and she didn't ask.

She knew he'd unwind after she jacked him off, but she wasn't sure he was ever going to give her the chance. When he rolled onto his back, he started telling her about the chemist who figured out the structure of the benzene ring. She had no idea what the benzene ring was, but there wasn't any stopping her gasbag client to ask for an explanation. "This chemist had a dream in which a snake swallowed its tail," he said, "and they told him, 'That's kind of easy, you just fall asleep and figure something out.' And he replied, 'Visions come to prepared spirits.'" Then it was time for the gasbag's hand job.

He gave Jenny a hundred-dollar tip and called her "a very bright young woman." She accepted the tip and the compliment while she was trying to determine whether his story fit into her life somehow. She would have asked him for guidance—he didn't seem like someone who denied many requests—but he was more interested in meeting the other girls. So it was that Cookie, finished with her shift and headed to an outcall, and Sierra, who had shown up late, both received fifty-dollar bills, big hugs, and sloppy kisses on the cheek from their manic benefactor.

"He ever stop talking?" Nick asked when it was safe for him to step out of the master bedroom.

"I don't think so," Jenny said.

"Even when he came?" Sierra asked.

"I didn't notice," Jenny said.

Sierra laughed. "Concentrating on his dick?"

"No, thinking about something he said."

The ringing phones saved Jenny from having to explain about visions and prepared spirits. L.A. seemed to have an endless supply of horny guys with money to spend. One of them was Barry, who asked Jenny if he could have her last appointment. She would have preferred a real date, but she still had a lawyer to pay. She'd see him at eight.

Scott showed up half an hour before Barry was supposed to. Jenny didn't think much of it. He was probably just starting his weekend early. If he had something else on his mind, Sierra was there. She'd seen her last client of the day, and she was the only one of the girls who could tolerate Scott on a regular basis. Jenny couldn't remember the last time he'd said anything to her except hello. That was fine with her.

Ten minutes later, DuPree walked in, nodding his head, eyes like ice, talking in the monotone that Jenny had learned to find so terrifying. He had a dog with him, straining to get out of its leash and explore its new surroundings. At least that was all Jenny hoped it wanted to do.

"Hey," Scott said. "You brought White Fang."

"Name's Blanco," DuPree said.

Jenny tried to think of what kind of dog it was. She'd always preferred cats, would have had one, in fact, if her landlord allowed them, and this dog—squat, thick chest, pink eyes, undershot jaw—was butt ugly. Even with its tongue dangling happily from the corner of its mouth, she couldn't help thinking it must have been a candidate to be drowned at birth.

"Does he bite?" Sierra asked.

"Pet him and find out," DuPree said.

"Oooh, I don't think so," Sierra said, forcing a giggle.

That was when something in Jenny's head clicked. "It's a pit bull, right?" she said.

"You one smart little China girl, ain't you?" DuPree said, turning his eyes on her for the first time, his face devoid of emotion.

Jenny thought he was making himself sound ghetto to frighten her, to remind her of their time alone. But she still found it in her to say, in a voice she hoped was loud enough for him to hear, "I'm Korean."

"That mean you ain't smart?" DuPree was smiling now.

"I recognize what kind of dog Blanco is, that's all."

"Then maybe you want to pet him. You know, since you're the dog expert."

Silence smothered the apartment.

✤ ✤ ✤

It was the smirk on DuPree's face that pissed Nick off more than anything, that haughty I've-done-time-and-you-haven't look that thugs always seemed to fall back on at moments like this. The dog just added to DuPree's sense of menace, scarred by the cruelty that warps too many pit bulls. He could hurt you bad, even kill you, and DuPree was using the pit's reputation the way he would have a gun in a robbery.

Nick took a deep breath and said, "Knock it off. She's not interested in the dog."

"That so?" DuPree looked at Coco. "The man speaking for your true heart, Miss Saigon?"

"I'm a cat person," she said.

No one laughed but her.

"Sorry, I just am."

DuPree kept his eyes on Nick standing by the room divider. "How about you? You a cat lover too? Or you just like pussy?"

"You're missing the point," Nick said.

"Yeah? What point is that?"

"I don't like assholes."

DuPree's eyes narrowed. "Say what?"

"You heard me."

"Last motherfucker called me that, I put out a cigarette in his eye."

Blanco growled and Scott looked like he'd gone into shock. It was all he could do to say, "Not in here, guys. Guys?"

But Nick wasn't paying attention to him. It didn't look like DuPree was, either.

"You want to try your cigarette trick with me, you don't have far to go," Nick said. "Otherwise, get your dog out of here."

"Just on account of you said so?" DuPree said.

"I knew you'd figure it out sooner or later."

"I don't think you askin' nice enough."

"Okay. If you don't do what I told you to, I'm going to throw you out the window. Then I'll take your dog someplace to grow old peacefully instead of making you think people are supposed to shit cupcakes when they see you with it. Is that nice enough?"

DuPree put on a phony grin.

"I get it," he said. "You afraid of the dog. That's what it is, ain't it? You about to mess your drawers worryin' my man Blanco gonna chomp down on your ankle, make you scream like a bitch."

"If that's what happens, you won't see it," Nick said. "You'll be somewhere between the third and fourth floor."

"Sheeee-it," DuPree said.

"Quit stalling. Make up your mind."

DuPree started toward Nick as Blanco barked and lunged ahead of him.

Nick held his ground, thinking he would try to kick the dog away first, maybe bring down the divider on its head, before he went after DuPree.

"Goddammit, no!" Scott shouted, sounding like he'd finally found his balls. "You're gonna have the cops all over this fucking place."

DuPree looked like he couldn't believe his ears. "So this punch-drunk faggot can just stand there and disrespect me like he wearing motherfucking Kevlar? I hope that is not what you are telling me."

"All I'm saying is I'll get my ass thrown in jail," Scott said. "That would pretty much fuck up what we talked about, wouldn't you say?"

"Plus my next client will be here in, like, ten minutes," Coco said. "You want him to walk in and see your dog going crazy? We'll get great reviews on the Internet for that."

"She's not bullshitting, dude," Scott said.

Sierra nodded robotically, stunned that one of her sisters in the sex trade had dared to speak up.

Nick watched it all, not caring about anyone's worries, not even Coco's. He knew he was going to fight DuPree someday—it was practically written in stone—and he figured they might as well get it over with now.

But there was DuPree pulling the dog toward the door, and Scott padding after him, saying, "I'm sorry about this, bro, really I am."

DuPree looked past Scott and fixed his prison-yard stare on Nick. "I'll see you again, motherfucker."

"I wouldn't miss it," Nick said.

✤ ✤ ✤

On the way down in the elevator, all DuPree thought about was kicking that security cocksucker's head in, leaving his brains all over the goddamn floor, and then tearing that rice-paddy cunt up with his cock. "Motherfucker," DuPree said, punching the wall and getting a growl out of Blanco. DuPree was for sure going to fuck the pussy out of her when he ripped off Scottie's lame-assed operation. Next week, he told himself; he'd do it then, and maybe fuck Scottie up too, fucking doughboy pussy. Right now, though, with the elevator door opening, he just hoped he had some hash back at his crib.

When he and Blanco stepped off the elevator, there was a middle-aged white dude waiting to get on: trim, handsome, lots of gray in his hair, going for a casual look in a teal-and-cream-colored sweater that DuPree figured must have cost him four bills easy.

"Evening," the white dude said, staying mellow at the sight of Blanco, maybe not even recognizing a pit bull when he saw one.

"What up?" DuPree said, still in ghetto mode.

It was only when the elevator door had closed that DuPree thought about the briefcase the white dude had been carrying, wondering what was in it and where he was taking it. DuPree yanked Blanco to a standstill and watched to see where the elevator stopped.

Eighth floor.

How about that shit? DuPree thought. The dude was for sure going to see the Oriental bitch. Now DuPree understood why she was worried about scaring off a trick, if he looked like that much money. It would be nice, DuPree thought as he walked Blanco out into the night, if the dude was around when he took down Scottie's apartment. Might turn a nice score into a big-assed score. And then DuPree saw a Rolls-Royce convertible parked out front. Had to be the trick's. Just like that, it was more than a three-hundred-thousand-dollar car; it was an inspiration.

❖ ❖ ❖

Barry started to say hello as Jenny closed the door behind him, then stopped when he saw her press a finger to her lips. He looked puzzled, but she didn't explain, just guided him toward the master bedroom, away from wherever Nick was, away from Scott and Sierra listening on the other side of the dividers. She knew she was forgetting Barry's donation, but she didn't care.

As soon as she closed the door behind them, he wrapped his arms around her and moved in for a passionate kiss that died on her lips. He pulled back and gave her a puzzled look. "Not glad to see me?"

"Sorry," Jenny said.

And she was, really and truly. He looked so good and smelled so nice that any other time she would have been on him before he could jump her bones. She knew he was already hard—she could feel his thing when he hugged her. But even that wasn't enough to ignite her now.

"It's been really weird around here today," she said. "Like you wouldn't believe."

"You're all right, aren't you?" he said.

That was what she liked about older guys. They always wanted to protect you while young guys, if you told them the exact same thing, would say that giving them head would take your mind off your problems.

It felt like the most natural thing in the world for Jenny to lean into Barry and let him hold her. "I'm all right," she said, "but I feel about as sexy as, I don't know, a bowl of oatmeal or something."

"If you were oatmeal, I'd eat you."

Not cool, Jenny thought, *not now*. But sometimes even older guys made tactical errors, so she forced a small laugh and hoped Barry hadn't felt her recoil. She didn't want to chase him away. She just wanted to take the conversation in a different direction.

"What do you think?" he said. "We could talk a little about what's got you so upset, and then I'll give you some kisses on your sweet place, the way you like them, and we can see what happens."

There wasn't enough time left in the day for Jenny to tell him everything, mainly because she'd never told him anything. Barry didn't know about the robbery or the rapes or the translucent man or DuPree or Scott or the business of getting naked for strangers whose cocks you would soon hold in your hands. All Barry knew was that she was a cute little Asian girl he wanted to fuck, and that she wanted to fuck him, too. At least she had until today. And maybe she would tomorrow. But not now, when it was Nick who dominated her thoughts. She hadn't told Barry about him either, and she wasn't sure how she would, mainly because she was still figuring out what Nick meant to her.

"Would you mind if we were just quiet for a while?" Jenny said.

✤ ✤ ✤

The fear slowly ebbed from the place where Nick kept it stored deep inside him. It had grabbed his heart and his gut the instant he had seen DuPree's dog, but he had known he couldn't run no matter how much he wanted to. He had to stand firm and put on the same executioner's face he had worn in the ring, all the while remembering what Cecil had told him the first time he fought a genuine badass: "Never show fear—make fear work for you. Make the motherfucker across from you feel it." It was advice easily comprehended by an uncluttered mind, but Nick's mind now was a warehouse of bad memories.

They came wrapped in gauze, and were filled with vague figures moving in slow motion and speaking in voices he had to strain to recognize. He thought he heard his mother shouting—yeah, it was her for sure, shouting at a dog to get away from them. There was barking too, and growling. And a little girl's screams. And her blood. She was Nick's playmate, three years old, maybe four, from the two-flat next door, and her blood stained the last snow that fell in Chicago that year.

He could still see it, even though he couldn't remember the girl's name, or her face, or what became of her. He thought she had moved, she and her family, to get away from their memories of the dog and the blood. But there's no escaping what is carved in your memory. There is only enduring it. Why Nick had been able to succeed this time, he knew he would never say aloud. It was Coco. She gave him a reason to care and a purpose beyond chasing away unwanted suitors and cleaning up after two-hundred-dollar assignations. She gave him a reason to hold his ground. The hell of it was, no matter how tenderly she treated him, he still wasn't sure she saw him as anything more than a slab of meat.

✤ ✤ ✤

How do you spell his last name? she kept asking herself. It wasn't like they wore name tags—where would she pin one when she was wearing something low cut, except on one of her boobs? The only time she'd heard Scott say Nick's last name, he'd been mumbling. So everything she was doing now at her kitchen table was pure guesswork. B-A-V-K-O or B-A-V-K-A, or did it start with a P?

Jenny's fingers flew over the computer keyboard as she fed the possibilities to Google. She hadn't bothered at first because she'd decided that a man with such sad eyes couldn't possibly be a danger to her. Of course he might have turned out to be a disaster at providing security even if he had been a boxer, but he reminded her of a bird with a broken wing, and she didn't believe in abandoning wounded birds.

The Nick she'd seen call DuPree an asshole—an asshole! How great was that?—couldn't have surprised her more if he'd come to work in a fishnet dress. He'd kept it together the whole time, his voice real low, every move cool and economical, and when DuPree started toward him with that dog, it looked like that was what Nick had been hoping for. He was, like, totally fucking dangerous.

Jenny had never slept with someone who was dangerous or anything close to it. She hadn't slept with Nick either, but it was a possibility if she could just learn something about him. But she still couldn't figure out if his last name started with a B or a P. What about that V? Should it be an F?

A few keystrokes later her computer screen glowed with the tortured life of Nick Pafko, the street kid from the northwest side of Chicago who chased his dream as a boxer all the way to the ring, where it died when Alonzo Burgess did. It was an accident, a hazard of the trade, the kind of terrible mistake that other fighters had found a way to get past. But Nick was stuck in the quicksand of tragedy. And here was Jenny trying to decide if she should totter into it with him on four-inch heels.

24

It rained on and off for three days, which didn't do anything to improve DuPree's mood. Fuck the rain when he'd just had his Beemer detailed and it was almost June and he had work to put in. It was hard enough driving in the goddamn city when it was dry and motherfuckers weren't sliding all over like the streets were covered with ice. Maybe if it rained more, they wouldn't be reacting like they pissed sitting down. Things the way they were, though, the best DuPree could do was to tell himself the dude would be so busy keeping his Rolls in one piece that he'd never notice a brother on his ass.

The Oriental bitch had called him Barry, and DuPree knew he'd had it right in the lobby when he saw the two of them come out of the building, the bitch smiling up at him all dreamy and Barry eating that shit up. DuPree thought their next stop would be the man's love shack, but he kissed her goodbye at her car and went his own way. DuPree was right there behind him with Blanco on Friday night, and then by himself Saturday, Sunday, and Monday. He wasn't even tired by the end of it. The prospect of a big-assed score had him juiced, even if he had to bring his lame white boy Scottie in on it.

Fucking Scottie, whining about the cops just when DuPree was ready to fuck that boxer man up good. Whining like a bitch. DuPree was never going to get past that shit. But that was all right, because he had a surprise waiting for Scottie. Then Scottie could whine all he wanted.

Right now DuPree was pacifying his mind by driving home through Hancock Park, thinking about stealing enough someday to buy one of those get-a-load-of-me mansions right there in the middle of the city. Only problem was, just on the other side of Wilshire it could get rugged, what with gangs more interested in shooting each other full of holes than heeding the call of the profit motive. Maybe he could get himself an ocean view instead, something in Marina del Rey. He planned on giving it some serious thought once he fired up a spliff in his apartment on South Mansfield, the one he'd decorated when he was dating that Ethiopian model, a sleek, long-legged bitch who dumped his ass for an architect. A *white* architect. Not knowing why he'd started thinking about that motherfucker, DuPree headed straight for the bedroom where he kept his stash in a ceramic Buddha with a lift-off top. He was greeted by some unholy shit.

The room had been shredded, bedspread ripped and torn, pillows spilling goose down, curtains yanked from their rods so the streetlight shined in to make sure DuPree got a good look at the wreckage. And here came Blanco, the wrinkles on his face folded into a welcome-home smile, as if that would keep DuPree from noticing the immense turd that sat in the middle of the floor.

"Motherfucker," DuPree said.

His tone slowed the dog's approach.

"Cocksucker."

The dog stopped and retreated a step, its smile replaced by a look of shame.

"Goddamn motherfucking motherfucker."

DuPree wanted to hit him, kick him, beat his head in with a hammer. But from the depths of his rage came a warning signal: Raise a hand against a pit bull and you'll lose it. Motherfuck it. He'd shoot the fucking dog, put a bullet right through one of its pink eyes. He was imagining how much he'd like to see the back of the dog's head splattered on the wall when he thought about his neighbors for maybe the first time ever. They were from India or Pakistan, one of those snake-in-a-basket countries. They dressed funny and cooked food that smelled like his old man's dirty drawers. Ordinarily, no sane brother would have wasted an IQ point thinking about those sandal jockeys. But DuPree knew they'd for sure call the cops if he put a bullet in Blanco, and the thought of the cops convinced him to drop to one knee and act like the chump the dog expected him to be.

"Come here, motherfucker," he said. "What you acting all shy about?"

The dog looked at him suspiciously for a moment, then caved in the way he knew it would, trotting over, showing off that happy tongue again.

"Shit, you know I take good care of your ass."

The next day he gave the dog to his old man. Onus DuPree Sr. reacted pretty much the way his son expected him to: "What the fuck I want with a goddamn pit bull?"

"You need a pet," DuPree said.

"Pit bulls are for common niggers," Onus Sr. said. "I ain't no common nigger."

"Just a lonely one, isn't that what you told me last time I was here?"

"You saying this motherfucker can talk?" Onus Sr. pointed at the dog on his front porch, sounding like he wasn't interested in letting it advance an inch farther.

"Why you asking me crazy shit like that?" DuPree said.

"Because the only kind of company I need is the kind that can talk."

"Well, maybe you can teach him."

"Don't get smart with me, boy."

"Yeah, teach him to talk and yell at the neighbor kids and bitch at people that park in front of the house. Or maybe he can just bite them. You'd probably like that better, wouldn't you, you grouchy old motherfucker? You can't sink your own teeth in their asses—can't run fast enough to catch them, fat as you are—but your dog here, he can do the job for you."

The old man started to smile.

"Look at you," DuPree said. "Shit, you love what I'm tellin' you. You and this dog going to be tight as motherfuckers."

"He got a name?" Onus Sr. asked.

"Blanco."

The old man nodded thoughtfully. "Like this cat I played with in Tampico one winter. Francisco Blanco. Mexican fella. Smoothest swing I ever saw. The Cardinals wanted to sign him and he got drunked up and a truckload of chickens ran over his ass. Chickens. Goddamn."

DuPree, not knowing what to say, said nothing.

"All right," the old man told him. "Blanco can stay."

❖ ❖ ❖

Scott hadn't expected DuPree to call. He thought he'd have to be the one to pick up the phone after the thing with the dog and Nick. Fucking Nick, didn't he know he wasn't supposed to get all hairy-chested when it was DuPree he was talking to? Scott would have to straighten him out, teach him about the goddamn chain of command. Coco, too. But the thought of chasing off his best moneymaker and a guy who, to be blunt, scared him shitless was more than he could deal with at the moment. Good thing DuPree had been cool about it, but he still had to have been pissed. Scott hadn't exactly had a McQueen moment, that was for damn sure.

Anyway, DuPree made the call and Scott tried not to say yes to a meeting so fast that it sounded like he was queer for him. Now DuPree was on the other side of a corner table at Aunt Kizzy's, a soul food joint in the Marina where there was no other soul that Scott could see. DuPree had asked the woman at the door if they could keep some space between them and the other customers;

said he had some music contracts to talk over with his pale friend. Scott had been here with DuPree once before, on a Saturday when Little Richard strutted in on high heels fresh from his Seventh-Day Adventist church, looking so weird around the eyes that he had to be wearing mascara. This was where L.A.'s black bourgeoisie came to get in touch with their high-calorie roots, and Scott was all for it, tucking into his meatloaf and macaroni and cheese, promising himself he wouldn't order peach cobbler for dessert and knowing his promise meant nothing.

For DuPree, who picked at his fried chicken, this was obviously about business, not pleasure. He said he'd been following the dude from the other night, the one Coco had been so worried about missing. Couldn't help himself when he saw the dude's Rolls.

"He drives a Rolls?" Scott asked.

"Man, you got to start paying attention to your clientele," DuPree said. "No telling what kind of fish those ho's of yours got on the line."

"Yeah?"

"Yeah. Like this dude, he's living up there in Laurel Canyon, just off Mulholland. Nice place—modern, lots of glass—but it hangs off the side of the hill, you know, looks like one good earthquake would send it sliding. Man, that shit jangles my nerves."

"I hear you," Scott said, though he didn't believe DuPree's nerves ever got jangled and, to be honest, didn't agree with him. Scott would have donated a testicle to a network executive who was missing one if it meant a house in Laurel Canyon.

"But we're not burglars, so what the fuck, right?" DuPree said.

"Right," Scott said, liking his use of "we."

"We're businessmen seeking opportunities, and the first thing I notice is this motherfucker—"

"Barry."

"You got it. This motherfucker Barry looks like he has himself a wife and kids that visit weekends. I mean, he's getting his nut with your Oriental cooze one night, and the next motherfucking morning, there's the wife and kids pulling into his driveway, climbing all over him, lots of kisses and hey, Dad, let's get our asses to Chuck E. Cheese."

"And you want to blackmail him," Scott said. "Put a tape recorder in the room when he's with Coco, maybe walk in taking pictures when they're—" He stopped when he saw DuPree looking puzzled. "What?"

"That bitch give it up for you?" DuPree asked.

"She didn't for you?" Scott asked him back.

They both knew the answer instantly.

"Goddamn," DuPree said.

"Maybe she's got it sewed shut," Scott said.

"We can fix that shit."

"Fuckin' A. But first we got some blackmailing to do, right, bro?"

"Fuck, no."

"What, then?" Scott asked, hoping he hadn't stepped on his dick.

DuPree gave Scott a no-parole stare. "If you'll shut your damn mouth and listen, I'll tell you."

"I'm listening."

"All right," DuPree said. "We rob the motherfucker."

Scott wanted to grab a gun and get to work. He also wanted to get the fuck out of there, run, and never look back. Scott wanted to ask DuPree if it was normal for an apprentice criminal's instincts to be heading in two directions at once. But Scott also wanted DuPree to keep talking, so he uttered not a word.

"We're going to put a gun to his fucking head and make him open his goddamn treasure chest," DuPree said. "'Cause he got one, this motherfucker. You see that bag of his? That leather briefcase? It must have cost him three grand."

Scott shook his head, still afraid to speak.

"Oh, that's right, you're too busy with that Hollywood shit to check out all the money walking through your door, just begging to get taken. But I got your back on this one, man. See, I bump into motherfucking Barry when I'm leaving out of your trick pad the other night, me and my dog that started all that unnecessary drama. And I see his briefcase and I just got to know what's inside. I mean, I'm curious that way, understand? So I start following this motherfucker, not just up to his house but all over the fucking city. Do you have any idea how fucked-up traffic is on Sunday? Even when it's not raining? Makes me understand why I like working nights—at least you got a shot at getting some-goddamn-where. But I stick with the motherfucker, all right? I persevere, just like my pops taught me. And you know where the motherfucker keeps going back to? Even on Sunday? The motherfucking diamond district."

"He sells diamonds?" Scott asked, unable to contain himself any longer.

DuPree shut him up with a look.

"Better than that," DuPree said. "I think maybe the mother-fucker's got something illegal going on. Stealing them, smuggling them, fencing them—some kind of shit that's got him down there when every other place is locked up tight."

"That's good for us, isn't it?" Scott asked cautiously. "If it's illegal, there's less chance of him going to the cops when we . . . you know."

DuPree smiled. "You been wasting your time acting and shit. You're forgetting your dinner, too." He pointed at the feast that had grown cold on Scott's plate.

"That's all right," Scott said. "I want to ask you, shouldn't we know for sure what he's up to before we move?"

"You're not afraid of the unknown, are you?" DuPree was still smiling. "I mean, you're not going to tell me that now and break my heart."

"Fuck no."

"So we're just going to roll with it. See what's in the briefcase, maybe let motherfucking Barry take us downtown to meet his friends. All in all, just generally terrorize his ass and walk away with a serious goddamn score. You're up for that, aren't you?"

"Hell, yes. I'm in, bro. You know I am." Scott took a breath, summoning all his courage. "But I've got to ask you one more thing."

DuPree's smile vanished. "What?"

"We're not going to jump him at the apartment, are we?"

DuPree started smiling again. "Relax, dawg. This isn't about getting your ass thrown in jail. It's about our financial betterment. We're going to grab the motherfucker outside. Out in the street."

"I should have known you'd plan it like that," Scott said. "Sorry."

"No big thing," DuPree said.

But it was to Scott. He felt like eating again. Cold meatloaf wasn't so bad. Cold mac and cheese wasn't, either. And now he was damn sure he'd have some peach cobbler. He was looking to flag down the waitress when he heard DuPree say, "Tell me something." Scott put down his hand and turned back to DuPree.

"That bitch Sierra smart enough to do us a favor?"

25

"Sleep with both of them," Maria said on the phone. "What's the big deal?"

"I can't do that," Jenny said.

"Sure you can. All you have to do is lie back and spread your legs. Unless you prefer cowgirl or—"

Jenny erupted in laughter. "Maybe you could."

"Oh, so I'm a slut, is that it?" Maria was laughing too. "Just because I like ten inches of hard cock daily? Hourly if I can get it? Listen, sweetie, sometimes it takes two guys to give me that much."

"You're crazy."

"No, I'm horny."

"I'm hanging up now."

"Don't you dare," Maria said, laughing so hard she could hardly get the words out. "Do you hear me, Jenny? Do not—"

Jenny put down her cell feeling better than she had all weekend. Unfortunately that would only last until she went back to work on Tuesday, and then the tug of war in her head between Nick and Barry would resume.

She'd made a point of not telling Maria that Nick had killed somebody when he was a boxer. It seemed pretty strange when she thought about it afterward, protecting the guy who was supposed to protect her, but that was how she felt about him now.

On the other hand, it was strictly out of self-protection that she'd neglected to mention that Barry hadn't called her in two days. Here she was a half-step from sleeping with—oh, please, enough euphemisms—from fucking him, and all she knew was that he was in Santa Barbara. At least he'd been open enough to tell her he'd kept his place there. But couldn't he have taken her with him if he liked her as much as he said he did? Couldn't he have found time to slip away for a romantic dinner? On a Saturday? Come on, whatever it was he did to afford his Rolls—he was still pretty vague on the subject—it had to shut down sometime.

The weight of her skepticism made Jenny feel worse than ever no matter how good she was getting at *Tiger Woods*, an absolute killer with the joystick. Clients were supposed to get hung up on masseuses, not the other way around. On top of that, she'd told Barry her real name.

Nick still knew her only as Coco. She wasn't supposed to get hung up on him either. A security guy? Especially one with the past that Nick had? That was beyond ridiculous, no matter how sweet and sad he seemed to be. And seriously tough, too. She could never forget that, especially after hearing Maria talk about what had gone down in Los Feliz. It was those same guys again. This time they'd done a number on a couple of Thai girls working nights out of the back of a beauty shop. If push came to shove, maybe she'd have to place practical considerations ahead of romantic impulses.

Jenny was wondering what it would be like to have Nick save her when she met Sara and Rachel at 14 Below in Santa Monica that night, the first time she'd seen them since their poetry final. When they'd called, they sounded like they never expected her to say yes, probably because they assumed that her life was filled with men. She guessed it was, but not the way they imagined. Still, she made a point of leaving her cell at home in case Barry did call. Let him wonder where she was.

The beer was cold and Sara and Rachel supplied the diversion Jenny needed. She knew they were using her as bait for cute guys, but so what? She was out from behind her computer and away from her nagging thoughts of Barry. She drank, and Sara and Rachel got asked to dance, and when the live music started a little before eleven, Jenny actually found herself liking it. No punk, no metal, no emo. Just a guitar player from Texas and a couple of his steady rocking friends, real loose, lots of laughing and promises that they'd learn all the songs by next week. Sara said the guitarist used to play in Bonnie Raitt's band, not that Jenny knew who Bonnie Raitt was. But she liked the guitar player as soon as she heard him sing, "She ain't a dish, she's a whole set of china." The lyrics made her smile for the next two days, until it was time for her to work the evening shift on Tuesday.

She still hadn't heard from Barry and the first person she saw was Nick. Just like that, the cosmic joke was on her again. Barry's silence was a humiliation even if nobody else knew about it, but Nick was as reliably strong and silent as ever. All she said was, "Been busy?" And all he said was, "No, kind of slow."

It was one of those rare shifts when Sierra saw more clients than Jenny, and Jenny found herself feeling jealous, wishing she had worked Monday. Mondays were almost always off-the-tracks busy, the kind of day she needed if she was going to finish paying her lawyer, but Scott had given the shift to Pamela, his newest blonde. Jenny assumed it was her punishment for making that smart-assed remark about being a cat person.

The thought of it brought her back to Nick and what she now knew about him. It was hardly the kind of thing you bring up casually, like asking if he'd seen one of those TV shows everybody but Jenny watched. Anyway, they were following their usual post-vacuuming routine, him with his sports page and constant picking up, her with the two novels she had brought. She tossed aside *The Catcher in the Rye* after twenty pages, puzzled at why so many guys had recommended it to her when they discovered she had a brain. Holden Caulfield was the kind of whiny, self-absorbed jerk she had always hated. The polar opposite of Nick.

"Thanks for the other day," she told him.

"I didn't do anything," he said. "I didn't think he was going to, either."

"Really? Because I was like this is crazy, he's totally going to turn his dog loose."

"No, he looks to me like the kind of guy that takes things right up to the edge, then pulls back after he sees how you react. If you're scared or weak, something like that, then he's dangerous."

Jenny hoped she didn't look as surprised as she felt. She'd never heard Nick string that many words together. More than that, he was practically analytical.

"Wow, you've really thought about him, haven't you?"

"You fight for a living, that's what you learn to do. You don't want to get your clock cleaned because you didn't study the other guy. If he's better than you, hey, more power to him. But if you were lazy, you deserve a beating."

"I hope you never have to fight him," Jenny said.

"Guess we'll just have to see," Nick said.

He stared off into the distance. Jenny waited for him to come back and tell her what he saw, but he just said he was going downstairs to check the laundry. The only sound in the living room after that came from the pages Jenny turned in *The Way We Live Now*. Its author, Anthony Trollope, was a genius and everything—he'd finish writing a novel in the morning and start a new one in the afternoon—but he couldn't keep Jenny from thinking about Nick.

The silence wasn't broken until Sierra came out of her only session of the day, a doctor from Cedars. "What a douche," she told Jenny. "Never smiled, hardly said anything besides 'Take off your clothes,' and then he expects full service. Practically orders it. I told him maybe that works with his nurses, but not me. And I've got a fucking car payment coming up."

Sierra picked up her cell phone and started texting, then stopped.

"Oh, yeah. Barry called."

Jenny tried not to look too happy about it. "I didn't see anything written down," she said.

"It's around here someplace," Sierra said. "Anyway, he wants to see you tomorrow, at seven. You're working then, right?"

"Yeah," Jenny said. "Did he leave a number?"

Sierra smiled. "You mean you don't have it by now?"

"Somewhere in my backpack, I guess."

"Don't worry, I got it."

"Thanks."

Sierra busied herself loading her outsized purse for the trip home, striding confidently on the high heels she wore off-duty and on. She shouldered her purse and opened the door to leave, then stopped and walked back toward Jenny.

"Did he say anything about Friday?" Sierra asked.

"Who?" Jenny said.

"Nick. You're the only one he talks to."

Right, Jenny thought, *because I'm the only one who doesn't turn around and blab it to all the other girls.* But she said, "He hasn't brought it up, actually."

"I thought you guys were, like, closer than that," Sierra said, smiling as if she imagined their soiled sheets.

"Well, we're not," Jenny said.

"Uh-huh."

"Look, just because I treat him like a human being doesn't—"

"He's an animal," Sierra said.

"He is not."

"Yeah? Well, what would you call someone who kills a guy in a fight?"

Sierra looked smug and mean. No way Jenny could let the bitch one-up her. "I'd call him unlucky," Jenny said. "He could just as easily be the one that died, you know. It wasn't like Nick had this dirty trick that made the other guy fall and break his neck. It was a freak accident. Nick knocked the guy down and the guy hit his head on the rope and—"

Sierra couldn't hide her surprise.

"You don't know what happened, do you?" Jenny said. "You just thought—no, you didn't think anything. You never do. You heard Nick killed some guy when they were fighting, and instead of checking it out, you decided he was, I don't know, an animal, like you just said. Or a monster. And that really sucks, you know that, Sierra? And it's really stupid. And . . . and . . . "

"No wonder you're sleeping with him," Sierra said. "He's got control of your mind."

"I am *not* sleeping with him."

"Right."

Sierra turned and marched out the door.

"But I'd rather sleep with him than Scott," Jenny shouted after her. "Do you have to watch Scott's old TV shows too? Do you, Sierra? Do you?"

Jenny was angry. Jenny was laughing. Jenny was being pulled in so many directions by her emotions that she had to sit down before she fell down. The front door Sierra had left open would have to stay that way for a moment. Jenny had other things to think about, like what she was going to say to Nick, or if she was going to say anything at all.

❖ ❖ ❖

"I should have told you," Nick said.

Jenny looked up, as if she'd forgotten he'd be back so soon. When she started to say something, he cut her off.

"I was out in the hall when you two were yelling at each other."

"I think I was the one doing all the yelling."

Nick grinned. "I didn't know you had a temper. From the looks of Sierra, I don't think she did either."

"Did she see you?"

"No, she was too busy escaping."

Nick and Jenny looked at each other, uncertain of where to take the conversation next.

"I'm sorry," Jenny said at last.

"For what?"

"For . . . I don't know . . . "

Nick watched Jenny shrug uncomfortably.

"I don't want your pity if that's what it is," he said. "I don't feel sorry for myself, so there's no way in hell you should feel sorry for me. What happened in that fight is for me to deal with. I know it's gonna stay with me until the day I die—I can't change that. I used to think I could at least make up for it. The guy had a family and I took him away from them, and how do I make that right? I've lost a lot of sleep trying to figure that one out. I can't do it, can't even come close."

"Is that why you work here?" Jenny asked. "Like protecting us is some kind of penance?"

"No, I need to make my rent," he said with a small, sad smile.

She smiled back at him. "Tell me about it. I've got a lawyer to pay."

"So you know how it is. You put one foot in front of the other and do the best you can—although I've got to admit I never thought I'd end up in a place like this."

"We need you," Jenny said. "The girls, I mean. I don't know if any of them have ever told you, but you're the one reason we feel safe."

"Hearing it from you is enough," he said.

"But you made it sound like you hate it here."

"Not when you're around."

Nick kissed her, and Jenny let him know she liked it with her tongue. They kissed wet and hard and deep, and then he slid off her negligee as if it were a rumor. The buttons on his shirt were a struggle for her, so he yanked them loose himself. When they were both naked, his first impulse was to carry her into the master bedroom, but fuck it—too far to travel.

The train they were riding wasn't going any farther than the sofa. He made a mouthful of each of her breasts, his tongue teasing her lush, dark nipples until they were erect, then worked his way past her stomach until he could bury his face between her legs. She was clean and smooth down there, and he heard her moan as he tasted her for the first time. She grabbed his hair and bucked and writhed, and when she came, she screamed.

He raised his head and saw her smiling at him, her eyes gleaming with pleasure, her lustrous hair fanned out on the sofa's cushions. She looked more beautiful than ever when he mounted her and she took his stiff cock in her right hand. But even passion couldn't blind him to her size, her fragility, so he rolled the two of them until she was on top of him. She seemed surprised at first, and then pleased as he entered her creamy sex and she began to ride him, up and down, slowly at first, then faster and faster, back and forth, round and round. For an instant, nothing more, he would notice that her hair framed her face now and her lips and breasts were there for him to kiss. Then she would throw back her head and say, "Fuck me, fuck my pussy," and he would pump harder and harder.

They found a rhythm they didn't lose even when they tumbled onto the floor in slow motion. Now he was atop her, trying to go deeper and deeper until he touched her heart. He knew she was ready to explode when he heard a catch in her breath and she grabbed his arms. She came a heartbeat later, and then he did too, both of them with cries that had their origins in primordial ooze.

But his cry was louder, like that of an explorer who had just made the discovery of a lifetime.

Later, as they sat on the floor, still naked, their backs against the sofa, she smiled at him and said, "By the way, my real name is Jenny."

"Jenny."

He said it as if it were something to savor.

"It's nice to meet you, Jenny."

26

DuPree rang the bell and didn't get an answer. Rang it again. Still nothing. He knew the old man had to be around somewhere. His Ford Taurus was in the driveway, needing a wash as usual, and Onus DuPree Sr. never went anywhere unless it was in his ride. DuPree thought the old man should take up walking, fat as he was getting, but he didn't even run his fucking car all the way into the garage, just parked so it was a shorter trip to his front door.

DuPree stepped off the front porch and walked across the lawn to the driveway that led to the backyard. Halfway there, he heard the old man saying, "Uh-huh, uh-huh, you a motherfuckin' ball hawk, that's what you are." He sounded like a younger version of himself, the one who had his name in the newspaper, a wife who loved and scolded him, and a son who had yet to bring him shame. DuPree didn't think about those days very often—no money for him in the past—but when he got to the wooden fence that separated the backyard from the driveway, he couldn't help it. He saw the old man throwing a torn, dirty baseball toward the cinderblock wall at the rear of the yard and Blanco chasing after it, past the Chinese elm and across the patchy grass that was still damp from the weekend's rain.

The old man laughed as he forced himself into a squat and waited for the dog to return so he could wrestle the ball out of its mouth, pet its scarred head, and rough up the stubs of its ears. Then he slowly stood and drew back his arm to do it all again, the years falling away to a time when the white paint on the fence wasn't chipped, the roses weren't dead or in need of tending, and Onus DuPree Jr. was the one chasing down the ball.

"Hey," DuPree said, staying on the driveway.

When Onus Sr. looked over and saw who it was, the joy vanished from his face.

"What you want?" he said.

"My dog," DuPree said.

"Shit, he just got here," the old man said.

Blanco was by his feet now, looking up at him expectantly, waiting for another wrestling match over the ball.

"It's only until tomorrow," DuPree said.

"What for?" Onus Sr. asked, his yellow eyes narrowing with suspicion.

"Maybe I miss him. You ever stop to think of that, you selfish old motherfucker?"

"You never missed nothing, boy. Not another living creature, anyway."

DuPree nodded, his mouth twisting into something resembling a smile. "You must not have heard there's a first time for everything."

Onus Sr. didn't respond as he squatted to take the ball from Blanco's mouth. The dog was ready to go again in an instant, but this time the old man kept the ball by his side when he stood.

"I'd like to know what the hell you're up to," he said.

"I told you you'll have the dog back tomorrow," DuPree said. "That's all you got to know."

"No, it ain't. But come on in while I get his leash."

"Just bring it out front. I'll meet you there."

DuPree headed back down the driveway without waiting for a reply. The old man watched him go, then walked to the back door and opened it for Blanco. "Come on, you got a road trip," he said. After the dog padded into the house, the old man turned around and heaved the ball, trying to get it over the cinderblock wall and falling two bounces short. "Shit," he said, and followed the dog inside.

✤ ✤ ✤

The fucking carbs were going to kill him. Scott knew it even as he shoveled another fork full of warmed-up Pink Dot pasta Alfredo into his mouth. He told himself the only reason he was eating this shit was to make sure he had fuel in the tank. He'd be venturing into the unknown when he and DuPree saddled up, making the kind of move that could land him in the headlines next to that pussy-addled moron Robert Blake, and he didn't know when he'd get his next shot at food. Chewing thoughtfully, wondering if he should eat that cold piece of garlic toast too, he was starting to convince himself everything would be cool.

He had scored a .38 Smith & Wesson detective special from a props guy he used to drink with. It was a cold piece of blue steel with a snub nose and no serial number, and it made him forget about McQueen and feel more like Robert Mitchum or Lee Marvin back when film noir had hair on its ass. To go with the gat—a great fucking word even though DuPree probably hated it—he had butterflies, the kind he used to get before auditions and on his first day on the set. Butterflies were good. They told him he cared.

Showtime was 7 P.M. Sierra had said Barry was coming to see Coco then. Right on top of things, that Sierra, surprising Scott by calling as soon as she found out, giving Scott and DuPree almost a whole day to get ready. They'd grab Barry when he came back outside, all relaxed after getting off, not thinking about anything except the girl. Scott worried that she'd be with him. That was the only thing about DuPree's plan that hung him up: Coco might convince Barry to turn their session into some kind of a date. Coco looked to Scott like she could be pretty fucking convincing. But DuPree didn't seem to give a shit about her, thinking she was one of those responsible girls who would finish her shift before she reconnected with Barry. If she didn't, if she decided to play hooky with Barry, then they'd just roll with it. Scott could get her out of the way by acting like he needed to talk to her before she took off. And if she actually climbed in the Rolls with Barry, then fuck it, the surprise would just have to be on her.

Every time Scott arrived at that part of the plan, the part where Coco would undoubtedly see their faces, he got something worse than butterflies. He started wondering what DuPree would do then, and whether it would be ugly, and if he wanted to be in a movie like that. Naturally DuPree had said there was nothing to worry about, just thieves robbing another thief, the kind of thing that happened all the time and never got reported to the police. He'd even told Scott a story about how he had robbed a drug dealer who made house calls. It never made the news, and those sorry TV motherfuckers had their noses open for anything to fill the time when they weren't showing car chases.

Scott crumpled the container his pasta had come in and lobbed it at his kitchen's overflowing wastebasket. He missed and didn't care. That was how good a mood he was in, twenty past four, getting ready to head to his meet with DuPree. Then Sierra spoiled it by calling to say Coco hadn't shown up for work.

"You got to be fucking kidding me," Scott said.

"And she's not picking up when I call her," Sierra said.

"That fucking cunt. You leave a message?"

"Yes. I'm not stupid."

"Jesus fucking Christ."

"Well, I never liked her," Sierra said, relegating Coco to the past tense. "It was you guys that were so fucking hot for her, and she just thought you were a bunch of rice chasers."

"Shut the fuck up."

"Hey, fuck you. I'm trying to help, okay? I don't get why you're so interested in Coco and this Barry guy anyway. Are you, like, jealous or something?"

Sierra wasn't in on the plan. DuPree had made sure of that, warning Scott that if she became anything more than their spy, he'd fuck her up good. At the time, it was the last thing Scott wanted—Sierra was always agreeable about banging the boss—but now he wanted to kill her himself.

"Analyze me some other time, okay?" he said. "Where's she live?"

"I don't know," Sierra said.

"You're serious? You really don't?"

"It's not like we were friends, you know."

"Then what fucking good are you?" Scott said, and heaved his cell phone against the living room wall.

He stood there seething, blind to the dent he had put in the wall—what the hell, he'd dented it before—and then he moved to pick it up as fast as the pasta in his belly would let him. He needed the goddamn phone to call DuPree and break the bad news. Okay, it was in one piece. He started to dial, then stopped. He had to throw up.

✣ ✣ ✣

"First thing I need to ask you," DuPree said on the phone, "before we get down to any of this shit you're telling me: You're going to hang onto your nuts, aren't you?"

He was already convinced there was no way Scottie could do it. Scottie was a fucking actor, all the time growing stubble on his chin and talking tough so those Hollywood fools would think he was some kind of badass white boy. It wouldn't be any different now that DuPree had posed the question. Scottie would give him the only answer he could under the circumstances. Scottie would put on his act.

"Fuck yes I am," he said. "Don't worry about me, man. I'm your dawg—you know that. Shit, you ought to see this fucking gun I got. It is so fucking cool. A snub-nosed .38, you believe that?"

DuPree wanted to say he bet it shot real bullets and shit. He restrained himself.

"It's just that now I'm worried I got it for nothing," Scott said. "I mean, if Coco's not there and Barry calls and finds out—you know, if he doesn't show—we're shit out of luck, it seems to me."

"No, man, we aren't at all," DuPree said.

"You sure?"

"Hell, yes. It just got more interesting, that's all."

"Interesting? Maybe I'm missing something."

DuPree toyed with the idea of telling Scottie what a clueless motherfucker he was, and then held off because he could still be of some use. Not for any heavy lifting, but this was definitely a job for two men now—and a dog. DuPree just wouldn't let him know about Blanco yet. There wasn't anything to be gained by saying the goddamn dog was locked in the bedroom again, probably chewing the shit out everything it hadn't sunk its teeth into the other day. The important thing was to focus on this two-man job DuPree had in mind, and how one of the two men didn't have to be worth a shit. That was where Scottie came in.

"Okay," DuPree said, "we each got someplace to be. You got the trick pad, I got where she lives."

"You know where she lives?"

"I know all kinds of shit. Just listen, all right? If Barry shows up at her place, I'll call you and you get your ass over there. If Barry shows up at your place—"

"The trick pad," Scott said helpfully.

"Yeah. If he shows up there, you call me right away, and then you got to make sure he stays there. You clear on that? The motherfucker cannot leave before I am on the scene. Cannot. If he gets away, we got a handful of empty, and that would be seriously fucked up, you hear what I'm saying?"

"I'm with you, bro." Now Scottie was starting that bro shit again—DuPree wanted to tell him to cut it the fuck out. "But there's something I'm not clear on."

"What's that?" DuPree asked.

"How exactly do you want me to stop Barry? You know, if he shows up at the apartment—the trick pad, I mean—and then he starts to leave?"

Of course Scottie would want to know what to do. The motherfucker was an actor. He couldn't figure things out for himself. He needed direction. And it didn't matter that they weren't even to the criminal part yet. It didn't matter any more than all the times Scottie had talked DuPree damn near deaf about the directors who had fucked him over and how he was thinking maybe he should try directing himself. The motherfucker still needed help with his process. DuPree thought that was what Scottie called it anyway—his process.

"Just speak to the dude," DuPree said. "Stroll up to him outside the building and say, 'That's a fine sweater, my man. Where'd you buy it at?' Or ask him about his car. A motherfucker with a Rolls? With another white man acting like the car makes him a goddamn hero? Shit, sounds to me like you'll have a captive audience right there."

"But he'll see my face," Scott said.

"It don't matter, dawg," DuPree said. "How many times I got to tell you that? He's outside the law. When we take him down, he can't go running to the cops. All he can do is go home and watch your reruns on TV."

"I don't think they show them," Scott said.

"Whatever."

Goddamn, DuPree thought, *he better not start whining about his motherfucking residuals.*

"And we're not really sure he's a criminal."

"Your nuts, Scottie. You're hanging onto them, aren't you?"

"You know I am, bro. I'm just trying to get this right, okay? So let me ask you another thing."

"Hold on a minute," DuPree said, wondering if he should just call the whole thing off on account of this motherfucker. "You got to be straight on one fact, all right? The man is a criminal. He's the perfect score. Just keep telling yourself that, you hear? The perfect score."

"The perfect score—got it," Scott said. "But this is what I want to ask you: What if he blows me off? What if a stranger coming up and talking about his car, or his clothes or whatever, makes him nervous and he tries to get the hell out of there?"

"Then you got to ram him."

"With my Porsche?"

Scottie was whining now. Nothing pissed off DuPree more.

"That's right, unless you got another car. You got to sacrifice your Porsche for the greater good. Locate where he's parked at and make sure you're right there in position to T-bone the motherfucker. No, fuck it, a little fender bender will do. Just make sure you give me time to drive over so we can make our move."

A moment passed before Scottie said, "Okay, if you say so." He didn't sound convinced. "And then one last question: What if Barry doesn't show up at all? It happens all the time, you know, clients flaking out on girls."

Just thinking about it set off a buzz in DuPree. No way he could walk away from this no matter how fucked up Scottie was. No way in hell.

"Then we'll track his ass down," DuPree said.

27

As soon as he realized he hadn't been fucking just for the sake of fucking, Nick knew he was in unfamiliar territory. He wondered if Jenny was trying to get a handle on what had happened, too. He found hope in the fact that there had been no rushed, almost embarrassed parting the night before, and no straining to remember her name when he awoke the morning after. "Jenny," he said out loud, and liked the way it sounded so much that he said it again. But everything still seemed tilted at a weird angle because, when he thought about it, love and a jack shack didn't belong in the same sentence.

All the way to work he wondered if he even knew what love was. *Christ,* he thought, *I'm getting soft in the head.* Life had been easier when all he had to do was punch the man in front of him or throw another suitcase off a plane. Now he found himself wondering what he and Jenny would say to each other or if they'd just trade secret looks. And how would he feel the next time Barry came to see her? And what about that snake Sierra? She was always looking for something to gossip about, something that would give her leverage over the other girls.

The strange thing was, Jenny was running late for her turn on the evening shift, which tied a knot in Nick's stomach. At leaslt Sierra hadn't started bitching about it yet. She was too busy reading a text that made her so happy she practically pissed herself. "They got the motherfuckcrs," shc told Nick.

"Which motherfuckers?" he asked.

"The ones that raped all those massage girls. Those two assholes."

"Police catch them?"

"Actually, somebody blew their fucking brains out and stuffed them in the trunk of a car. The cops didn't find them until they started stinking."

"I didn't see anything in the paper. How'd you find out?"

"A girl I used to work with is screwing some cop. He likes to talk, I guess."

"And this cop, he's sure it's the same guys?"

"Yeah, the cops knew who they were, but somebody got to them first. Cool, huh? Like in a fucking movie."

Sierra's thumbs flew over her cell phone's keypad. She stood when she was finished and gave Nick an icy smile. "I hope you're not getting too comfortable around here," she said. "You may be out of a job. And guess what else? If your little friend Coco doesn't show up pretty soon, her ass may be out the door too."

Sierra waltzed off to the bathroom while Nick tried to regain his bearings. If the job was over, the job was over. He'd socked away enough money to cover rent and expenses for a couple months, and maybe his luck would change when he went looking for work again. Jenny was a different story, though he didn't know how the story was going to end. Maybe she hadn't shown up because she'd been thrown off-balance by what happened between them too. To find out, he needed to see her again, talk to her again, maybe even make love to her again.

Jenny was still consuming his thoughts an hour later when Sierra answered the phone and began pacing the living room and pretending her panties weren't in a knot. "No, I'm sorry, sweetie, Coco isn't here yet," she said. *Sweetie* was a word that made Nick cringe, a cheap endearment the girls seemed to slide into every telephone seduction.

Then Sierra said, "Oh, sure, Barry, I recognize your name," and Nick started paying more attention. "I'm hoping she didn't, like, have an accident, you know?" Sierra said.

Nick had an idea what would come next.

"If you're still interested in some company, though, I'm available. My name's Sierra—blonde, thirty-fourC, all natural."

Barry must have shot her down instantly because the next thing Nick knew she was uttering a curt goodbye and tossing the phone onto the other sofa like it was diseased. "Asshole," she said. "Fucking rice chaser."

She glared at Nick. "God, I could use a bump. You don't have any coke, do you?"

"No," he said.

"That's right, you just clean shit up."

He wanted to tell her he'd never get all the shit cleaned up as long as she was around, but the ringing telephone kept him from saying a word. Sierra picked up and right away her tone of voice changed. It had to be Scott.

"Yeah, I just talked to that douchebag . . . No, he's not coming here . . . I don't know, maybe Coco set up something with him at her place. I always thought she was a sneaky little bitch . . . Why are you asking so many questions about her? Are you turning into a rice chaser too?"

Whatever it was she heard next stunned her.

"I don't believe it . . . Are you fucking crazy?"

It was all she could do to keep her voice down. She glanced at Nick uneasily, as if he knew what Scott was saying.

"Don't tell me any more, okay? . . . Because I don't want to know, that's why. Besides, it's not . . . Yeah, exactly . . . No, you know I won't. Later."

Sierra hung up and walked to the kitchen without another look at Nick. He watched her go, wondering what Scott had called about, knowing he was up to something, worrying that it involved Jenny somehow. Maybe Barry too, but the hell with him. Jenny was Nick's only concern, especially after Sierra asked Scott if he was crazy. Crazy meant DuPree was involved too. It had to.

Nick bolted out to the kitchen and found Sierra lifting a glass of Two Buck Chuck to her lips. He grabbed her arm before she could get a taste of it and spun her around to face him.

"What the fuck are you doing?" she said, trying unsuccessfully to wrest free of his grip. "Let go of me."

"I want to know what's going on," he said.

"Nothing's going on."

"Don't lie to me."

He squeezed her arm tighter and she dropped her glass. It shattered on the floor, splashing white wine on her bare feet and his shoes.

"Fuck you," she said. "If you want to know so bad, talk to Scott."

"I'm talking to you."

"No."

"Talk, goddammit."

"He'll kill me if I say anything, honest to God he will. Him or that psycho DuPree."

"Then you're catching a break because all I'm going to do to you is this."

He yanked her toward the shattered glass and she screamed as she went up on her tiptoes. Then he yanked her in a different direction and she stepped on two pieces at the same time. Now she had something to scream about.

"Okay, okay," she said, hopping on one leg as she tried to check her gashed foot.

"Worry about that later," he said, pulling her away from the blood, wine, and broken glass and depositing her at the kitchen table. "Talk."

"They're going to rob Barry. They think he's rich or something. And they're going to use DuPree's dog, those twisted motherfuckers."

"Scott's part of this? I thought he was an actor or something."

"Or something. The fat asshole got fired from his last acting job. Tried to talk some makeup girl into blowing him, like he doesn't get enough freebies from the girls here."

"That doesn't make him a robber, just—"

"An asshole, like I said. And he's an asshole that can't get work in Hollywood anymore. You don't need to be a genius to figure out why. So he talked DuPree into letting him tag along when they rob Barry. Like being a fucking pimp on the side isn't enough for him."

"Scott told you this?" Nick asked.

"Some of it," Sierra said. "The rest I heard when he was on the phone. Once he starts talking all badass to impress DuPree, he forgets I exist. You know, I really need take care of this foot."

She started to get up.

"Sit down," Nick said, pushing her back into her chair. "Now I want to know what you haven't told me."

Sierra hesitated.

"Okay, time for another walk," Nick said.

"Jesus Christ, you're crazy."

"You're right."

Nick yanked her to her feet. She howled with pain when her wounded foot touched the floor.

"No, no," Sierra said. "He's got a gun, all right?"

"Who does? DuPree?"

"Probably, yeah. But I'm talking about Scott. It's one of those old-fashioned guns, like some cop used on TV back in the day. *Drag*-something."

"Jesus Christ. How about"—Nick had to stop himself from saying Jenny—"Coco? You tell her what's going on?"

"She's not picking up."

"You could leave a message."

"I've left a shitload of messages. She doesn't call back."

Nick didn't need to ask if the messages contained a warning. He knew the answer just by looking at Sierra.

"You know where Coco lives?" he asked.

"Kind of."

"Fuck 'kind of.' You do or you don't."

Nick saw Sierra's eyes go wide and realized he had her backed against a wall. He knew he should give her some room, but he couldn't make himself do it, not even when he heard her saying, "Hey, take it easy."

"Tell me where she lives," he said.

"Shit, I said I would. But how about some fucking space?"

"Goddammit—"

"It's on the other side of, what is it, Sawtelle? Like two blocks over. Between Santa Monica and, you know, Olympic. I picked her up one day when her car wouldn't start. She said everybody told her the building where she lives is, like, the color of baby shit. You'll see it, trust me. It's right on the corner."

Nick headed for the door without another word.

He could hear Sierra behind him, asking, "Are you hung up on Coco, too? Is that what this is about? You want to be her fucking hero?"

That was part of it. The other part would have taken too much time to explain.

✤ ✤ ✤

What had she been thinking about? Sleeping with a guy who killed somebody? Come on, you know? Even if it was an accident, what kind of sport would let someone do that? And what kind of guy would—no, Jenny wasn't going to start on Nick. He had too many scars already, the ones she could see stitched on his face and the ones she knew were on his soul just by looking into his sad eyes. But she couldn't handle seeing him today, not when her head was a ball of day-after confusion.

Sleep was Jenny's favorite pastime. She was going to stay in bed as long as she could, the way she had after her mother died, when she was just trying to keep it together, no family in America to fall back on, only an old lady who rented her an apartment above a garage. Six years later, with the covers over her head, moving in and out of sleep, it felt as though trouble couldn't find her. There were none of the stories she'd read when she Googled Nick, the tragic ones about what he'd done to another boxer and the heroic one about his punching out a gangbanger who tried to rob him when he was delivering beer.

Jenny was still wondering what that was all about when she climbed out of bed as afternoon crept toward evening. He hadn't told her anything about himself, really. Maybe he was worried that too much talking would start him thinking about the man he'd killed, the man Jenny couldn't get off her mind. Every time she thought about him, it brought her back to her questions about Nick.

A check of her caller ID told her that Maria had phoned—they always unblocked their numbers for each other—and that the fifteen other calls had been anonymous except for Rachel from school. She guessed that Sierra had made at least a half-dozen of the calls, and she hoped that Barry was among the others. It was the first time he'd been more than a passing thought since she and Nick got horizontal, and here Barry had been a viable candidate to become the epicenter of her life. But she had finally given in to the realization that this wasn't the time to be thinking about anything resembling a relationship. She worked in a jack shack, she wasn't trolling on eHarmony.

With that in mind, Jenny put off checking her voicemail until almost six-thirty, deleting her e-mail unread, flipping through books without focusing on the pages, watching just enough reality shows on TV to remember how easy they were to hate. She saved Maria's and Rachel's messages for later without listening to them, but she couldn't resist playing the increasingly hysterical pleas Sierra had left, the gist of them being that Scott would be really pissed if she flaked out. Sierra called her Coco, a name that already seemed to belong to the past. Jenny shed it like cheap lingerie every time she left work, and now she wasn't sure she ever wanted to put it on again.

She was behaving as if she'd given up massage. It surprised her, but it felt right. Everything about the business now seemed too weird and complicated for her to handle, and if that meant her lawyer would have to wait for the rest of his money, she was sure it wouldn't be the first time for him. The important thing, she decided, was for her to stay home and chill out, to make a cup of tea and give some serious thought to what she was going to do with the rest of her life.

Her phone rang again. Another blocked number. She checked for a message almost reflexively and found herself listening to Barry say he was on his way over to make sure she was all right. "No," she said aloud, and barely heard her teakettle whistling.

Now she hated herself for letting him this far into her life, in a weak moment brought on by the illusion of romance, an urge to hold a man's heart in her hands, instead of his johnson. Her first impulse was to leave. She was already wearing jeans and a sweater; all she had to do was grab a hoodie and step into her sandals. She could come up with an excuse later—or pretend Barry never happened. It wouldn't be anything she hadn't done before.

She was wondering if this time would make her feel worse than the others, when someone buzzed her from the building's outer door. Barry already? Well, too bad if it was. She wasn't answering for anybody. She would just wait until the buzzing stopped and the unwanted visitor gave up. When she finally checked the water for her tea, she felt lucky it hadn't boiled away. She filled a cup, the heat from the steam stinging her hand, and put in a tea bag, hoping whoever was downstairs would leave soon. She was in no mood for games, and she didn't care who—

The pounding was on her front door now, shattering whatever resolve her pep talk had provided. It had to be the same person who buzzed. He must have kept trying apartments until a tenant who just wanted the damned buzzing to stop let him in. Funny how she automatically assumed it was a man. It could just as easily be a woman who thought she was a bitch or a whore or a husband thief. But the way her life had been going lately . . .

And then she was sure it was a man because he was calling for Jenny. It wasn't Barry, though. And Mark, the lurker, had to be too scared to follow her home after Nick—wait, that was who it was. *Oh, God,* she thought, *is he going to be one of those guys who thinks he's in love with me just because I slept with him?*

Jenny moved cautiously to the door and looked at Nick through the peephole. His expression was as desperate as his voice: "Jenny? Open up, Jenny! Come on, you got to open up!"

She knew he was right, though for a reason that likely hadn't occurred to him. She had to open up or the apartment manager would yell at her. He might even call the cops.

"One second," she said, keeping her voice down.

When she opened the door, Nick skipped hello and said, "You all right?"

"Yeah, sure," she said. "How did you find out where I live? I never—"

Across the hall, behind Nick, she could see one of her neighbors peeking out at the commotion, a Russian woman barely six months in the country. She was trying to hold back her two small children while she satisfied her curiosity.

"You better come in," Jenny said.

"Yeah," he said, taking a last glance over his shoulder before he entered. "But not for long."

"What are you talking about? I mean, why are you here, anyway? I never told you my address."

"Sierra described your building and I started hunting for it. Now come on, you got to get out of here. You and Barry if he's with you."

Nick's eyes swept the living room and kitchen with a frantic intensity that unsettled Jenny. She was starting to feel like she'd taken bad acid.

"Well, he's not," she said. "Not that it's any of your business."

"Look, I don't care if he is here," Nick said, eyeing the closed door to the bedroom.

You don't? Jenny thought, surprised that she was disappointed. But what she said was, "I'm not lying."

Nick looked back at her, holding up his left hand as if he were trying to stop the hostility. "I'm sorry, all right?" he said. "I just came to take you someplace safe."

"You're not making any sense," Jenny said. "Why would I, like, run off with you?"

"Scott and that guy with the dog—"

"DuPree."

"They're going to rob Barry, and if you're with him when they do, you could get hurt."

It was all Jenny could do to say, "You really expect me to believe that?"

"Sierra says Scott's got a gun."

"And you believe *her?*"

"This time, yeah, I do. DuPree's probably got one too. You want to hang around so you can find out how crazy those two assholes are?"

"Come on," Jenny said. "I like you, Nick, I really do. But all I did was fuck you. I didn't, like, pledge my undying love."

Nick didn't flinch.

"Congratulations," he said. "But this isn't about that. It's about your life."

"Right."

"You believed I was going to take care of you in that goddamn jack shack, didn't you? When those psychos were out raping massage girls?"

"Yeah."

"And you remember me chasing away poor fucking Mark and looking after you when DuPree shook you up so bad?"

"Yeah."

"Well, what's coming down with DuPree and Scott is worse than all that shit combined. You hear what I'm saying?"

Jenny felt helpless, the carefully tended components of her life suddenly thrown into a centrifuge.

"Jenny," Nick said, "we got to go now."

Her head spun worse than ever, and everything else about her was paralyzed.

"Dammit, please," he said.

His tone made her focus again. It went beyond the fear generated by the moment and the sorrow in which he preserved his past. It was as if he were telling her he finally had a chance to do something good within his reach, if only she would let him do it. She didn't know what he would ask in return. She didn't know if it mattered.

"Okay," she said, in a voice so small it barely registered on her own ears.

The next thing she knew, he was wrapping a hand around her arm and steering her toward the door. Her first steps seemed awkward, almost robotic. She wondered if the rhythm of escape was in her.

28

They would have run down the front steps and around the corner if Jenny hadn't been wearing those damned sandals. They kept slipping off, but even when she started carrying them, her bare feet weren't much of an improvement. The irritation Nick felt must have shown in his face because she told him, "I'm going as fast as I can." He didn't reply. He was looking up and down the street for a car he was afraid he wouldn't recognize until it was too late.

He'd parked his pickup in the entrance to an underground garage on the other side of Missouri, uncertain which building was Jenny's until he'd climbed out and seen that dirty-diaper brown up close in the fading light. Now there was someone in a black Toyota Camry stopped behind him. As soon as he saw that it was a woman honking her horn and moving her mouth angrily, he put her out of his mind and resumed looking for DuPree and Scott, who would kill him rather than curse him.

"This is mine," he told Jenny when they got to the truck. "Get in."

"What about that lady?" she asked.

"Just get in."

Nick watched Jenny scoot to the passenger's side. When she had the door open, he began to climb in, only to be stopped by the sound of another horn honking. He spun toward it and saw a Rolls-Royce that had to be Barry's, white ragtop, pale yellow body. He tried to remember if the guy at the wheel was the one he'd seen through the peephole. Yeah, it was, and he was pulling to a stop behind the woman in the Camry, powering down the passenger window and leaning across the seat, shouting, "Jenny!"

"Barry!"

Nick turned and saw Jenny hurrying toward the Rolls. "Dammit," he said, and moved after her.

The only time the woman in the Camry stopped honking was to lean out her window and yell something at him as he passed her. He couldn't hear what it was, but he nodded anyway. Anything for a few seconds' peace. By the time he reached the Rolls, Jenny was at Barry's open window, telling him, "I'm serious."

The look on Barry's face said he wasn't buying it. He glanced at Nick and, in a voice both weary and snotty, asked, "Who's this?"

"This is Nick. He's helping us."

"Yeah, but who is he?"

"I don't know what you mean."

"Okay, if I have to spell it out, are you—"

"Shut the fuck up," Nick said, "or we'll leave you here."

"What do you know, he talks," Barry said.

Nick smacked the hood of the car with an open hand and Barry recoiled, wide-eyed. "You want to be an asshole, fine," Nick said, "but there's two guys looking to rob you, and they've got guns."

"You sound pretty sure of that."

"I am. And don't even think about going home and closing the curtains until this is over. That's the first place they'll look."

"But my wife and kids—"

Barry caught himself and looked at Jenny. Her expression betrayed nothing. It was the woman in the Camry who was visibly pissed off as she resumed honking, the expression on her face suggesting she was on the verge of living out a violent fantasy.

"Come on," Nick told Jenny. "We're going."

He wrapped an arm around her waist and started moving her toward his pickup, never looking back at Barry. That was for Jenny to do as she tried to keep pace with him.

"No, wait," Barry said. "I believe you, okay? Just give me one second here."

He grabbed his black leather briefcase and scrambled out of his Rolls, leaving it half-blocking the entrance to the parking garage. He took one last sad look at it and hurried to catch up with Nick and Jenny while the woman in the Camry shouted out her window at him.

Barry wouldn't look at Jenny when he found himself wedged between her and Nick in the pickup. *He really is a weasel,* Nick thought, but it was the wrong time to make an issue of it. Nick pulled out and sped two blocks, blowing stop signs at both, before he turned left on Sawtelle, into the rush-hour slog. No one uttered a word until Jenny pointed at a restaurant called the Blue Plate and said, "This is far enough."

Nick angled the truck to the curb and Barry looked at Jenny, disbelief contorting his face. "So close?" he said. "For Christ's sake, they might drive by and see me."

"Not if you're inside," Jenny said.

Barry looked at Nick desperately. "Come on, pal, you know this isn't right. You're feeding me to the fucking sharks."

"Just go in like she told you and call a cab," Nick said. "You'll be fine."

When Barry finally started to move, Nick snatched his briefcase. "No," Barry said, struggling to hang onto it until Nick rapped him on the nose.

"Ow!" Barry said, grabbing his beak, tears coming to his eyes.

"Shut up or I'll hit you again," Nick said.

That got his attention. Jenny's too.

"Is what's in this thing worth dying for?" Nick asked. "Maybe getting Jenny killed, too? Tell me. I want to know how much you value life."

Barry remained silent, as if he were afraid he'd choke on what he would say.

"I had a manager like you once, when I was fighting," Nick said. "The only thing he ever cared about was the money. So here . . . " Nick thrust the briefcase back at Barry. "Take what you'd get us killed for. But I'm keeping the case. We clear on that? The case is mine."

Barry started working on its combination lock.

"Faster," Nick said.

At last, hands shaking, Barry slid a plain four-by-six manila envelope from the briefcase, then gave it back to Nick.

"Now get out," Nick said.

Jenny opened the door and stepped onto the curb so Barry could exit. "Fuck me," he muttered as he stalked off toward the Blue Plate. When Jenny jumped back in the pickup, she called after him: "Tell your wife I said hello."

✤ ✤ ✤

Traffic was a motherfucker. Seemed like it messed with DuPree every inch of the way. He hadn't expected Wilshire to be worth a damn, but Olympic should have been better. That was how he remembered it from the last time he'd been fool enough to try driving at rush hour. Besides, at a quarter to seven, he'd thought rush hour would be easing up. He knew how wrong he was as he crawled along with the rest of the fools, all that muscle under his Beemer's hood and no room for flexing it, not even in that little stretch through Century City with only one light. Nas was doing "Life's a Bitch" on the Blaupunkt and DuPree was telling himself, *Yeah, no shit,* and wishing he had some weed. Nothing to do but slam his fist on the steering wheel and promise himself he'd take it out on Barry and that bitch Coco. In the passenger seat, Blanco looked at him like he was crazy.

When DuPree finally turned onto Purdue—after taking what felt like a goddamn hour just to get past the 405—it was almost seven-thirty and he thought for sure they'd blown it. But he went into a slow crawl just the same, eyeballing every car jammed along the curb on both sides of the street. When he paused at the Missouri intersection and looked both ways, there it was on the left: Barry's Rolls.

He speed-dialed his man Scottie: "Get your ass over here. We got him."

Now DuPree had to find a parking place and wait, him and Blanco. If Barry came out before Scottie showed, no problem. DuPree had his Glock; he could take care of business himself. He just wanted to get situated with a good view of the Rolls and the building where Barry was undoubtedly enjoying some of that fine Oriental pussy. Ten minutes later, DuPree was still driving and looking, thinking good parking places were as hard to find as a break in the motherfucking traffic.

✤ ✤ ✤

They drove down Beloit, with the parking lot that was the 405 on one side of them and apartment buildings and an occasional single-family home on the other—bare-bones shelter for people simply trying to survive another day in L.A. Jenny felt like she was being reminded just how hard survival was every time Nick checked his rearview mirror or braced himself at an intersection. Once or twice Jenny tried to see what he saw, but mostly she kept her eyes straight ahead and wondered what was waiting in the gathering night.

When Nick hung a U-turn and parked between a tatty convertible and a pickup that had been converted to a camper, she shifted anxiously. She wanted to run, she wanted to stay with Nick as her protector, she just wanted to come out of this alive.

"Jenny?" he said. "You got anybody you can call?"

"Call?"

She expected them to be out on the street by now, racing toward a hiding place, fleeing DuPree and Scott and the guns

Nick said they had. Instead, she was sitting here trying to figure out what he was talking about.

"Friends or somebody," he said. "People you could stay with."

"Like, hide."

"Like that, yeah. Somebody that doesn't have anything to do with all this."

She couldn't help smiling. "You mean that doesn't know I'm a—"

"You're Jenny, okay? Just Jenny."

Even though she'd told him to call her by her real name, it felt strange to hear him say it. And then she felt something else, absolution maybe, or forgiveness, though she hadn't sought it. He was letting her know that Coco no longer existed for him either. Now she was a girl he had just met, a fresh face no matter how her secret life had collided with his. But there was no time to unspool all the words she would have needed to thank him for his kindness, his bravery. All she could do was nod before she dug her cell phone from her purse.

"Let me call around," she said.

Nick opened his door.

"Where are you going?" she asked.

"To talk to them." He nodded at three men in work clothes by a worn-out truck across the street. "Make your call."

She watched him trot toward the men as she dialed Maria and got her voicemail. No surprise there. No time to wait, either. She dialed Rachel, got another voicemail, and felt fear clutch at her stomach. Her hands shook as she dialed a third number, thinking, *Be home, Sara, please be home.* And Sara was, instantly deciding that they should grab dinner at Babalu, where they served this incredible banana cream pie, not that Jenny ever ate dessert. "We'll see," Jenny said.

She climbed out of the pickup and walked across the street, wondering if this was how it felt to be inside a video game. The first thing she heard was one of the men telling Nick, "*Sí.* Is no problem." The speaker was the eldest of three Mexicans, easily twice the age of the other two. When the guys with him saw Jenny, they grinned and whispered to each other in Spanish.

Nick turned to her and said, "Did you get hold of somebody?"

"Yeah."

"Good. My friends will take you there."

"I thought you were taking care of me," Jenny said.

"I am."

She shot a glance at the young Mexicans that said she didn't believe him.

Their elder statesman read it instantly. "You'll be safe," he said. "Your friend helps us, now we help him. To where are you going?"

"Santa Monica," she said.

The elder Mexican opened the door to his truck and motioned for Jenny to climb in. But before she could let herself do that, she had to ask Nick, "What about you?"

"I'm home," he said.

He pointed at a shabby building that looked like it had been laid on the block sideways. The door to his apartment must have been down the narrow walk on the north side. It was half grown over with untended oleanders that rendered the two lights out front all but useless. If there were more lights in the rear, Jenny couldn't see them.

"Is there someplace for you to hide?" she asked.

"Worry about yourself," Nick said.

"But how will I know you're all right?"

"I'll figure that out later."

"You don't have to do this, you know."

"Just get going."

Jenny wanted to kiss him more than she had ever wanted to kiss anyone in her life, but she couldn't even hug him or offer a simple thank you. He was already hurrying toward his apartment with Barry's briefcase in his left hand, and there was nothing she could do but get in the truck. As they drove away, she was still looking back, wanting another glimpse of Nick and hating the idea that he had been swallowed by darkness.

✥ ✥ ✥

So far Scott loved everything about his new gig as a criminal: DuPree buzzing all the apartments until somebody let them in, then going to Coco's place on the first floor and not even knocking, just kicking the fucking door in. DuPree had his gun out and Blanco by his side when he checked the closets and behind the shower curtain. Nobody home, but he did find out the teakettle was still warm. Scott should have known enough to check it after playing so many cops on TV, but it was DuPree who did, and said Barry and Coco must have just split. And then he said knock it off when Scott looked like he was ready to trash the little bitch's computer and fuck up her books. Anybody else and Scott would have been pissed, but DuPree was strictly business, a real pro. Scott told himself to remember it all—and to pull his gun next time. DuPree needed somebody who had his back.

On the way out of the building, DuPree scared the shit out of a woman across the hall when she looked to see who was making the noise. Just said, "Boo," real soft and put on his penitentiary face. Maybe Blanco helped too. Whatever, she shut her door in a big fucking hurry—and the man was just getting warmed up for when they sniffed around Barry's Rolls. It was blocking half the entrance to the apartment garage across the street, like fucking Barry had abandoned it and taken off on foot.

They asked each other why a guy with enough brains to make the money he had would be so goddamn dumb. Shit, almost eight, rush hour had to be over by now, and you never wanted to be a pedestrian in L.A., particularly when there was somebody looking to rob your ass.

The answer appeared in the form of a woman who came out of the building over the garage yelling, "Is this your car? Is it? You tell me right now." She looked like she taught school or sold clothes at Macy's, middle-aged, plain, probably no man in her life, but she wasn't going to let herself get pushed around. Didn't give a shit about any damn pit bull either. She said this was the second time the entrance had been blocked since she came home, and she was fed up. The first time there were two men with an Asian girl maybe half their age, God knew what that was all about, the three of them going off in a dreadful old truck and leaving the Rolls behind. Except the woman called the Rolls "this car," as though it meant no more to her than Blanco did.

"We'll take care of everything," DuPree told her, sounding as calm and rational as the therapists Scott had when he could afford them.

"You will?" the woman said.

"Yes, ma'am," DuPree said, and kicked in one of the Rolls' taillights.

"Oh my," the woman said.

"Maybe you shouldn't get involved," DuPree said, still using his voice of reason.

"I think you're right," the woman said, backing away as if he were a cobra.

Scott watched with the kind of awe he was sure Steve McQueen would have been too cool to feel. But fuck McQueen, he'd never been part of something like this, DuPree laying out how Nick had somehow figured out pretty much everything. "I'll bet that treacherous fucking Sierra told him," Scott said. But DuPree refused to be sidetracked. He stuck to the subject, theorizing about Nick and his sorry pickup and how he'd used it to help Barry and Coco get away. Scott kept agreeing with him until his cell phone rang. He checked the caller ID and then, doing his best to sound cool, said, "We have lift off."

"What the hell you talking about?" DuPree said.

"It's him."

"Your boxer man? Give me that." DuPree jerked the cell out of Scott's hand and didn't bother saying hello to Nick. "You finally give up on this running away bullshit?"

Whatever Nick said back made DuPree smile.

"I was thinking more like the motherfucker's briefcase and the little China girl, you feel me?" DuPree said. "But we can negotiate that when we together, being reasonable men and whatnot."

DuPree nodded at what he heard next. "Uh-huh, uh-huh." He flashed Scott a twisted smile. "Nah, man, I don't need your motherfuckin' address. I know where you live. See you in a couple."

He tossed the cell to Scott and headed for his car. As Scott ran after him, a troubling thought made its way through the rush he was feeling. After all those years as a star, even a fading one, he was now a sidekick, and the thought of how far he had fallen touched off a yearning for what he used to be.

❖ ❖ ❖

TV sounds drifted in from one of the other apartments, and music floated on the soft evening air. Nick strained to hear what the song was, but couldn't. He shook his head and tried to think of the last time he'd played something from his own collection. His CDs were stacked in the corner, *The Essential James Carr* on top. He was dead, James Carr, but his music lived after him, at least for those people who had carried it with them through the years. *A righteous memorial for any man,* Nick thought, and then there were footsteps coming up the walk that brought him back to the moment.

He knew it was them even though they moved quietly and the curtains were closed. He wondered if he should turn off the table lamp beside the sofa where he sat, the lamp with a hole in the shade that let out more light than he wanted when he watched TV. But no, he'd be damned if he'd hide in the dark.

The footsteps stopped outside his door. He imagined the door would get kicked in next. That was what always happened in movies, and movies provided the cues for almost every hard case he had known. The dangerous ones were those who made their own rules. When he heard the doorknob moving slowly, almost politely, he realized what he was up against and stood to face it.

The black guy stepped inside first. *DuPree,* Nick told himself. The white pit bull was at the end of the leash DuPree was holding. The dog held Nick's interest only until he heard Jenny's voice, tiny and frightened—"Nick"—and then there she was, as Scott muscled her inside.

DuPree picked up on Nick's surprise instantly. "That sorry-assed truck she was in broke down," DuPree said. "Good thing me and Scottie came along or she would have missed the party."

"You okay?" Nick asked her.

Jenny nodded.

He looked back at DuPree. "No deal as long as she's here."

"In case you failed to notice," DuPree said, "you ain't exactly operating from a position of strength."

"I know where the briefcase is. You don't. What would you call that?"

"I call that a reason to let this goddamn dog chew your motherfuckin' balls off. Ain't that right, Blanco?"

The dog barked and strained to break free of the leash, its Mike Tyson chest and shoulders looking more powerful than ever. DuPree, strong as he was, struggled to keep the dog under control, but he made sure the effort wasn't obvious. With him it was all about style points.

"Or maybe I turn the dog loose on her," he said. "Think that might get you talking, fighter man?"

Nick answered with a stare.

DuPree gave him a cold smile, then told Scott, "Take a look around, make sure they ain't hiding Barry in the fucking toilet."

Scott did as ordered, dragging Jenny with him.

"It's up to you," DuPree told Nick. "Yes or no."

"I hope your dog isn't going to pee in here," Nick said.

"Keep talking shit and that dog's gonna have your China girl for lunch."

"She's Korean. Get it straight."

Scott stepped out of the bathroom with Jenny, saying, "All clear," the way a cop angling for a promotion would. "My man," DuPree said, not bothering to hide the smile that cranked Scott up higher than he already was. "Don't fuck with us, goddammit," Scott told Nick, and pulled his gun from beneath his wash-faded safari jacket.

"Be cool, man," DuPree said.

"Fuck cool. This motherfucker's keeping us from a righteous score."

The dog barked and resumed tugging angrily at its leash, but the amused expression remained on DuPree's face.

"You're just glad to be here, aren't you?" Nick said to Scott. "Like being on TV, only real."

"Fuck you, acting like you don't give a shit about anything," Scott said.

"I give a shit about her," Nick said, nodding at Jenny. "As soon as she walks out that door, I'll tell you where to find what you came for."

"I was thinking she should party with us first," DuPree said. "First me and my man Scottie, then the dog."

Nick's stomach tightened. "Not today."

"Not ever," Jenny said. "You assholes."

"Shut the fuck up!" Scott said, and backhanded her across the face.

She went crashing into a wall and sank to the floor, dazed, maybe unconscious.

Nick came flying off the sofa at Scott, who whirled to pistol-whip him. Out of the corner of his eye, Nick could see the dog lunging at Scott too. "No!" DuPree yelled. "Goddammit!"

Everything after that, no matter how loud and angry, was muffled as Nick raised his right arm to block the pistol that Scott brought crashing down on him. Nick felt a bolt of pain shoot through his arm. He thought it was broken, and then the thought was wiped away by the sound of Scott screaming, "Get the fucking dog off me!"

Scott pitched forward, twisting in a vain attempt to wrest free of the dog's jaws. Nick saw the opening and threw a left hook that landed on the bridge of Scott's nose. It broke with a snap, blood spurting from both nostrils and Scott finding one more thing to scream about as he clamped his left hand to his face.

Nick shoved Scott out of the way and started toward Jenny, who still hadn't moved. But DuPree dropped the leash and punched him above the left eye. Nick fell to one knee, thinking DuPree's fist felt like a brick. He was cut now and blood blurred his vision, but his right eye was still good enough to see the gun in DuPree's right hand. *Another pistol-whipping motherfucker,* he thought.

And then he heard Scott scream, "DuPree!"

DuPree couldn't resist glancing at his partner and the dog that sounded like it was making a meal of him. The growling and chewing noises were punctuated only by thuds that must have come from Scott pounding the crazed Blanco, pounding, pounding.

Nick seized the moment and drove a right hand into DuPree's belly. More pain shot through Nick's arm. He wondered if he'd puke, and if DuPree would too, folded up the way he was, arms in tight to his ribs as he gasped for air that wouldn't come.

Nick pushed himself to his feet with his left hand and tried to clear his head. DuPree, still doubled over, bull-rushed him, driving a shoulder into his chest and sending the two of them into the sofa. It skidded backward and its cushions came off, revealing where Nick had hidden Barry's briefcase. Nick would have sworn DuPree smiled before he made a desperate grab for it.

But all DuPree got for his trouble was the cheek that Nick carved open with a left hook before they tumbled to the floor. And still DuPree wound up on top of him when they rolled into the displaced sofa and came to an abrupt stop. *Jesus, he's big,* Nick thought. The only way to unhorse him was to club him on the ear, and fuck the pain in Nick's ruined right hand. It was better to rupture the son of a bitch's eardrum, better to hear him howl and make him forget the punch he'd been about to throw.

As Nick shoved him over onto his back, there was a crash and the room went dark, save for the light through the open bathroom door. The lamp beside the sofa must have been a casualty of the fight it sounded like Scott was still losing to the dog. His screams were coated with liquid now, and the dog kept chewing, the only living creature in the apartment convinced of victory.

Nick pounded away at DuPree's face, his fists growing slick with blood. He threw punch after punch, his right hand throbbing too much to inflict serious damage, until DuPree reached up to fishhook Nick, tearing at the corners of his mouth. Then DuPree was on top again, raining punches down on him, merciless punches, heavy punches, heavier than any Nick had thrown. Many more and he would be out. More than that and he would be dead.

His left arm snaked upward and he dug a thumb into DuPree's eye, soft and moist and sensitive enough to arouse a shriek that DuPree had likely not known he was capable of emitting. Nick dug his thumb in a little deeper and hoped the fucking eyeball would be on the end of it when DuPree fell away from him.

There was a gunshot behind them and the dog howled, short and sharp. Then another gunshot, and another. Then nothing but wet noises.

Nick struggled to his feet and wiped the blood from his left eye. He looked for Jenny first and saw her stirring. Then for Scott, and saw him bathed in gore, pinned beneath the dog's lifeless body and moaning in agony. Then for DuPree, and saw him getting up two steps away, driven by meanness or maybe just by the confidence that came from the gun that was back in his hand. Before he could do anything with it, Nick closed the distance between them and threw the right hand that pain told him not to and that instinct told him was his only prayer. He hit DuPree right on the chin—*Oh, Christ that hurt, oh, sweet mother of Jesus!*—and DuPree toppled backward, hit the wall and went as still as a pillar of salt.

Nick bent at the waist, his hands on his knees. He could hear the sounds of his own breathing and the blood from his split eyebrow dripping on the floor. He turned on the overhead light and saw DuPree lying at the base of the wall. His head was twisted at such an impossible angle that Nick didn't need a doctor to tell him it was a broken neck. And don't blame it on the goddamned wall. He had killed another man with his fists.

"Nick?"

Jenny was doing her best to stand, one hand braced against the wall, the other feeling her bruised face. "Everything's okay," he said, and started toward her.

He was stepping over a toppled chair when he saw Scott struggling to raise the bloody pistol he'd used to kill the dog. He was pointing it in Jenny's direction, his face a picture of hatred. "Bitch," he said in a death-rattle voice, using the last of his strength to squeeze the trigger.

The gun went off an instant after Nick threw himself at Scott. The slug hit Nick high in the chest, left side, like a sledgehammer, but it was his back that felt suddenly wet and warm as he landed on the floor. He barely heard himself grunt over the sound of Jenny's scream.

Everything around him was a blur now, like someone was fucking with the picture. But he knew she was beside him, leaning close, saying his name, telling him she was sorry. He tried to form an answer out of his scrambled thoughts and gave up when his mouth filled with the copper taste of blood. Then her voice began to fade. Now someone was fucking with the volume, and he couldn't do anything about it. No picture, no sound. He knew what came next.

29

She rose from the kiss she'd given Nick wondering if he'd lived long enough to feel it. Only then did she realize she was standing in a pool of blood that had painted her bare feet red. Nick's blood. She screamed louder than ever and began stumbling toward the door before the wail of sirens in the distance stopped her. *What,* she wondered, *am I going to tell the cops?* She looked around the slaughterhouse that Nick's apartment had become. Looked at DuPree and Scott in hideous repose and at the dog, its ferocity made grotesque by the bullets that had torn it apart. Looked at Nick one last time and realized that she was on her own now.

And then Jenny ran, just as she had from the rape-scarred trick pad that once seemed to have propelled her out of this secret life. Ran because what she faced now surpassed her darkest imaginings. Ran without giving a damn about her suspended license or the lawyer who would be even scarier when he was pissed off at her than he was when he was on her side. Ran because the fragile foundation of her life had been shattered and there was nothing and no one to cling to.

She hid in shadows when a police car raced past her, its siren howling and more sirens behind it. She stubbed her toes on broken sidewalks, splashed through puddles left by lawn sprinklers, dodged traffic that treated her more like a target than a pedestrian. The sight of her apartment building offered her a sense of security until she raced inside, found her front door kicked in, and was hit by another avalanche of terror.

A note from the building manager said he would have someone repair the door in the morning. In the meantime, he had put strips of blue painter's tape across the space where her door had been, as if that would pacify Jenny or keep intruders out. She ripped away the tape, but when she stepped into her apartment her anger vanished, replaced by the jackhammer pounding of her heart and skittering nerves that had her ready to bolt. She turned on the lights and found books and magazines strewn around the living room. Her teakettle lay dented on the kitchen floor. But that was it for signs that two killers had been there. They hadn't even touched her laptop.

She would need it wherever she went, though she had no destination in mind, just the urge to put L.A. far behind her. She would become another particle in space floating through the unknown, and how, she asked herself, do you pack for that? She began by dragging two canvas duffel bags out of a closet and putting her book of Elizabeth Bishop's poems in one. Her laptop, jeans, a sweater, and some underwear followed. A Hello Kitty notepad, too. But her toothbrush, socks, and a pair of running shoes were forgotten, lost amid her fractured thoughts.

And then she wanted a shower more than anything in the world, wanted to feel hot water cascading down on her so she could wash the blood off her hands and feet and everywhere else it might be. But not with the front door kicked in, no, never. The best she could do under the circumstances was to rinse her hands and arms in the kitchen sink and wipe her feet and legs with a wet towel. It would have been so simple, so basic, if the blood on the towel weren't Nick's.

She wept until she ran out of tears, and then she turned practical. She needed money, even wished she'd taken the cash DuPree and Scott were carrying. They didn't need it anymore, those bastards. But there was no going back, nor could she milk enough out of ATMs to take her wherever her next stop might be. She would have to empty her safe-deposit boxes, but the banks weren't open until morning. A long night awaited her, a night she would rather spend anywhere but in the apartment where everything had begun unraveling.

It was around eleven when she lugged her duffel bags, one full, one empty, downstairs to her car and then eased out of the garage checking for cops, for thugs, for crazy shit she was afraid to imagine. Her ringing cell phone startled her. A glance at caller ID told her it was Sara, no doubt wondering where she was. *In limbo, that's where,* Jenny thought, but she wasn't going to tell that to Sara, who would tell Rachel, and then they'd probably post something on social media and the whole fucking world would know. It was inevitable, but Jenny wasn't going to help.

She drove aimlessly on surface streets, from Venice to Century City and then down to Manhattan Beach. When she'd killed a good ninety minutes, she headed north on Pacific Coast Highway, out of Santa Monica and into Malibu, the ocean on one side of her, low-slung mountains on the other, but seeing none of either in the after-midnight darkness. She made it to Ventura an hour away, turned around and went back to Santa Monica, did another one-eighty and returned to Ventura. Nature caught up with her on her second visit.

Eyes bleary, bladder bursting, she had no choice but to make a pit stop at a Denny's. Before she got back in her car, she caved in to weariness and ordered coffee to go.

"You all right, miss?" a waitress wearing cat's-eye glasses asked her.

"I'm fine," Jenny said too quickly.

"There's something on your sweater that looks like blood. Right there, the elbow on your left arm."

"Oh."

Jenny strained to find an explanation and kept turning up images from Nick's apartment—blood-spattered walls, dead men and a dog, and Nick, always Nick. She fought the impulse to cry.

"Must be from the little boy I babysit," she said at last. "He gets lots of bloody noses. Allergies, I think."

As soon as the waitress went to get her coffee, Jenny was out of there.

She cried in the privacy of her car until she fell asleep. When she awoke, she was still in the Denny's parking lot, scared to death the police would be there any minute. Not until she was making her way out of Ventura did she realize it was almost four. Only five hours until the banks opened. But as she rolled toward L.A. on the 101, she dozed off again and would have missed a curve in Agoura Hills if a trucker's blatting horn hadn't awakened her.

The tears and close calls had abated by the time she curled onto the 110 through downtown and exited to drive back and forth across the city on Olympic Boulevard until she thought she would lose what was left of her mind. Then she switched to Pico and did the same thing, waiting for hazy morning sunshine to spread itself over the L.A. basin like rancid butter.

Just before nine, she pulled into the parking lot at the first of the three banks on her list. The drill would be the same at each of them: take the money out of the safe-deposit box and put it in a paper shopping bag from Ralphs. She'd transfer the money to the duffel bag when she got back to the car, but she wouldn't count it until later. She just wanted to be gone.

By a quarter to eleven she was heading north on the 405. Half an hour after that, she was on the 5, weaving in and out of the big rigs that turned the highway into an obstacle course, trusting her instincts to tell her when she found a safe haven. Or maybe she'd never make it there. Maybe the cops would pull her over. Maybe DuPree had friends who would kill her because he was dead and she wasn't. She turned on the radio to drown out the voices in her head and got an earful of country music, Spanish-language stations, and crackpot preachers. When the news came on, she turned it off and drove on.

Her trip carried her beyond fatigue and into country green and cool and lush. It felt safe there as the afternoon shadows grew long, safe enough for her to crash at a motel on the edge of a town she would forget as soon as she left it. But her sleep was restless, wracked with dreams. They were like crumbling photographs that reminded her of how much she missed Nick, and after every one of them, her tears returned.

What she longed for was some tangible reminder of his presence in her life. A shirt with his scent on it, perhaps, or maybe a note he'd written. But there had been no such things in their short, unlikely time together, so she would have to create one. She checked the room's desk and found three sheets of cut-rate stationery alongside a ballpoint pen well on its way to going dry. She picked up the pen and began to write:

Too early the parting
Too late the awakening
And I am left with—

Her search for what came next turned empty and unsatisfying. She kept putting words on paper and crossing them out, and soon enough she found herself hoping Nick hadn't come into her life just to rid himself of the ghost that haunted him. She hoped there were other things he would have told her, and that she would have heard him out.

But she would never know, and now the clock beside the bed was telling her to get back on the road even though it was barely after midnight. She folded her unfinished poem and tucked it in a hip pocket of her jeans. Then she threw the pen in one of her duffel bags, zipped up everything but her churning imagination, and headed for the door.

On the street that led to the interstate, she drove past gas stations and fast-food joints closed for the night, and neon lights made seductive by wisps of mountain fog. The neon came from two bars, their parking lots half-filled by pickup trucks and workaday cars. Beyond the bars was a sign Jenny hadn't expected to see so far from what she'd left behind: MASSAGE. It was there and gone as she hit the gas, and once more Nick consumed her thoughts.

He'd told her there was a good guy in every story, and then he'd become the good guy in hers. He had died so she could live. That was his gift to her, and she yearned to repay it with the poem she could feel in the beat of her heart. The words she needed to finish it hadn't come to her yet, but they would. She was sure of it. They would come if she just drove far enough.

Acknowledgments

Oh, the stories I could tell you about agents. I had one in Hollywood who said, "At Columbia they're calling me the Antichrist." At least he was good for a laugh. Not so my last show-biz agent, who left me in a ditch by the side of the road. Imagine my surprise, then, when I realized that the first person I want to thank here is my literary agent, Farley Chase. Without him this book doesn't exist.

Farley came into my life after *A Better Goodbye* had been ushered onto the showroom floor by the legendary Sterling Lord. Though I still have the greatest respect for Sterling, we eventually drifted apart. Just as I was about to stuff the manuscript in a drawer, there was Farley, a mellow soul with a fighter's heart, ready to run with it, knocking on doors all the way.

He struck gold when Ben LeRoy answered his knock. Ben is a literary adventurer, embracing long-shots and defying the publishing industry's predilection for books that are easily categorized. Aided and abetted by the sharp-eyed Ashley Myers, he provided a home at Tyrus Books for the lost souls I created and, by extension, for me. Saying thanks to someone like that is hardly sufficient, but it is the best I can do.

John Ed Bradley, Mike Downey, and Leigh Montville—old friends from my press box days—may not remember encouraging me to take a shot at a novel, but I will always remember gratefully that they did. Likewise, my ex-wife kept telling me I could write one even after we'd washed up on life's rocky shoals. Maybe not a novel like this, but the thought was what counted. Thank you, Paula Ellis.

Once I began putting words on paper, it was an act of courage to phone me because I was damn sure going to read the caller whatever I had just written. Mark Kram Jr., who never backs down in his journalism, remained a steadfast and generous sounding board throughout. Jim McCarthy, a friend since we were kids with baseball dreams, did the same. Not a day passes that I don't wish I could call and tell him the novel he always asked about finally made it into print.

I shamelessly inflicted early drafts on friends far and wide. To Alex Belth, Sonja Bolle, Tom Boswell, Rob Fleder, Jacob Epstein, Susan Haeger, Michael Hill, Christopher Hunt, David Israel, George Kimball (RIP), Paul Levine, Ron Rapoport, Steve Smith, Ken Solarz, Kip Stratton, Jane Shay Wald, and Eddie Wilson, I say thanks for not getting a restraining order.

When I sought criticism, I turned to Clyde Edgerton and Paul Hemphill first, never imagining that Hemp would soon be gone. Gerry Howard offered a single suggestion that inspired me to rewrite a third of my book, which must be some kind of record. Kathy Tomlinson kept everything noir with notes like this: "Nick sounds like a weenie here." (Not anymore, Kathy.)

Most everything I know about boxing can be traced to Johnny Lira, the former lightweight contender who was never braver than in his losing fight against liver disease. For doses of real life, I couldn't have had better sources than Ted Branson, Ken Caputo, Don Fischer, Jim Nielsen, and Galen Yuen.

And then there were the massage girls who stepped out of the Internet ads and the back pages of *L.A. Weekly* to reveal themselves as flesh-and-blood human beings. Two in particular proved far better than the stereotype that traps them all—bright, insightful, articulate, funny, charming, and irreverent. No names, of course. Just my boundless gratitude.

JOHN SCHULIAN was a nationally syndicated sports columnist for the *Chicago Sun-Times* before moving to Hollywood to write and produce TV dramas. *A Better Goodbye* is his first novel. He is a co-creator of *Xena: Warrior Princess*, a long-time contributor to *GQ* and *Sports Illustrated*, and the author of three collections of sports writing. His short fiction has appeared on the websites Thuglit and The Classic and in the *Prague Revue*. He lives in Southern California.